I0569806

JEFF MADISON

AND THE

SIEGE OF BYLLERAZ · BOOK V

First edition 2025

Jeff Madison and the Siege of Bylleraz
ISBN 978-1-945709-29-6

Copyright © 2025 Bernice Fischer
BerniceFischer.com

All rights reserved. No part of this publication may be reproduced, stored in a retrieval system, or transmitted, in any form or by any means, with the prior written permission of the author.

Edited by Maya Fowler-Sutherland
Cover illustration by Mirela Barbu

DISCLAIMER
All names and characters appearing in this work are fictitious. Any resemblance to real persons, living or dead, is purely coincidental

When the afterglow of day dwindles to an end
and twilight hurries the sinking sun over the bend.
As moonrise unleashes its first beam of light,
that's when the magical hour will ignite.

Musings of Ruogh

Acknowledgements

Thank you to …

Mirela Barbu, for the phenomenal cover … it's where the magical journey begins.

Maya Fowler-Sutherland, for editing and polishing until the story sparkled.

Andre, for keeping me grounded when whimsy took flight.

Angie … for providing the ugly pink sofa and the goggles. We are going on an adventure!

1

Nequam threw his hands in the air. "Phoebe, what are we waiting for, let's go!"

Phoebe looked up from her trimmed nails and glared at Nequam who stood in front of her with his eyebrows drawn together.

Nequam was a tall, scrawny looking boy with brown hair styled in a Mohawk, his head smooth and shiny either side of the strip of hair. He was also a shape shifter and had spent many years looking for a girl called Lyric who had disappeared from the forest within his home world, Bylleraz. He was so convinced Phoebe was this missing girl, that while Jeff was trying to avoid capture from the dreamons, Nequam impersonated Jeff and enticed Phoebe away from her home town of Little Falls. When they got separated, the two evil witches Zorka and Wiedzma captured her.

Now, Nequam tossed a pebble down the cobblestone street and watched it bounce on the rounded stones. "Your essence has been successfully sewn back into your body," he said to Phoebe. "That transparent ghost-like look is all gone, and you're back to normal."

Phoebe's encounter with the two Drakmere witches, Zorka and Wiedzma, wasn't that long ago. Zorka's horrible plan was to use Phoebe's life essence to give her immortality. So she and Wiedzma cast an evil spell that separated Phoebe from her life essence. The rescue team, consisting of Jeff, Madgwick, that crazy witch Angie, and Watroc the water dragon, managed to save her just in time and bring her back to the spell weavers in Sandustian who spent months weaving her life essence back into her body.

No one knew what happened to Wiedzma but Zorka was turned into a frog by Angie during a temper tantrum and then Phoebe squished her ... by mistake. Zorka was Wiedzma's mother but she didn't seem too upset that her mother got squashed. Wiedzma disappeared soon after, fearing what the good witch, Angie, would do to her in retaliation.

Now, listening to Nequam, Phoebe shrugged her shoulders and stuffed her hands into her jeans pockets. She wore a pink jacket and a white T-shirt. Her curly brown hair bounced on her shoulders, and her voice was soft and musical as she spoke. "I don't even know if I want to go to Ballywhatever. *And* I don't think I am this girl *Lyric* that you claim me to be."

Nequam sighed and closed his eyes. "Bylleraz, the place is called Bylleraz, and it's not just any place. It's the place where you were born, where you belong. Your home before you disappeared in the forests when you were just ..."

"Three ... so you said, blah blah blah blah," muttered Phoebe and wrinkled her nose.

"Maybe if I call you *Lyric* you will start remembering a bit of your early life," Nequam said with his hands on his hips and a scowl on his face, his eyebrows almost touching. He jammed his hands into his pockets, pulled out the linings, then with a shake of his head he shoved the linings back into the jeans. He did not have any extra clothing when they arrived in Sandustian so Jeff's mother gave him some things from Jeff's closet. He really liked the pants Jeff called "jeans," they were comfortable and hardy. He wore a red "hoodie" also from Jeff closet, which was also cool, except his Mohawk was too long and did not fit into the hood. Much to his disgust, Upijer, one of the senior warriors, recently gave him a hectic brush cut to ensure the hoodie fit properly. He brushed his hand over his very short, almost non-existent Mohawk.

"I doubt it and I like my name just as it is," Phoebe retorted as she glanced up the road again. She breathed in deeply and smiled. The air had a soft fragrance of orange blossoms that lingered in the breeze.

The little Sandustian road was dotted with cottages hugging each other; each had a brightly painted door and quaint cottage-style windows. Flower pots with dainty flowers of bright pink and blues decorated doorways and the cobblestones were different shades of grey. So crooked and skew were the houses that their brick red roof tiles looked ready to tumble off. The houses continued until the road curved out of sight. It looked like a picture from a fairy tale.

Nequam lifted his thin yet muscular arms into the air as if pleading. "Just a visit, *Lyric*, meet the people. If you don't like it then I will personally bring you back."

"I am already arguing about going and coming back, and don't call me Lyric!" Phoebe retorted as she narrowed her chocolate brown eyes.

"We'll leave the minute you say you want to come back. So what do you say … we can leave now?" Nequam raised his eyebrows.

"No," Phoebe said and crossed her arms.

"No? Why?" Nequam grabbed his face with both hands. His jaw clenched and unclenched as if he were chewing gum.

"Watroc told me to wait for him. We can go when he says we can go," Phoebe said.

"What is this bond you have with this water dragon? Do you *have* to do everything the lizard says?"

Phoebe slapped her thigh. "Do NOT call him a lizard. I'm not going to explain something that you won't be able to understand anyway – Watroc and I are more than friends, we are *linked*. You know he stopped the witches from finishing their spell on me by holding onto my life force. I won't go without Watroc."

"And you will not be going without us either," a voice said behind them.

Nequam turned to find Horrigan, the Sandustian warrior, standing with his arms folded against his broad chest.

Phoebe spun around with a squeal and a clap of her hands. "Horrigan ... are you coming too?" Her voice rose with glee.

Horrigan's muscular arms bulged as he brushed his hands over his shiny bald head. A tattoo of a dagger with an intricately patterned handle ran down the side of his face, with the tip of the blade ending at the point of his chin. His eyes gleamed dark purple and he looked mean and intimidating in his black leathers and muscle shirt.

Nequam groaned, "Great, so who is *us* ... who else is going? Please don't tell me it's that crazy witch Angie."

"Angie is *not* crazy, just a little out there," Phoebe snapped.

Horrigan scratched his chin as if his tattoo itched. "I personally do not think that witch has all her moonballs in the basket, but no, she won't be joining us. She left for important witch-like business, which only a witch could have. A warrior called Nyx will be joining us; she is receiving her orders from the warrior Kojo now."

"So when she gets here, we can go?" Nequam asked, his eyes wide and his chin pushed forward. Although Phoebe did not believe she was the lost girl Nequam thought she was, she and Nequam had the exact same chocolate brown eyes that sparkled with gold specks like stars in the night sky.

"No, we have to wait for Watroc," Horrigan replied.

"Why?" Nequam whined and his head dropped back as he stared at the blue sky.

"Because he instructed us to wait and you would be wise to follow a dragon's order without any arguments. They do not like to be ignored or crossed. Just putting it out there ..." Horrigan said with pursed lips.

Nequam threw his arms up in the air and turned away with a heavy sigh.

"Do you know where Watroc went?" Phoebe asked as she peered over his shoulder in case the dragon in question appeared.

Horrigan rubbed his head as if he was thinking. "Not sure ... but all three dragons, Azghar, Calidus and Watroc, said they had something important to do."

"And Jeff, can he come?" Phoebe asked.

"When he gets back he has to start the new term of warrior school with the other recruits, so definitely not. We won't see him for a while." Horrigan did not meet her eyes but studied the dragon engraving on his leather wrist band.

"I thought they would be back by now and everyone is being really secretive about what is going on," Phoebe said and bit her nail, studying Horrigan.

"I am sure they will be back soon," Horrigan said and then quickly turned to Nequam as if just noticing something. "What happened to your hair?"

Nequam opened his mouth to answer when a cheerful voice called from down the lane.

"Hey Horri!"

Horrigan closed his eyes and dropped his head.

Phoebe spun around to see who had called; her mouth dropped open.

A warrior was walking towards them with a wide smile and deep purple eyes. Her black hair was tied in a low braid that hung down her back and swung from side to side with each stride. She wore a short black leather skirt with a brown and black striped blouse and a snug brown waistcoat fashioned with bronze hooks down the front. Her black cloak was fastened at her neck and flew behind her as if caught in a wind storm. Thin straps wrapped around the base of each of her calf-length brown boots.

"Did she just call you Horri?" Phoebe asked with a grin. Her braces flashed in the sunlight.

"It's Horrigan, not Horri. If you are coming with us then at least get the name right." Horrigan growled as he cracked his knuckles.

Nyx winked at Phoebe. "So, I am Nyx, and I am going with to ensure your safe return journey from Ballyhoo."

Nyx was one of the many woman warriors within the Sandustian force. She had rosy cheeks and a dimple on her left cheek. Just below her left eye was a thin white scar from a previous battle. Her lips were full and rosy. Her eyes shone in a soft shade of purple.

Nequam sighed and rolled his eyes at Horrigan. "It's Bylleraz, not Ballyhoo. Why would she not be safe with me?" He frowned, as if the whole idea of Phoebe being in danger was ludicrous.

Both Nyx and Horrigan turned to stare at Nequam with raised eyebrows.

Nyx opened her eyes wide in mock innocence while stating the obvious, counting on her fingers as she listed: "Taken into Torturra that could have burnt her to a crisp, being captured by not one but *two* evil witches, being separated from life essence, almost getting sucked into the nothingness. I get it. Fee-ee was *totally* safe with you." She finished with a wave of her hand.

"Her name is Phoebe," Horrigan started.

Nequam spoke at the same time, "It's Lyric, her name is Lyric."

Phoebe grinned at the warrior who looked energised, hopping from one foot to the other, rearing to go. "I totally like you," she said.

"Aw thanks Fee, I like you too. Not so sure about Quamie there ..."

"Nequam, my name is NEquam." He turned to Horrigan to grumble. "Is she always like this ... getting the names wrong?"

Horrigan muttered out of the corner of his mouth, "She does it on purpose, just to irritate us. She tries to break us down. I am sure of it."

Nyx turned to Horrigan, "Any news?" she whispered.

Horrigan shook his head. "Kojo has instructed us to continue as normal in the meantime."

Phoebe was about to ask about this when her eyes widened, she spun around on her heel and gazed down the still empty road. "Watroc is coming!"

6

"I don't see anything," Nequam muttered.

"Wait for it," Phoebe whispered, the gold specks in her eyes starting to sparkle with excitement. She took a deep breath and closed her eyes as a whiff of sea breeze floated on the air.

With a flash Watroc appeared and stomped with heavy thuds toward Phoebe, his talons clicking on the cobblestones. His eyes were bright green with yellow irises, and as he moved his scales gleamed. It looked like shimmering jade liquid flowing from one scale to the next, moving and evolving, seeping from one to the next. The sunshine added a mother-of-pearl effect. Mighty white spikes ran down the length of his spine all the way down to his tail, which twitched from side to side like on a frustrated cat. Two white horns protruded from his forehead. Watroc shook his wings; the edges looked like seaweed and fluttered in the breeze. Green stream puffed out of his nostrils in large white round circles as he passed the staring Sandustian villagers.

One villager feebly waved at the dragon. But Watroc, bad tempered as always, ignored the villager.

"Phoebe," Watroc growled as he reached her side, his head moving from side to side. A large white tooth jutted over his lip as if he were grinning at her.

"Great. We can go now." Nequam clapped his hands.

Watroc's eyes narrowed as he growled, "Only if Phoebe *wants* to go." Then he turned to stare at Horrigan and Nyx with one penetrating green eye. Slowly, as if awaiting an explanation or introduction, he blinked.

Horrigan lifted his chin and swallowed before waving his hand towards Nyx. "This is Nyx, she is coming with us to help ensure Phoebe's safety and return journey."

"Only if Lyric *wants* to come back," Nequam stated loudly.

Phoebe rolled her eyes as she grinned at Watroc. She rubbed his scaly nose but was careful to stay clear of the steam that still wisped from his nostrils.

Watroc lowered his head until one piercing eye was level with Nequam's head. "Her name is not Lyric, it is Phoebe." He snarled and pulled his lips back to reveal his first row of teeth.

Nequam gulped and stepped back but pressed his lips together and muttered, "We will see about that when we get there."

"Erm, so we should go. We have a long journey ahead of us and it may take several weeks to get there," Horrigan said with his hands on his hips.

Watroc lifted his head. "Several weeks? Phoebe and I are not travelling several weeks. We will fly. We will meet you there."

Horrigan and Nyx exchanged glances. "I wish Rig or Angie were here." Horrigan held his hand over his mouth as he muttered to Nyx. Rig was one of the few warriors that Watroc would listen to, perhaps because Rig was normally as bad tempered as the dragon. Then of course, *everyone* listened to Angie unless they wanted to be turned into a frog …

Nyx smiled at Watroc and swayed from side to side as if chatting to a friend. "Well considering that Horri and I have been appointed to keep Fee safe and to ensure she *can* come home … perhaps we should travel together. I've heard a lot about your power and I've been told you are super fast." She gave Watroc a wide, winning smile and blinked a few times.

Horrigan stared at Nyx and then at Watroc. His mouth dropped open in disbelief: this tactic was actually working.

Watroc's head snapped up as if he was unsure what to make of this girl warrior Nyx. "Fee? Feebe … Fee… I like it." He snorted and steam shot out of his nostrils as he laughed. "Okay you and … *Horri* can fly on my back."

"It's Horrigan," Horrigan muttered under his breath but he bent over to study his boots to make sure his comments were not really heard by the dragon.

"And Quamie … I mean, he knows the way. Maybe he can also come with us?" Nyx asked with a little shoulder lift.

Nequam groaned. "My name is Nequam," he barked and frowned at

Nyx.

Watroc snorted, huffed and puffed. "This is priceless ... Quamie ... I like that too!" The dragon jerked and a puff of smoke popped out of his nostrils as though he had hiccups.

Nyx clapped her hands and tossed her braid over her shoulder. "Alright then – let's go – this is going to be so exciting. Ballyhoo, here we come!"

Phoebe stared up at Watroc's neck. "Uh Watroc ... where should I sit? I mean the last time was with Angie on her sofa ..."

"No, no. No sofa. Angie is not here, we do not need the sofa. Not happening."

"Oh. Okay." Phoebe looked around, searching for ideas on how to sit on Watroc's back.

Watroc stared at Phoebe's fallen face and downcast eyes. She curled a piece of hair around her finger as she thought.

He jerked again and a puff of smoke shot out of his nostril. "Arrrrghhhhh, I hate that sofa! It's so ugly, and I look terrible, not frightening at all."

He closed his eyes and mumbled half under his breath. With a green flash, a double-seater sofa appeared strapped to his back. It was Angie's dull dirty pink sofa. It looked about 150 years old with fluff and stuffing popping out of the seams. Suddenly the dull pink was covered with bright yellow and green flowers splattered all over. Dragons had their own powerful magic after all.

Phoebe squealed and flapped her hands. "Oh I love that sofa, it looks tatty but it's so soft and comfortable. You gave it some new colours. Looks great!"

"I added a few flowers," Watroc mumbled and lifted his head. He was obviously pleased with Phoebe's delight.

Nequam burst out laughing when he saw the sofa. His laughter ground to a stop when he saw Horrigan frantically shaking his head and making a cut motion across his throat with his hand, but it was too late. Watroc's

9

eyes narrowed and his bottom lip jutted out.

Horrigan helped Phoebe into the sofa and nodded with approval when the daisy-print safety belts secured her in place. Nyx shrugged and settled in next to Phoebe with a wide smile. Horrigan turned to secure Nequam to a large spike behind his chosen spike when Watroc spoke. "Not there ... further down."

With rolling eyes, Nequam moved two spikes down.

"Not there either, still further," Watroc said with a jerk and a puff of steam popped into the air.

"Why? Lyric can you please talk to him!" Nequam whined.

Watroc's head spun around and his jaws snapped as he hissed. "Her name is Phoebe! If you want to fly with PHOEBE and me then go down to the last spike. This is my back, my spikes and *that's* where you can sit."

Horrigan shook his head at Nequam and thumbed towards the last spike at the end of Watroc's tail. "Hop, it's probably about the balance," he said, trying to smooth over the seating arrangements.

Nequam's lips were tight and his jaw clenched as he took his place at the last spike. "Balance my butt," he muttered.

Horrigan secured him with his magical dust and returned to his own spike in front of the sofa and announced, "Ready to go."

Watroc nodded and stretched out his wings; a few rough grey barnacles were flung aside and bounced against the cobblestones. He craned his neck into the sky. "We will travel through Drakmere," he announced.

"We don't need to go via Drakmere, that's the long way," Nequam yelled from the bottom of the tail and pointed in a different direction.

Watroc wagged his tail viciously like a dog shaking water from his coat. The momentum tossed Nequam from side to side until he was gasping and groaning for the dragon to stop. With both arms he clung to the spike, muttering about keeping his teeth.

"I know the way to Bylleraz, and I have decided to fly through Drakmere," Watroc said.

"Besides, we will need water for his wing chambers," Phoebe told Nyx in a chatty voice.

"Water for his wing chambers, what do you mean?" Horrigan asked as he twisted and craned his neck to see Phoebe. His eyes went wide.

"Oh it's so much fun. You'll see," Phoebe replied, flicking her hair over her shoulder with a laugh.

The dragon flapped his wings a few times and launched into the air. Within minutes, Watroc and his passengers were just a tiny speck in the sky and in a blink of the eye they vanished.

Dragons, you see, have their own doorways from one world to another.

2

They soared through blue skies dotted with cotton-ball clouds. In the distance white snow-capped mountains stretched into the horizon and below was a sea of forest with different shades of green, waving and winking as they flew overhead. Rivers and streams snaked around valleys and meadows covered in pinpricks of colourful flowers. The sun was bright and the air almost seemed aglow with sunshine. Drakmere was beautiful but as Rig, a warrior from Sandustian often said, *don't trust anything in Drakmere.*

Phoebe leaned over the side of the ugly pink sofa and screamed "I DON'T SEE IT!" She peered around and into the distance; she blinked rapidly to clear the water from her eyes. Her voice sounded wobbly from the wind.

Watroc swung his head from left to right. "It is coming, up over that hill."

"What are we looking for?" Horrigan yelled as he craned his neck. His head snapped left and right – he didn't want to miss a thing.

Nyx hung over the edge of the sofa as she too stared into the distance.

Nequam yelled from the bottom of the tail, "This is so stupid. We do not have time for detours. We could almost have been there already if we had gone *my* way. Why are we listening to a lizard?"

Watroc dipped his head and growled. His eyes narrowed and a thin green flame jetted out of his nostrils in a steady stream.

"We are looking for Lake Therror," Phoebe yelled into the wind.

"There is a lake called *Therror*?" Nyx asked Horrigan with raised eyebrows.

"I do not know; this is my first time in Drakmere," Horrigan shot back.

"You have never been to Drakmere before ... seriously?" Nyx screeched at Horrigan.

"Well ... have you?" Horrigan yelled back and glared at her until she looked away.

"Um, Watroc, what kind of creatures live in a lake called Therror?" Nyx asked with a shake of her head.

"Terrifying creatures," Watroc snorted.

"Wonderful," Horrigan muttered.

"Don't worry, we will look after you! This is practically Watroc's home ground ... and we only saw two scary monsters in the lake. They called us 'meat sticks.' They fled in fear after they realised who he was. They raced away when Watroc threatened to eat them." Phoebe said, and she threw her head back and laughed.

"I bet he was *really* scary," Nequam said and rolled his watering eyes.

"Scary enough for the monsters in the lake called Therror, so I would be more careful of what I say if I were you!" Nyx snapped. She drummed her fingers on the sofa's arm rest, her nerves shot with the prospect of landing at Lake Therror.

"I see it Watroc! It's to the right," Phoebe screamed and pointed.

The bright blue spot grew larger as they flew closer; the surface sparkled and twinkled like diamonds glittering in the sun. The water had small little waves with white crests dipping and diving.

Nyx and Horrigan leaned to their right, stretching to see the lake in the distance.

Watroc dipped sharply to the left. His tail whipped violently, making Nequam screech as he clung to the spike on the tail with both arms.

"Right, hard right," yelled Phoebe, jabbing her finger in the opposite direction.

13

"Oh ... right." He dipped to the right, twisting his body so that his tail snapped the other way.

Nequam screamed and grabbed the spike.

"Oops. Wrong direction ... my bad ... is *Quamie* still with us?" Watroc asked almost hopefully, with a jerking movement which made everyone bounce in their seats. Watroc was laughing.

Nyx twisted around and saw Nequam draped around the spike. His head nodded and drooped to his chin. "He is still there, barely holding on ... looks a bit green. I think he is going to get sick."

"DO NOT get sick on me!" Watroc roared and pulled his lips back.

"I am glad we are landing. I am quite thirsty and a stretch of the legs would be welcome," Horrigan said as he gazed at the blue, shimmering lake.

"Watroc needs to fill his water chambers but that doesn't necessarily involve landing," Phoebe said, her smile wide. The gold specks in her eyes sparkled as if she was waiting for something exciting to happen.

"If we are not landing, then how is he going to fill his chambers?" Nyx asked with a frown. She glanced at Horrigan and then back at Phoebe.

"Can we get off first ... please? I think I am going to be sick," Nequam croaked from the bottom of the tail.

"Are you ready, Phoebe?" Watroc growled.

Phoebe settled back and stretched her hands in the air as if she were on a rollercoaster. "I am ready. Come on Nyx, put your hands in the air, it's more fun that way," she yelled.

Nyx automatically lifted her arms in response to Phoebe's excitement and asked with a little shake of her head, "What's more fun?"

They were so high that Lake Therror looked like a blue saucer beneath them. Without warning Watroc dropped his head and dived straight on a collision course with the water. His wings folded back against his sea green scales.

Horrigan started to scream and Nyx gasped. They were heading towards a direct impact!

"We are going to die," Horrigan mumbled.

Phoebe squealed with delight and laughed.

"AAAAARRRRRGGGGHHHHHH," Nequam screamed.

"Go Watrooooooc!" Phoebe screamed with her arms waving above her head.

Seconds before impact Watroc pulled up and performed a violent belly flop on the water, the impact of the massive belly making the water rise on either side like concrete walls. The dragon bounced like a pebble skipping across a smooth lake. Phoebe squealed with delight and hunched her shoulders in a feeble attempt to stop the water from splashing over and down her back.

Horrigan and Nyx screamed as a wall of water cascaded over them.

Watroc snorted, having a wonderful time was thumping his tail up and down as he relished the feeling of the water's resistance with every blow. Every now and then a weak scream was heard from Nequam as Watroc slammed his tail repeatedly into the water. Watroc skidded and pounded with his tail. The rush of water sounded like turbines. Watroc reared his head into the air and with a loud POP like a plug being pulled from a bathtub, he rose out of the lake and into the sky. Water poured off his scales as they glistened in the sun. The seaweed that trailed at the tips of his wings flapped in the rush of wind.

"Whoop! That was so much fun," Phoebe laughed as she wrung the water from her hair. She shrugged out of her wet jacket and hooked it over the back of the sofa to dry.

Horrigan was silent, his eyes wide and his mouth hanging open as the water ran down his face and arms. His arms were wrapped in a bear hug around a spike and his knuckles were white from his death grip. Nyx was still pressed back into the sofa, her hair plastered across her face, her clothing hung like wet drapes and she opened and closed her mouth, unable to find words. Her arms were still stretched into the air.

Phoebe chatted away as she unclasped Nyx's cloak, wrung water out of it and hung it beside her pink jacket to dry. "That was just brilliant. So unbelievably cool." As she was leaning over the sofa to secure the cloak, she looked for Nequam but not see him. "Watroc, Quamie's gone!" she yelled.

"And just when I thought today could not get any better," Watroc said, a lilt of laughter in his voice.

A thin voice came from beneath Watroc's tail. "Here … I am here." He slowly dragged himself back over the tail. Horrigan's dust rope was unbreakable but the force of the tail slamming against the water had dislodged Nequam until he hung to the side of the tail. He looked bruised and shaken.

"No, it's okay, he is okay, still there," Phoebe said with a sigh.

"Oh yaah ... I am so relieved," Watroc growled.

"Uh Watty, how much flight time do we have before we have to do that again?" Nyx asked, trying to keep her voice soft and casual.

"Oh my water chambers can last a long time. I did not really need the refill, but I know that Phoebe totally loves it, and my name is not *Watty*."

Horrigan hung his head and started muttering to himself.

"Ah ha. Phoebe *totally* loves it." Nyx nodded as if this made complete sense.

"Watroc, you did that just for me? You are just awesome," Phoebe gushed as she leaned forward and patted the only part of Watroc she could reach.

3

Watroc had reached a steady height and headed towards the sun. "The doorway to Bylleraz is in this direction. Not too far."

Nequam groaned but said nothing; he was still hanging onto the tail with no strength to argue. If not for Horrigan's rope of magic dust he would have fallen off by now.

Phoebe narrowed her eyes as she peered into the distance. "Looks like we're heading into a storm. Look at those dark thunder clouds."

The clouds were thick and puffy, billowy and shaped like cauliflower. They were dark grey, almost black in some places. The weather looked ominous and frightening.

Watroc gazed ahead then snorted, "Those are not thunder clouds. Those are shimmers."

"Shimmers?" Nyx sat forward, suddenly very interested. "I have never seen so many in one place before."

Horrigan flexed his muscles and rolled his shoulders as if preparing for a fight.

"What are shimmers?" Nequam yelled weakly from the bottom of the tail.

"So …" Horrigan replied, "there is an evil witch called Wiedzma, and she rules parts of Drakmere from Drakmere castle. And these are her evil, horrible pets."

"That's the evil witch that tried to kill Lyric!" Nequam screamed. "When do we pay *her* a visit?"

"I am starting to like him ... wait ... the feeling just went away. I still do not like him," Watroc muttered.

"Rhed told me about the time the shimmers attacked him and Jeff. He said it was like having a nightmare wide awake. He said it felt like he was being eaten alive, like they were trying to bite, suck and lick his skin off," Phoebe said and then bit her lip.

Watroc slowed down so that they were gliding and only flapped his wings now and then. "We will not be able to pass them unnoticed because they are stationed directly in front of the doorway to Bylleraz," Watroc said.

"I wonder if they are here by chance or if they are guarding the doorway," Nyx said.

"Well," said Horrigan, "Wiedzma *was* working with the dreamons in Torturra; she fled when Angie turned Zorka into a frog. But she might *still* be working with the dreamons, with Zorka gone ..." His purple eyes gleamed as they remained glued on the shimmers ahead.

"What do you think we should do?" Phoebe asked as she gripped the armrest.

Nequam yelled in a muffled voice, "We plough through them like a bulldozer. They will scatter in the path of this ferocious dragon. This huge dragon, with his overactive tail ... I can't take anymore."

"The only other choice is turning around," Watroc said. "The shimmers do not scare me but I don't want to take a chance with Phoebe's safety."

"They have to get through us to get to Phoebe!" Nyx declared.

"I'll be fine, let's go through them," Phoebe said, nodding at Nyx and Horrigan.

Watroc spoke: "We will proceed so prepare for a fast and furious fight. I'll make a dash for the doorway, creating a mist to mask our arrival but cannot do much more without depleting my wing chambers. Maybe we should quickly do another refill?" Watroc asked.

"NO REFILL!" Nyx and Horrigan shouted at the same time.

"We will be through before they know what hit them," Horrigan yelled.

Horrigan opened his fist and a blast of sparkling dust raced to Phoebe and fashioned a silver glittering helmet.

Nyx nodded and with a smile shot her own dust at Phoebe to cover her eyes with round glittering goggles.

"Get ready, warriors." Watroc started to exhale steam through his nostrils, and the air thickened until a heavy mist enveloped them. The mist took on the colour of blue sky, thus camouflaging the dragon and his passengers.

Phoebe moved to the middle of the couch and sat with her legs tucked under her. The sofa safety belts moved with her and strapped her in. With both hands she held onto the straps.

Nyx was standing on the backrest of the sofa. Her dust had anchored her to Watroc and her weapons glittered in her hands.

She looks very cool and I love that corset and those boots! I want to be a warrior like her, Phoebe thought as she gazed up at Nyx.

Horrigan had also risen to his feet and jumped from spine to spine until he was closer to Nequam and in a better position to provide protection for Watroc. His lips were pressed in a thin line and his eyes glowed purple.

Watroc sped up until the ground passing below blurred. Due to the dragon's powerful magic, the mist moved swiftly with him, disguising both dragon and warriors. At the speed they were going, no one could talk.

I think my cheeks are going to pull away from my face, Phoebe thought.

She stared ahead at the dark clouds churning and twisting lazily. Every now and then she saw the pinpricks of red eyes, and she rubbed her arms and shivered. *Ugh, they give me the heebie-jeebies,* she thought.

At the last second Watroc opened his mouth and roared, releasing a mighty green flame that incinerated the shimmers directly in his path. Without slowing down, he shot through the small hole that his flame had just created. The mist evaporated and the shimmers closed around them.

Phoebe, sitting on her sofa, could see the fight from all angles; she watched Watroc snap at the shimmers as they rushed past. Into his mouth the shimmers vanished.

Just then Watroc roared, "ARRRGGGGHHH!"

Without missing a beat in her fight, Nyx yelled, "What's wrong? Have you been bitten already? We've only just started!"

"No one told me the shimmers were so tasty, NO ONE. They were keeping that information away from me on purpose!" Watroc howled.

"Shimmers are tasty?" Phoebe asked with her tongue sticking out.

"They are soft and light … and melt on my tongue, sweet like honey and they taste like ... like ..." Watroc could not find the words.

"Honeycomb?" Phoebe yelled.

"Honeycomb! Nyx hit more my way! I am hungry!" Watroc yelled.

Nyx moved left and right, not pausing, as shimmers exploded around her from the thin glittering blade she sliced through them. Now and then her dust turned into a bat and connected with a shimmer which flew past Watroc. He neatly turned his head and gulped it down.

"YUM," he roared while he snapped at shimmers that came near him.

Nyx twisted and turned on the back of the sofa. A silver boomerang flew from her hand with a flick of her wrist, cutting the shimmers in half and making them evaporate before rushing back into her hand. All the while, she had a bright smile on her face.

Phoebe watched with wide eyes. Nyx did not even seem to be watching for the return of her boomerang – she just knew when to grab it and flick it out again.

"SEND SOME TO ME," Watroc yelled to Nyx.

Phoebe twisted to check on Horrigan and gasped as she watched the warrior somersaulting over a shimmer and slicing it overhead. Horrigan landed on Watroc's back in a crouch before leaping up and running along the length of the dragon's body. While he ran, his blades sliced and dispensed with shimmers on either side. His dust released and reconnected him like a bungee cord allowing him freedom to jump, dive and race around the dragon.

Those shimmers didn't stand a chance against Horrigan. She stretched further until she saw Nequam, who was lying flat on his stomach, still tied to Watroc's tail spikes. Her eyes widened but then she saw Nequam was pretending to be helpless but as the shimmers came in close, he used his legs to fling them closer to Horrigan's ruthless charge.

"WATROC!"

Phoebe whirled around when she heard Nyx scream.

Watroc dropped his head but said nothing.

"WATROC, HAVE YOU SLOWED DOWN?"

"No. Not really," he muttered.

"YOU HAVE! We're working ourselves to death to keep these monsters away and you are SLOWING DOWN TO EAT THEM?" Nyx shouted.

"Oh alright! I like them. They are sugary and I am hungry!" Watroc roared and then promptly snapped at a shimmer which disappeared into his mouth in a flash.

"THE DOORWAY. RIGHT NOW. WATROC," Nyx yelled and stamped her foot on the sofa.

Phoebe flew back against the sofa as Watroc shot forward with a grumble.

"Hold on, we're going through," Nyx yelled to Horrigan and Nequam as they passed through a ring of white clouds.

Phoebe's mouth dropped open as her reflection stared back at her from hundreds of mirrors, big, small and all different shapes. Most of the reflections were green due to Watroc's size. Then just as suddenly the illusion was gone and they pushed through another white cloud ring and straight into Bylleraz.

Phoebe stared around this beautiful world. Snow-capped mountains towered on either side as they flew. "Wow ... it looks a little like Drakmere except for the sky and sun ... odd but pretty, like twilight back home."

The sky was a light purple and high above the sun shone a bright red. The sudden warmth made Phoebe lift her face into the sunshine and smile. She looked down and saw a multicoloured green carpet of treetops that swayed gently in the breeze as if welcoming her to their world.

"Something is wrong," Nequam said.

"What do you mean?" Horrigan asked as he turned around sharply to see if any shimmers had managed to get through.

"There is always a loud GONG that reverberates around Bylleraz when a doorway has been used for entry – be it friend or foe."

"I did not hear a gong," Horrigan said as he rubbed his tattooed chin.

"There *was* no gong."

4

"Jeff? What in fireballs are you doing here?" Madgwick asked, blinking rapidly. He leaned to the side to see if anyone was standing behind Jeff.

Jeff stared at Madgwick. How could this be – he was dead, he was bleeding and DEAD. He shook his head as the thoughts tumbled around his head.

The warrior standing before him looked strong and healthy with no signs of the ghastly trauma he had suffered in the dark chamber of Gridmoor. The blood that had left snail-like trails over his brutalised torso was gone; the puncture wounds from the weapons they had used on him had vanished. He looked exactly as he did the last time Jeff saw him, in the forest when he had given him and Tricket, another student at the warrior academy, some pointers with their training. He was wearing a very loose coarsely woven cream shirt half open. He still wore the tan pants but they were filthy with dark brown and black blotches. His boots were the same boots from when he lay on the slab in Gridmoor. His black hair seemed like it was caked in gel and stood in all directions.

Jeff gasped at Madgwick's startling blue eyes.

Madgwick always had shiny purple eyes, but not anymore. His eyes changed. Madgwick sent his dust to safety when he was captured by the dreamons. And it was the magical dust that gave the warriors their purple shiny eyes.

Madgwick gripped his arm and dragged him forward towards the glow of the fire. "Are you alone?"

23

"Are we dead?" Jeff asked softly as he stumbled after Madgwick, who pulled him forcefully towards the circle of fire.

"He is in shock. Bring him closer to the fire," a familiar voice urged. "Quickly ... you are too far away from the light."

Jeff twitched and inhaled deeply. "Khrow? Is that Khrow?" he gasped he narrowed his eyes in an effort to see further.

"Madgwick! Come NOW!" The abrupt order sounded just like Khrow.

Madgwick moved behind Jeff and pushed him forward forcing the boy to move his legs.

Jeff's feet felt like they were stuck in mud as he staggered forward and moved with the force of Madgwick's momentum.

Madgwick is here and that voice I keep hearing in my mind ... that voice that made me wonder if I was crazy because I was hearing a dead person: That voice is Khrow. Finally it was making sense. *Yes. This proves it. I am dead. I died in the chamber. I saved Rig, Angie, Trezz and Harley just like Ruogh told me I would. But I died doing it.*

Jeff had been told by a magical being that "he would save them all."

When Jeff was attacked and a dreamon placed inside him, he tried to leave in fear that he would lead or grant the dreamons access through the magical barrier that protected Sandustian. So he left his friends and family and by pure chance ended up in a dark, misty swamp where he met the mystical Ruogh. It was a place where magic was created. It had no name, no one could find it and no one was welcome. Even if he tried, Jeff could not give a clear description of Ruogh because all he saw were lights, and a warm feeling of "rightness." Nevertheless Ruogh allowed Jeff entrance into this mysterious magical swamp. There he called for Calidus, a fire dragon who happened to be Jeff's friend, to fetch him. Ruogh told Jeff that he would save *everyone*, but Jeff could not save Madgwick – when they arrived in stone village called Gridmoor, Madgwick already lay dead on the slab. *But* here he was and seemingly alive.

Now, beside the fire, the minute they reached the circle and embraced by the orange glow of the flames, Jeff turned and hugged Madgwick. He was so happy to see the warrior. They hugged like long-lost brothers.

Then Jeff turned away from Madgwick and slammed straight into Khrow. "I am so happy to see you. If I have died then this is the best place to be – with you two," Jeff muttered. Khrow lightly tapped his back then dragged him closer into a bear hug. Now was not the time to be a macho warrior.

"Are you okay?" Khrow asked gruffly. His eyes were a deep brown as he glanced around them as if watching for something or someone to appear.

He looked exactly the same as the last time Jeff had seen him, except he was wearing a light cream shirt, very similar to the one Madgwick wore. His sleeves were ripped off at the shoulders, revealing muscular arms that bulged. His skin was a smooth black that shone in the fire light. The biggest change was that his eyes were brown. Again, this was a change from the shining purple eyes of a warrior. In Khrow's case, his magical dust had left him the day he saved Jeff: To save Jeff's life, Khrow had gifted his dust to the boy in the tunnels of Torturra.

Jeff nodded. "What is goi …" he started to ask but Khrow held his hand up to halt any further questions.

"There's a lot to say and learn but *NOT* now. We are in danger and we have to move. Can you run?" he asked with eyebrows raised at both Madgwick and Jeff.

Jeff nodded and swallowed hard. He stared at Khrow's grim face. Judging by the clenched jaw and firm lips pressed together, things were going to get rough.

"Okay. There's no time to explain everything so listen carefully. We do not have time for questions, so don't ask any. We have to reach the castle sanctuary called Dunargh. I have placed fire stacks at intervals en route to the castle. Right. The fire stacks will give us safety while we are in the fire glow. Each one will be lit before we get there to assist us on this race for survival." Khrow took a steadying breath. "We are running from strange creatures called wuunacks. They will suck you dry within minutes ... the only thing that keeps them away is daylight or the glow of fire. We have to reach the next fire stack before they catch up – and they are fast. If we are caught by the wuunacks, it's over. We are dead." Khrow dropped his head and stared at Madgwick, then Jeff. "That's it in a nutshell ... are you ready?" It was not a question; it was more of a fact.

"What's a wuunack?" Madgwick asked.

"But we are already dead – aren't we?" Jeff asked at the same time.

"What did I just say about questions?" Khrow barked.

Madgwick and Jeff snapped their mouths shut.

"Take a torch; we are going to move fast." He looked at Jeff. "You are the youngest, so stay in-between us and stay on my heels. If anyone falls you keep running; you cannot help them." He paused and then added, "Do not fall."

Madgwick and Jeff nodded and lit their torches. Jeff bit his lip. His eyes darted from Khrow to Madgwick. This was a bit frightening.

Khrow pointed. "We run that way, there is a path but it is narrow. Ready. On three. One-two-three. GO!"

Jeff copied Khrow and held his torch above his head. He did not dare glance over his shoulder at Madgwick but he could hear his footfall. No one said anything but the heavy breathing seemed very loud. As Jeff ran, he caught a slight movement out the corner of his eye, but he did not even try to identify what it was.

There was a loud clicking sound, like crickets, around them.

He kept pace with Khrow and made sure he did not stumble or trip his warrior friends. This was life or death ... again.

After what seemed like forever, Jeff got a stitch in his side. He clenched his teeth and kept pushing his legs. He had no choice but to keep moving.

"Almost there," Khrow yelled.

They stomped around a large boulder and there ahead stood a blazing fire stack about three feet high. They ran into the circle of the glow and stopped. Jeff dropped the torch and bent over with his hands on his knees as he tried to catch his breath. Madgwick patted him on his back but he was also breathing heavily.

Madgwick gazed into the darkness to try and see what was chasing them.

Khrow turned in a circle also peering into the darkness. "Just a few minutes to catch our breath and then we are moving to the next one. Get ready."

No one spoke as they struggled to control their ragged breathing.

Jeff swallowed repeatedly, trying to get ready for the next dash.

Staring into the darkness, he squinted when he saw a flicker of movement, but it was too dark and he couldn't make out what moved but it seemed huge ... or a lot of whatever it was.

He glanced at Madgwick and saw him staring in the same direction.

Madgwick turned and met his eyes. He pulled his lips as if he wanted to say something but there wasn't really anything to say.

Khrow lit the new torches and handed them out. He pointed in a direction that led them further into the forest. "Are we ready? That way. Come on ... another run. Do not lose focus."

They were sprinting again. Jeff kept his focus on Khrow's broad back and tried to match his strides with his. The warrior never slowed down and he held his torch high above him. The trees flashed past Jeff as he ran but he took no notice – he ran.

"Torch up," Madgwick gasped, making Jeff realise he was dropping his torch.

He shoved his arm up into the air and was shocked to notice a black wave of movement surge beside him like a raging river. Shadows were all to be seen, but he could hear the loud clicking and screeching. He knew they were there and those creatures were watching him, just waiting for him to drop the torch again.

Jeff was dimly aware they were out of the forest: no more ferns brushing his legs as he ran and there was the crunch of stones under his shoes. He kept his focus on Khrow and tried to match his movements and direction changes from the warrior. He was aware of Madgwick right behind him and knew the warriors could go faster but were pacing themselves to him. He pushed himself harder.

His stitch was back and he battled to keep the torch above his head, almost stumbling. Just when Jeff thought he could not take another step, the darkness was broken with a blazing fire stack just like the one before.

Jeff fell to his knees and retched with dry heaves. He clutched his side.

Khrow circled round them. He was hardly breathing hard.

Madgwick, like Jeff, was breathing heavily but then in all fairness, he was recently tortured.

"The next stop is at Dunargh. We get past those gates and we will be safe," Khrow said and held his hand out to haul Jeff to his feet. "This is the last one. Have you got one more sprint in you? Come on ... after everything you have gone through ... you're going to let this bring you down? No! So, one more. Dig deep and let's go." He turned to Madgwick. "The last stretch is through a field. The ground is uneven. We must be careful not to fall."

Madgwick nodded as he took the torches that had been left next to the blaze and rammed them into the fire. They burst into flame. He gave one to Jeff and one to Khrow.

"Almost there. Let's do this," he muttered.

Jeff held his torch in front of him, dragged in a breath, straightened up and gave a single nod.

Khrow turned and pointed in the direction they were heading towards. "Over the field and before you know it, the castle gates will be there. They will open when they see us coming."

"Khrow," Madgwick said softly, "something's out there, but I can't

28

just see what they are."

Khrow grunted. "They are all here now. Our element of surprise is gone so one wrong move and they will be all over us. We will be toast. One more thing ... if one of us falls, keep going. Nothing can be done for the fallen because it will already be too late." He looked at Jeff and then at Madgwick, gave a nod and then said, "On three."

They were running again but this was the last stretch, which somehow gave them more energy. Jeff was in front this time and he kept his focus on his feet. He felt something next to him keeping pace. He knew it was neither Madgwick nor Khrow. He knew that if he turned to look, he would see teeth grinning at him ... so he did not look.

"Almost there," Khrow grunted from behind.

Almost there almost there, Jeff thought frantically. Then it happened ... he glanced to the side ... and yes. There was a mountain of shiny blankness ... so close to his face. *SHIMMERS!* Jeff tripped over a stone and tumbled to the ground, rolling over stones and grass. His torch flew to the side away from him. He opened his mouth to scream but he had no air in his lungs.

"JEFF!" Madgwick screamed.

"Noooo Madgwick – keep going," Khrow shouted and forced Madgwick to keep moving. Madgwick could not fight against the brute force of Khrow dragging him away from Jeff.

Jeff heard them run ... the sounds of their footfall moved further and further away. He could hear Madgwick saying "Jeff – Jeff – Jeff."

Then he was covered in hard things that seemed to be crawling all over him, like a carpet. He opened his lips to scream and within seconds, his mouth was filled with a hard crunchy substance. He spluttered and spat as the creatures tried to force their way into his mouth and nose. He could not breathe. The creatures moved around and beneath – so many that he felt himself lifted off the ground to be carried away like ants with their meal prize. When he felt the creatures crawling over his eyes, he squeezed his eyes shut. He brushed them away from his face and ears but there were too many.

In the distance he heard Madgwick screaming his name.

Jeff felt strangely calm. He was not being bitten as with the shimmers, which felt like your skin was been sucked off. And it was not as terrifying as the screatures with strings of black cloth trailing off them like mummy monsters.

His only thought was of his fiery friend, Calidus. He opened his eyes; the world was black as if he was blind.

"Calidus." He whispered the fire dragon's name as if the name itself would bring him comfort at the end.

Something strange happened. The whispered name had an immediate effect. The racing around him slowed and Jeff felt the ground beneath him. His fingers clawed the sand and grass. He pushed to his knees. Creatures were still hanging onto him.

"Calidus," he whispered again.

The creatures fell off him and scurried across the floor around him, darting in and out as the monsters tried to reclaim their prey.

Jeff frowned and then said the name again: "Calidus." And then he was standing. A veil lifted from his eyes. It was still dark but he could see.

He glanced around and saw his torch lying on the ground. The flame flickered and teased and then winked out.

He looked around trying to see the creatures swarming around. A large black object shot across the floor at him.

"Calidus!" he shouted and braced for impact but it veered away at the last minute.

They couldn't touch him when he spoke the dragon's name … Jeff turned in a circled and looked beyond the sea of black shining creatures.

"Calidus," he said again and the blackness shuffled and churned – away from him.

In the distance he saw a towering structure with a glowing light. Dunargh.

Taking a step forward, he muttered the dragon's name again. *They almost seem like beetles*, Jeff thought as the blackness moved with him.

Why could the blackness not touch him, and how did this have to do with Calidus?

I'm not sure how this works but be afraid, be very afraid of my dragon friend, he thought.

"Calidus," he said again and watched as the beetle-creatures recoiled.

Jeff took a step at a time, calling out the dragon's name when the beetles inched forward. He edged closer to the large wall looming in front of him.

The black beetle-like creatures moved with him ... step for step.

When he reached the wall, he shouted, "KHROW!"

Something hit his head from behind. He staggered to the ground in a daze. Another blow hit the back of his head, causing him to hunch and squeeze his eyes shut. White pain blasted through his head.

In the distance, he heard a voice whisper, so soft it sounded like a train receding.

Find me boy ... come find me.

Then the faint whisper was replaced by shouting. Madgwick?

He heard shouts beyond the wall. "It's Jeff. It's Jeff! Open the gate, bring the torches. Jeff, we're coming!"

He could hardly open his eyes from the blinding pain in his head.

A wooden gate opened slightly and it was as if the sun had just risen. Surrounded by the glow of light, he was hauled to his feet. With his arms hanging over shoulders, his feet scraped across the dirt as he was dragged towards the crack of the door.

The gate slammed shut behind them with a loud thunk.

5

Jeff was dragged through the gates; he left trail marks on the dirt road as his shoes scraped the gravel. He blinked at the faces as they gathered around him. Everyone was asking questions, all talking at the same time but he could not make out what they were saying. His head hurt. He tried to find his footing but could not gain his balance.

"Give him space. Give him space. SILENCE!" Khrow yelled. "Give the boy a chance to breathe. He will answer all our questions, but let him recover. There is time, okay?"

Khrow's yell for silence was met with grumbles and muttering as everyone lowered their voices to hushed tones. Hands flew left and right as they talked and whispered amongst each other.

Jeff's knees buckled and Madgwick tightened his grip, keeping him on his feet although not quite standing.

"Fireballs, I thought I lost you!" Madgwick muttered.

Jeff wobbled as he was finally able to stand. He lifted his hand to his head and stared at the bright red blood on his fingers.

Suddenly Jeff was spun around by his shoulders and hoisted into the air like a rag doll. Khrow inspected him while holding him in the air.

"Check, Madgwick ... has he got everything ... arms, legs," Khrow ordered.

"He has everything he arrived with and a lot more courage than most," Madgwick confirmed.

"Count his fingers!" A thin voice cried out.

"And his ears! Those nasty things sucked Jigsaw's ear right off," another exclaimed loudly.

Jeff tried to see who was talking. *Sucked Jigsaw's ears right off ... seriously ... Jigsaw?* he thought groggily.

Khrow seemed to be happy with his inspection and pulled Jeff into a bear hug. "I thought you were gone – after all this time of trying to keep you alive, I could not believe I would lose you to this place when you were so close to me." He muttered softly so that only Jeff and Madgwick could hear.

Khrow tilted his head to peer at Jeff's wound; a trail of blood gushed through Jeff's brown hair and down his neck.

"You are hurt. Someone bring me supplies. Sit, Jeff." He led Jeff to a grass patch aglow in lantern light.

Jeff reached up to touched his head where it hurt, but Madgwick slapped Jeff's hand away. The simple motion seemed so like Madgwick, such a normal action from the warrior that Jeff's lips twitched.

"Don't touch it, it will get infected," Madgwick scolded and clucked his tongue. He took the bag of supplies that had been deposited next to him and rummaged through it, pulling out a little red cloth and a small bottle of white liquid. He rolled his eyes. "This bag is pathetic; I miss my satchel with everything you could possibly need to cure any ailment or injury."

"Your bag also included frog vomit and snail snot ... and other disgusting potions. I don't miss any of those," Jeff muttered with his eyes closed.

Madgwick dabbed Jeff's head while Khrow hunched down in front of him and asked the questions everyone wanted answered.

"Jeff, I know your head hurts, but this is really a matter of life and death. How did you get away without being eaten?" Khrow asked.

Jeff could hardly move his head as Madgwick inspected his gushing wound; his eyes darted from face to face as they stared and waited for the answers. Some of the men had raised eyebrows as if keen to hear, but many stood with furrowed foreheads, straight lips and narrowed eyes as if annoyed that Jeff had managed to escape the wuunacks.

I don't know ... but these guys do not look friendly to me. They look angry. I don't know why Calidus's name kept those things away but I don't want to tell anyone about that right now. I'll tell Khrow and Madgwick later, he thought.

Jeff winced as Madgwick tapped his head and then said out loud, "I really don't know ... I thought I was a goner for sure, but I seemed to repel those things ... whatever they are. Then something hit me over the head."

The muttering and grumbling picked up at Jeff's words.

"Repelled them ... how?" someone behind Khrow whispered.

Jeff closed his eyes as Madgwick dabbed and brushed his head wound so he could not see who was asking.

"Not normal. This is not normal – I don't like this," someone else said and there were murmurs of agreement.

Jeff winced again and glared at Madgwick.

"Sorry Jeff, I am done." He turned to Khrow. "Looks like a surface wound. If we keep it dry, it should heal quickly. He is so pale that his freckles look like dots of ink. Also, all the dreamon veins are gone."

"Gone? We will talk later about that." Khrow stared at his feet as he nodded.

Groups of men huddled together as they whispered and pointed at Jeff.

Jeff ignored them and rubbed his face as if he could erase the ink-like freckles and glanced around at the buildings that surrounded the soft dark green patch of grass where he was sitting. The grass was so soft it tickled his hands. He could not see much through the crowd of men standing around him but nearby was a large tree covered in fist-sized fruit. The fruit looked yellow but it could just be the reflection from the lanterns hanging from the branches. Surrounding the grass were blocks of cream and grey stone walls with moss and ferns growing through the cracks. Lanterns and torches lined the walls, providing a soft golden glow. Some of the interior walls had crumbled and seemed to sneak into the shadows. Stones lay scattered on the ground. It looked like they were inside a fortress or a castle ruin. He looked up and breathed in the air sweetened by lemon blossoms. The black sky above was really odd and almost alien, and the dull yellow moon was so big it seemed flood the sky.

So close I could almost touch it, Jeff thought as he stared at the moon.

Beyond the moon were millions of pinpricks of stars ... but not white and twinkly as he was used to back home. The pinpricks were bright yellow and orange.

"Wow ... so this is where we end up when we die – in a castle of sorts. I kinda had a different vision in mind. And I somehow didn't think I would be running from something that wanted to kill me again," Jeff said to Khrow as he gazed around him.

"Die? Oh we are not dead Jeff, and neither are you," Khrow muttered as he looked around at the faces staring at Jeff and frowned as if he had also picked up that some of these faces were not all happy-to-see-you-alive faces.

Jeff snapped around to face Khrow, his nose wrinkling at the pain from the sudden movement. "What do you mean we're not dead? I saw you. I saw both of you and you were both dead. Sorry. But you were. Dead."

Khrow, a Sandustian warrior, had long ago saved Jeff from a dreamon attack but in the process was fatally injured by the dreamon monster. Then somehow the dreamons opened the gates of Torturra, a hidden land protected by fire. Jeff and Khrow fell through the gates ahead of a dreamon attack party. This land was so lethal that even the air would have turned Jeff into ash within seconds. And so, knowing he was not going to make it, Khrow used his dust to protect Jeff. Indeed, Khrow "gifted" his magical dust to Jeff to keep him alive until he was found and rescued by other Sandustian warriors.

Jeff was there when Khrow died.

So Jeff ended up being stuck in this beautiful and vivid world where everything was fire, from the green flames that formed leaves to the blue licks of flame that made up the feathers of the birds that chirped and darted from tree to tree. Everything was on fire yet nothing was destroyed. That is when he met and made friends with Calidus, a bad tempered fire dragon with short-term memory loss – bad news for those the dragon did not remember.

Khrow laughed but it was not the kind of hearty laugh that invited others to laugh along. It seemed bitter and strange. "Yet here we are. You are right – we *were* dead ... *there*. But not here, in *this* world, where we are alive. I thought I would be trapped here forever but then Madgwick showed up and a few hours later you did."

Madgwick brushed his hair off his forehead and said, "It's hard to understand. I can hardly figure it out myself. I arrived in this strange place to find Khrow waiting for me. Then he said someone else was coming, so we waited – and *you* arrived. What happened in the chamber?" Madgwick asked.

Khrow glanced around and hushed Madgwick with a movement of his hand. "We will talk about that later." He murmured and gave a small nod.

Jeff released his pent-up breath and stretched his eyes at Khrow. He did not want to talk about the chamber or Calidus in front of everyone either. Something seemed off here. Maybe he was wrong but not everyone seemed happy to see him alive.

Khrow sat down beside Jeff and passed him some water in a roughly carved wooden cup.

The others settled on the grass. At a rough count there were about fifteen men.

Keep it neutral, Jeff thought.

"What are those things?" Jeff asked as he wiped his mouth with his sleeve. The water was the sweetest he had even had.

"We don't really know – we call them *wuunacks* but their real names or how they got here is about as big a mystery as how *we* got here. They feed in the dark, so if you get caught away from the light at night you will be taken. This is the only safe place we know of," Khrow said.

"Taken?" Madgwick asked with raised eyebrows.

"Painfully," Khrow said with a nod.

"And this?" Madgwick asked.

"This is the only refuge in this whole place. It's called Dunargh although no one knows how it got that name. We know that for some reason the wuunacks cannot penetrate these walls or gate. It is amazing here. It's one of the most beautiful and tranquil places I have ever been to. Green and luscious with waterfalls, mountains, mist and glorious sunshine during the day. Water is fresh and sweet and food is of abundance. It's paradise with everything you could possibly ask for ... except for the wuunacks that come out at night. Once darkness falls you'd better be in Dunargh or you won't make it through the night. Don't actually know if there are any other predators in area and surrounding forests. It's only the wuunacks to be watchful of. That we know of."

"How did you know someone was coming?" Madgwick asked.

Jeff held his head as he sat, with his pounding headache he was quite happy to just listen to the questions and answers.

One of the men sitting on the grass closest to them spoke up. He scratched his red beard. His nose looked like it had a small balloon embedded in the tip. His shaggy long reddish-brown hair was tied behind his head. His clothing was brown and looked like leather. His eyes were a startling blue. "There is one who resides in the forest," he started.

"This is Srat. He has been here the longest," Khrow said and waved for Srat to continue.

Srat stared at Khrow for a moment and then went on, "He foretold that an arrival is due when the sky is brushed with yellow and orange streaks. It does not happen often. Khrow saw the sky turn, so we went and set up a light trail with fire stacks. The arrival location is always the same place – just inside the forest beyond. We don't normally fetch a newcomer as that is their fate to bear. If they make their way here then they are welcomed. If not … well that used to be the rule here," Srat said with a shrug and glanced at the nods among the others.

Madgwick's eyebrows lifted at Srat's tone.

"It caused a bit of a stir when the sky did not shimmer down – first time ever there were two arrivals within hours of each other. It was starting to get dark so I was not about to leave a newcomer on their own out there at night. It would have been murder," Khrow said with a shake of his head.

Another Dunargh inhabitant spoke up, "He was devastated when he thought he might have lost you. There's something different about you," the man said.

Jeff peered at the speaker; he sat towards the back of the group but had a large floppy hat which hid his features. The man kept his hand over his mouth.

"I don't know anything about that but Khrow and I have a history," Jeff said. He was a little groggy and sleepy but continued, "I cannot tell you why or how I got away but when Khrow spoke to me, it calmed me down. Then something hit me over the head … twice," Jeff said.

Even before he died, Khrow had an ability to speak to others through telepathy. It was not easy do but he had that gift. After he died, he often spoke to Jeff when he was in a tough situation. Jeff could never understand how he managed to hear Khrow but was always grateful with the knowledge Khrow was watching over him.

Khrow turned to look at Jeff with a frown. "I didn't talk to you tonight."

"I heard you." Jeff frowned as he tried to remember the voice. "It was you."

"No, Jeff … it was not me." Khrow's eyebrows were almost touching.

The man in the large floppy hat gasped and pointed between Jeff and Khrow. "*He* can talk to *you* … with his *mind*?"

"What did the voice say?" Madgwick asked, not giving Jeff a chance to respond to the man in the hat.

"Uhmmm ... something – called me boy," Jeff said and then he frowned. "No wait ... it was ... actually I am not a hundred per cent sure."

"Who would be able to talk to him here – and who hit him over the head?" Madgwick asked Khrow as if he had all the answers in this strange new place.

"I know," one of the men leaning against the tree said while he inspected his dirty fingernails. He did not even look up as he spoke. His features were in shadows.

"Who?" Khrow asked.

"It's that seer. He claims to be able to foretell the future," a Dunargh man grunted.

"And the past," someone else muttered and shook his head.

"And the present," another chimed in and everyone nodded and grumbled.

"Where does he stay?" Madgwick asked.

"We don't know and we don't care. He is such an annoying individual that we have banned him from living with us in Dunargh. He just causes havoc and we all wanted to murder him. He is the only one who would be able to communicate like that. The last person he was able to talk to was taken by the wuunacks."

"He wasn't that bad. I think he was just trying to improve on things," muttered the man in the floppy hat sitting right at the back and almost out of the glow of the lanterns. His voice was nasal.

Khrow shook his head. "I never met him; he was gone from here before I arrived. I assumed he had died from the wuunacks when you banished him to his fate. But why would he hit Jeff and then whisper in his thoughts ... he could have just spoken to him."

Jeff rubbed his temple with two fingers. His headache was getting worse.

Khrow gripped Jeff's shoulder and gave a little tap. "Let's call it a night. Tomorrow we can discuss what happened in the Gridmoor chamber, and other matters."

Jeff didn't even bother to find a spot; he toppled over and fell asleep, vaguely aware of someone covering him with a blanket.

6

Jeff leaned over the wall and stared down at the blue-grey waves crashing and tumbling over the dark jagged rocks like shards of black glass. The wall felt like sandpaper on his hands. The deep blue sea was endless like a clear photo of blue sea upon blue skies and no horizon. It seemed he was in a rundown castle perched on the very edge of a cliff. He walked around on the narrow pathway along the top of the castle wall. The breeze flirted around him and Jeff inhaled the fresh, salty sea air. As he navigated the wall, he had to leap over gaping holes, and he wondered what battle had left these scars. It was early and the sun was still painting the morning sky with hues of yellow and orange. He reached the other side of the wall and gazed into the distance, away from the sea. As far as he could see was dark forest, almost like the forests back home. Like a green swaying carpet. In the distance was a mountain range, almost grey-blue, so far off it was. The peaks were huge but not snow-capped like the mountains in Drakmere.

As he gazed at the mountains and the forest below, he caught a sharp flash out the corner of his eye. He squinted as he focused, sure he saw a light blink, like a mirror flashing from the sun. Something or someone was out there. He concentrated on that particular point when he heard his name called from within the castle.

With a final glance at the trees he hurried back to where Khrow and Madgwick were waiting.

"How's your head?" Madgwick asked as Jeff joined them. It seemed they were the only ones awake.

"It's fine, a little sore but the headache is gone – all good." Jeff grinned and ducked from Madgwick's fingers as he tried to part Jeff's hair to see for himself.

Khrow had a platter of fruit and nuts. The fruits were red and round and had a very tough skin which Jeff had to pull off with his teeth. Inside was a fleshy creamy texture so juicy he had to wipe away rivers of sap that ran down his chin.

"This is good!" Jeff spoke with his mouth full. He was hungry.

Khrow and Madgwick sat at a little wooden table under a large leafy tree that threw a huge circle of shade over the entire area. The shapes Jeff noticed last night were bright yellow and green fruit, like lemons.

"You seem a bit better. Your freckles don't look like they are popping off your face anymore," Khrow said as he studied Jeff in his new clothing. The cream shirt had a thin rope tying the front together. The sleeves were too long but Jeff had rolled them back, and the brown pants were held up by a drawstring. Everything was too big but it was all they had. Jeff could not stay in his lightning-singed clothing, burned, tattered and torn. His T-shirt was totally caked with blood from the blow from his head.

Jeff looked around for the other inhabitants of the castle and was surprised to see they were alone. *Great, we can talk freely*, he thought.

"Everyone has something that needs to be done; they will be back later or before nightfall," Khrow said when he noticed Jeff looking around with raised eyebrows.

Madgwick held his hand as if to stay the conversation. "First – news of Sandustian – did Trezz deliver the message … was Sandustian saved?" Madgwick, still in the dark about this outcome, asked.

Khrow held up his hand. "Madgwick filled me in on the mission from his point of view while we were waiting in the forest for the next arrival. I know Calidus. I have seen him in my visions when he was rescuing you from the nothingness. But who is Trezz? Is he the dreamon who tried to help you?" Khrow asked.

42

Jeff nodded and then continued, "We were lucky Trezz found us because the dreamon inside me was blocking the reverse beacon spell, so we didn't even know how to get to Gridmoor. Trezz whispered something to Rig and suddenly they stopped fighting. That's when he told us of the planned attack on Sandustian. I don't know if Sandustian was saved but Calidus sent an urgent message to Azghar and Watroc. Angie said it was out of our hands and that we had to move forward to find you."

Khrow nodded and then patted Madgwick's arm. "Azghar and Watroc would have answered the call. No doubt. Azghar is very fond of Sandustian. And Watroc will never let anything happen to Phoebe."

"Then? What happened in the chamber, Jeff? How did you end up here?" Madgwick asked.

"Well ... where do I begin?" Jeff said.

"The shortest version." Khrow placed his elbows on his knees as he leaned forward to rest his chin on his fists.

"We arrived in Gridmoor and were devastated to find you had died." Jeff shook his head as he thought back. "Angie took it badly. I thought she was going to explode! And Trezz – I have never seen anyone so angry as when he saw you lying on that slab. He was wicked, Khrow – just wicked. He killed dreamons just by looking at them – he dissolved into smoke."

"Smoke ... who is this warrior?" Khrow looked at Madgwick.

"Trezz is a Nytezard. He was captured by Uzas a long time ago and apparently I cracked the dreamon bond with an act of mercy in the Little Falls cemetery. Long story."

"A Nytezard!!! You befriended a Nytezard?" Khrow's elbows slipped off his knees.

Jeff carried on, "Then Uzas released lightning, which struck everyone down. I have or *had* a dreamon in me who said that the lightning would not affect me – so I intercepted the lightning and pulled the bolts away from Angie, Rig and Trezz, which helped them to escape." Jeff played with a soft twig as he spoke, tying it into a knot.

43

"The black veins are gone, but can you still hear the dreamon inside of you, can you sense if he is there?" Madgwick asked.

"He was with me until I took all the lightning – after that I have not heard from him again. And the elders had blocked my dream catcher ability so I could not use that. Anyway that's how I died. Saving everyone just as Ruogh told me I would."

Madgwick's and Khrow's mouths dropped open.

"Ruogh?" Khrow asked.

"Never heard of him," Madgwick countered.

"Well, he knew Calidus. He called Calidus to fetch me after the dreamon attack and put me into some kind of trance-sleep state. Calidus said he did some kind of spell that bound us together. That's how I was able to survive the fire when Calidus tried to fry the dreamons and screatures but got me instead."

"Calidus tried to fry you … dreamons and screatures?"

"It's part of the longer version." Jeff scratched his head.

Madgwick leaned over and slapped Jeff's hand away from his head wound.

"You survived Calidus's fire, which can only mean you have dragon fire in your veins. Maybe that's why the wuunacks could not touch you. Maybe that is the answer – no one has ever been able to repel the wuunacks before."

"I said 'Calidus' and they moved away. I didn't want to say this in front of everyone," Jeff said with a sniff.

"That voice that you heard outside the gates. Some of the people here think it's the seer who lives somewhere in the forest. We don't know how he keeps the wuunacks at bay, but he was ousted from this place before I arrived. I think he was a bit difficult," Khrow said.

"Can you remember what he said?" Madgwick asked with a raised eyebrow.

Jeff shook his head. "It happened so fast and I honestly thought it was

Khrow."

"We will have to find out what he wants. Maybe we can find a way out of here – back home," Khrow said.

Jeff's lips turned up. "I am sure I heard Calidus say something just before I left – it's on the tip of my tongue but I can't remember what it is either."

"We need to find this seer. He may have the answers."

"Jeff, concentrate – can you try and talk with him … try now?" Madgwick urged.

Jeff closed his eyes and concentrated on hearing the slightest sound. He waited. *Hello ... are you there* … he thought but heard nothing – just silence. "Nothing. I will keep trying."

"Can you access your dream catcher abilities now?" Madgwick asked as he plucked grass.

"No, I already tried." Jeff sighed.

They spent some time poring over a crude map that Khrow had drawn up during his stay there, trying to figure out where the seer would be. Jeff filled in the blanks with regards to his dreamon carry on. Madgwick laughed when he heard how Angie sat in her deck chair and gave him fighting instructions.

Jeff noticed that Khrow was very quiet when he spoke of using the dust. *He must miss his dust. I wonder if it's a punch in the gut to hear about his dust working for someone else. I will ask Madgwick.*

Jeff bit his lip. He had an idea but they were not going to like it. "I think I know how to contact the seer … he spoke to me when the wuunacks were around me – so maybe I should head out of the gates tonight and see if he will talk to me again."

"Jeff – are you mad? Calidus's protection may not work again. I totally forbid it," Madgwick said and shook his head. He stood up and walked in circles.

Khrow stared at Jeff and narrowed his eyes as he studied Jeff. "Have you had any success with trying to contact him today?"

Jeff pressed his lips together in a thin straight line and shook his head.

"Then I think you may have a point and it's something to consider." Khrow nodded.

"That's madness – he cannot go back out there!" Madgwick said with his hands on his hips.

Khrow stood up and turned in a slow circle and spoke in a low voice. "I know – I know but really Madgwick, what choice is there? It's that or stay here forever and it's not really forever because sooner or later you lose something within you and then wander out to the wuunacks or walk clean off the cliff on the other side of this castle." He waved his hands around at the ruins that had been turned into makeshift rooms. "They all want to find a way back home, but slowly yet surely they lose that drive and become complacent and *happy* where they are. When *that* happens, soon nothing makes sense anymore and then they end it. That is how it is here. I have never lost hope of finding a way out and you will not either! This seer left the compound a long time ago. I think there was a disagreement or something and he was ordered to leave but apparently he always spoke of visions. I never met him so I can't tell you anything more about him. But he *has* made contact with Jeff. We need to try it. We have to find a way out of here."

7

Just then a few men came striding through the gate. No one spoke and their glare was fixed on Khrow. Their faces were dark like thunder, scowls pulled at their features and they looked like they had been sucking on lemons. A few men broke off and headed into a side door and disappeared out of sight. The man with the red shaggy hair and red balloon-like nose didn't miss a step as he purposely strode towards Khrow. He stared directly at Khrow and ignored Jeff and Madgwick completely.

Khrow nodded at the man as he approached. "I am not sure if you were introduced properly last night. This is Srat."

"Khrow … we need to show you something we found in the forest – it has been taken into the basement. Come." He pointed to a small entrance into which the other men scurried.

Khrow got up and walked away, disappearing through the dark doorway.

Madgwick and Jeff sat on the grass, talking about his fighting skills and dust.

Five minutes later, a thin scrawny man hopped out of the doorway and almost ran to them. "Uhhh … Magic … Khrow says he needs you to come to the basement – needs your help with something … I think that's what he said."

"The name is Madgwick – not Magic." Madgwick rose effortlessly to his feet. He beckoned to Jeff to come with him but the thin man plopped down next to Jeff with a grin and said. "I will keep him company – so …

you are called Jeff," he said and stretched his legs out in front of him as he leaned back on his arms.

Madgwick frowned but made his way to the dark doorway. He kept looking back as if something was puzzling him.

Jeff stared at Madgwick as he disappeared into the darkness. *Something is off with these guys – they are separating us,* he thought.

Srat appeared and seemed as if he had just gone through a tornado. His leather clothing was torn and hanging skew. His hair was half undone and his lip was broken. His nose was bleeding and seemed bent out of proportion. The wooden bench sagged beneath his weight. He leaned forward with his elbows on his knees as he stared at Jeff.

"So … here is the thing. This is not personal and it does not mean we don't like you. But we don't like you. You arrived and everything changed. You are the only one to survive the wuunacks and now we hear you also got a message from the seer. We don't want your sort here. If you value your friends' lives then you must leave now. Right now."

Jeff's mouth dropped open. "They will never let me leave," he stammered.

"Which is exactly why they are staying locked up in the basement until you are gone. You must leave right now," he said with a curt nod as if all had been finalised.

"Where would I go?" Jeff asked.

"We don't know and we don't care but you cannot stay here – if you stay here then we will all die – we are convinced of this. Please." Srat almost looked desperate as if he truly believed Jeff was about to cause danger to rain onto everyone there.

Jeff saw he was surrounded. He looked at each one of the men who stood in front of him and not one would meet his gaze.

"I don't understand – you think I'm a threat?" Jeff asked with a frown.

"Yes, to everyone here. The seer spoke to you and the wuunacks could not touch you – that is something different and we don't do different – that is how we have stayed alive so long. We stick to what works, and that is not you. Please leave. If you value your friends and their lives, then you will leave. We are not asking."

"Can … can I talk with Madgwick and Khrow first?" Jeff asked.

Srat pursed his lips and shook his head. "No. We will explain once you are far away. Of course they will be angry but they will not be able to follow you. In the end they will understand that it's in everyone's best interests. Let's go." Srat stood up and pulled Jeff to his feet, leaving him no choice but to stand.

"But … but …" Jeff started. He glanced at the doorway, hoping to see Khrow and Madgwick. But they were not there.

He stumbled backwards as a large brown cloth bag was shoved into his chest with a gruff "Here, some food."

As if they could not bear to look in his eyes, the men turned away.

Jeff had no choice and clutched at the bag. Again he glanced at the place where Khrow and Madgwick disappeared and desperately hoped they would make an appearance.

"Khrow! Madgwick!" he yelled, hoping they would hear him.

"It's no use." Srat spoke gruffly. "They cannot hear you and we will not let them out until tomorrow – you should be long gone by then. And don't hang around the gate or we will put an arrow through you from the wall!"

Jeff tilted his head as he could faintly hear Madgwick calling and Khrow cursing.

"Don't make this difficult," the big man said. He gripped Jeff by his upper arm and marched him towards the gate.

"You are making a huge mistake. I'm not a threat. I'm with Khrow and Madgwick." Jeff tried to talk to the men but his reasoning was met with silence. "You guys better be prepared because I don't want to be you when Khrow and Madgwick get out and find you kicked me out."

He was met with silence.

Jeff felt his heart racing and he swallowed hard. He bit his lip. He was being kicked out and turned away into danger. *Crap – now what do I do?* he thought.

They marched him halfway to the forest, then stood in a line blocking the castle from view. "Do not come back. You are not welcome."

With that they turned away and stalked back into the castle. The gate closed behind them with a dull thud. The castle seemed to fade to grey.

Jeff stood staring at the castle gate, huge and impenetrable as it was. He dropped the bag to the ground. *I can't believe this is happening.*

From around the side of the castle, the man who gave him the bag of food appeared and headed swiftly into the forest, beckoning him to follow.

Jeff scooped down, picked up his bag and warily followed the man who had disappeared into the forest.

They were just beyond the tree-line, out of sight of the castle and anyone who may have been watching Jeff.

The man was old and bent over. His hair was grey and wispy as it fluttered in the breeze. His clothing looked wrinkled and too small for him but above all, his face was creased and his green eyes dull – he seemed … tired.

The man said. "I am sorry this happened. Please do not think badly of them. They are afraid." The man wrung his hands as if he did not know how to explain the actions of his fellow castle inhabitants.

"Ha – I'm afraid too and I'm a little younger!" Jeff retorted and crossed his arms over his chest.

"Yes. It frightens them when something happens that they don't understand. You survived the wuunacks and they don't understand how. You also heard 'the voice' and that was just too much."

"I would never kick someone out to be killed by creatures just because they are different. I would use that to search for a way out. Maybe surviving those wuunack things was just a once off – so thanks for that. I am really looking forward to a painful death tonight!" Jeff snapped and snatched the bag off the ground. He clenched his fist, wanting to hit something.

"No one wants to leave here, boy, it's just you and your friends that want to leave. Everybody else will and wants to stay here forever."

"Not even to escape the wuunacks?" Jeff asked.

"Not even for that … it's not painful like Khrow described – giving up is like going to sleep after a long, long day. It's a good choice for those who decide to give up."

He was quiet for a moment, then he looked at Jeff.

"Now … I can't help you get back in and you can't hang around here because you *know* Khrow and Madgwick will come out after you and *they* will not survive the wuunacks. You have to leave this area if you want to ensure Madgwick and Khrow stay behind those gates."

"But where will I go and what should I do?" Jeff whispered.

"Do? You have a big job to do, young man. You *must* find the owner of that voice. It is believed he knows where the exit portal is but won't disclose the location to anyone – not that I think anyone will leave anyway. I think he reached out to you because you managed to repel the wuunacks. There is something different about you and if he has made contact then he needs *you* to open the portal. Be mindful, because he won't just come out and tell you – he will not trust you enough for that and don't you dare trust *him*. Once the door is opened he may just try and leave you behind too. You will have to use your wits and wiggle the location of the portal out of him. Then once you know the location you can come and find your friends."

"Should I trust *you*?" Jeff asked.

"That's a very good point. At this stage only trust Khrow and Madgwick. That would be the wisest thing to do."

"Do you want to come with us?" Jeff asked as the old man stood bent in front of him.

"Oh no … this has been a long, long day and I am ready to let it all

51

go."

Jeff said nothing but just stared at his feet. The old man had given up like Khrow described but he seemed quite at peace with the decision.

He pointed to the mountain that Jeff saw earlier that morning while standing on the castle wall. "I don't know exactly where but a good place to start to find him is at that mountain. Now don't waste time. Go now, and good luck, boy."

Jeff watched the man hobble away back towards the castle.

He stared at the castle for a few moments. He knew the man spoke the truth. Khrow and Madgwick would come out after him if he was here and they didn't have the protection that he had – if he still had it.

Jeff bit his lip then turned and looked at the mountain in the distance.

"I can do this. I have to do this." Jeff threw the bag over his shoulder and walked further into the forest towards the mountain.

8

"Hold up Watroc, let's just talk for a moment," Horrigan said as he patted the spine he was tied to with his silver glittering dust. The dagger tattoo running down the side of his face from temple to chin glistened in the sunshine.

Silence filled the air; the only sound was the deafening WOP-WOP of Watroc's mighty wings whipping and flapping as the dragon hovered in one place.

Horrigan twisted to face Nequam. "Maybe the gong missed our entry."

Before Horrigan had even finished his sentence, Nequam started to shake his head rapidly. "Not possible – from the beginning of the existence of Bylleraz there has *always* been a gong. It has never missed an entry or exit, not even once."

"Should we go out and try again?" Nyx asked, her eyes darting from Horrigan to Nequam.

"No, if the gong didn't sound, it means that something is very wrong. The gong is always there – always."

"Like what?" Horrigan asked, twisting around and scanning the skies for movement.

"I don't know, this has never happened before but I am afraid ..." Nequam's voice trailed off.

"How far are we from the village?" Nyx asked as she too started peering around, watching for signs of potential enemies.

Nequam studied the tree-covered ground far beneath them, and then he looked at the mountains on either side as if to gain his bearings. "The village is over that mountain peak over there." He pointed into the distance where there was a dip between two large mountains that seemed to disappear into the heavens.

"Okay, so if you are so convinced something is wrong, then maybe it would not be a good idea to fly directly to the village," Nyx said with her eyebrows raised.

Horrigan nodded. "It would be like ringing a bell to announce our arrival. If the gong did not sound then it will be to our advantage to make a silent entry."

Phoebe knelt on the sofa as the warriors talked, and now she turned back to Watroc. "Watty, can you do that camouflage thingie again? Then we can fly over the village to see if anything is obviously wrong."

"I can do the camouflage *thingie* again, fly slow and low, but the warriors better keep their eyes open as I can only fly over once, then I need to refill my chambers," the dragon said with a snort and a puff of green smoke trailed out of his nostrils.

Phoebe turned to Nequam. "We can't stay at the village if something is wrong. Do you know of a safe place for us to stay tonight? We'll need water for Watroc."

"Well, maybe for us, but the overgrown lizard will have to ..." Nequam started.

Phoebe's cheeks brightened as if dabbed with a red paint brush and the gold specks in her chocolate brown eyes flashed. Her head snapped up, her lips in a firm straight line. "Nequam, if you don't stop baiting Watroc, then, irrespective of what is happening at *your* home, we will drop you off and go back to Sandustian. Watroc is with me and I am with Watroc. I go where he goes. Got it?" she snapped.

Nequam stared at the mountain peaks in the distance before he sighed and nodded. "Okay, I am sorry."

"So do you know a place big enough for *all* of us, or don't you?"

Phoebe barked, her lips still pressed together. Her frown had not left her forehead.

Watroc's teeth pulled up from his bottom lip as if he were grinning at how tough Phoebe sounded.

"Yes, there is a cave with a huge underground lake which is not too far; we can head there after we fly over the village." Nequam spoke in a subdued voice and gazed at the waving trees below.

The warriors were quiet and stared ahead. Both had a healthy respect for dragons, which Nequam still had to learn. If not for Phoebe, Watroc would have eaten Nequam long ago. Dragons were not particular about who they ate. Nequam was playing with fire, a fact a few Sandustian warriors had already told him.

"Good, let's go then." Phoebe patted Watroc on the neck.

Watroc lifted one wing and dipped into a slow turn as they headed for the peaks Nequam had pointed out earlier.

Concealed by his magic, the dragon with his passengers arrived at the village that was nestled at the bottom of a valley. Phoebe took a deep breath at her first view of Bylleraz.

Tall mountains laced with grey stone and white snow flanked the valley. A waterfall cascaded down in a sheet of white and blue that looked so inviting it seemed the water bubbled and beckoned for a closer and refreshing look. The base of the waterfall disappeared into a dark green forest. Pockets of forest trailed along and in between the patches of bright green grass that dotted the hillside. A raging river gushed inside a groove along the valley floor, its frothy waters churning and white as it raced along.

The houses were built very close to each other, the grey and brown cobblestoned passageways weaving among the houses. The houses themselves were very colourful with brightly painted slate roofs. Little stone bridges crossed the water canals that crisscrossed the village. Tied row boats bobbed in the water in the channels. In the middle of the village was a large open square with a beautiful fountain and a statue of a little girl holding a stone, offering it to the heavens as a gift. The stone was shiny and blue, like glass, and cut in the shape of a diamond. Brightly coloured flowers dotted the passages, the window sills and entrances of houses. A mass of colour surrounded the statue. The little village looked beautiful and empty.

Nyx and Horrigan leaned from side to side as they scanned the ground, looking for the slightest movement. Stunned, Nequam sat staring at what seemed like a ghost town. Phoebe kept her hand on Watroc's neck. It kept her calm as she gazed around. The village seemed deserted, although trails of smoke escaped from chimneys. House doors stood open, and carts were toppled, leaving the pathways littered with cabbages and scattered pumpkins. In the middle of a green park, an empty child's swing rocked back and forth under a large oak tree as if an invisible child was still playing happily.

"Watroc, can you go to the left?" Nequam whispered.

Watroc glided left and whipped his wings twice to keep his momentum going. They followed a cobblestone path that led away from the village towards an outcrop of mountain. Smooth circular steps carved into the stone rock-face disappeared into the darkness. On either side of the entrance were stone statues like guardians, with a sword in one hand and a red stone like sparkling ruby in the other.

No one said a word as everyone stared at the creepy and eerie scenes below.

"We must leave now. Which way?" Watroc growled.

"Follow the river downstream," Nequam whispered back but he twisted in a final attempt to try and see any kind of movement.

Watroc gave another two flaps of his wings and flew downstream; he flew so low over the water that Phoebe smiled at the light spray on her face. She closed her eyes and breathed in the sweet air. It felt so real after the ghost village they had just left.

Once they were out of earshot from the village, everyone sat up, realizing they had been hunched over the dragon as if to make their appearance smaller. Horrigan shook his head and Nyx kept turning around to make sure no one had noticed their silent fly-over. Phoebe released a heavy sigh. Nequam sat stunned as he stared at the plush green carpet of trees that flew by beneath him.

"Around the next bend you will see hanging vines covering the side of the mountain. Fly through the vines to find a large cave with the underwater lake. We should be safe there as it is not visited or spoken about," Nequam said quietly.

Watroc glided around the bend and over a pool of blue-green water that sparkled and twinkled as if diamonds were embedded into each droplet. Nyx and Horrigan cast out their dust to part the vines as they flew into the cave.

Watroc landed with a thump on soft sand. Phoebe looked around as she hopped off the dragon's back. Watroc shook his neck and the ugly sofa disappeared in a puff of smoke.

Horrigan produced a dust lantern that gave a soft yellow glow. Soft light bounced off the walls and ceilings.

"That was creepy, as if everyone left in a hurry – or got taken without warning," Horrigan said as he rubbed his bald head.

"Are we safe here, Nequam?" Nyx asked. She gazed at the vine curtain. The entrance was concealed but it could also be a trap.

"No one ever comes here or speaks about this place," Nequam said as he studied the lights dancing on the ceiling.

"Why?" Phoebe asked, turning around. It was dark and gloomy but as a cave goes, it seemed okay – not at all like that smelly pitch-black cave that housed that evil witch Zorka who had tried to steal her life force. This cave had a damp wet sand smell but it gave a sense of peace and security.

"I don't know for sure, but it is said to be haunted. Strange sounds can be heard here … although I have never heard them and I've spent a lot of time here. So, there is an underground lake full of fish that stretches under the mountain, down that way." He pointed down one dark tunnel. "The forest has plenty of berries, nuts and fruits. We should not go hungry." He paused, then looked at everyone. "So what do we do now?"

There was silence as everyone was deep in thought; the emptiness of village had shaken everyone.

Phoebe took a deep breath and puffed her cheeks before she blew the air out of her lungs. She held her hand up and counted on her fingers as she spoke. "Okay. We need more information than we got with the fly-over. I think we should head back to the village and have a look around – without getting caught. We need to scout the forest around the cave and find food to eat tonight. We need to explore this cave to see if there is another exit so that we don't get trapped. Watroc, you should go to the lake and take a rest, and refill your chambers in case we need to leave in a hurry." Phoebe sounded so firm and business-like that everyone stared at her with their mouths hanging open.

Nyx nodded. "Good idea. I suggest one warrior go with Quamie to the village, one warrior to scout the forest and get some snacks for dinner. Fee can stay here and explore for an exit."

"I will go to the village with Nequam," Horrigan volunteered.

"I will scout the forest and bring back some munchies," Nyx said.

"I don't like leaving Lyric alone," Nequam muttered as he drew a line in the sand with his toe.

"Fee is not going to be alone – she is going to be with Watty and like seriously ... who is going to mess with a dragon? He can go to the lake and refresh, fill those chambers and maybe scare some fish out of the water." Nyx smiled up at the dragon.

"Do not tell me what to do and stop calling me Watty. I DO NOT LIKE IT." Watroc growled and a thin stream of green fire flared out of his nostrils. His eye narrowed as he glared at Nyx.

Phoebe laughed and patted him on his nose and stroked a whisker. "I think *Watty* is a very cute name."

Watroc started to hum. "Fine. You can call me Waaa ... *that* name, but no one else!"

Horrigan slapped his thigh and said, "That's settled then. Right, we will meet back here. Stay out of sight – stay safe."

Horrigan and Nyx walked towards the curtain of green but then Nequam gave a low whistle and beckoned to the warriors – there was another way out of the cave without getting caught up in the dangling tentacles. They went around a corner and then they were gone.

9

Horrigan peered out of a narrow slit of the shuttered window and studied the street below. His eyes darted left and right, alert for the slightest movement. He grimaced at the potted flowers of orange and yellow that bobbed and nodded as a soft breeze weaved through the alleyways. On a normal day the flowers would have looked like a fresh sign of life – vibrant and bright ... but today, it just seemed overly dramatic.

This village was empty. He had been through every single house on this road and a few on the row behind. People had either left in a hurry or were forcibly taken but without any signs of struggle – *really odd*, he thought and bit his bottom lip.

Moving around the house, he paused at the doorway of a bedroom. Pictures hung askew on the walls, red and blue striped curtains floated in the breeze. Horrigan's eyebrows rose at the carelessly dropped tops and shorts that lay scattered on the floor. *Nobody even bothered to pack – a little messy,* he thought. In every room the visible signs of life screamed at him, people *lived* here, mothers, fathers, children. Toys and clothing were lying everywhere. To have the people vanished without any explanation was chilling and mysterious.

A tattered fluffy brown teddy bear with a missing nose caught his eye. He rubbed his chest as a strange sensation crept over him. While he stared at the toy lying forgotten on the floor, the voice of the keeper of runes echoed through his memory. *The runes have foretold ... Horrigan ... a family of your own ...*

Horrigan remembered how he stared at the magical wooden doors at the entrance of the Sandustian chamber. The doors were inscribed with magical moon runes that twisted and turned constantly, sometimes foretelling future events, sometimes reminiscing about the past. The keeper of the runes sat on his usual stool and recorded all events the runes chose to tell. Horrigan remembered how the old man stared up at him with his pale blue eyes and his shaggy grey hair that hung to his shoulders, and how a small smile played on his lips.

"I do not have a family," Horrigan had answered with a small shake of the head as if to say: *everyone knows that.*

"The runes are never wrong ... so it shall be," the old man replied with a shrug and turned back to transcribing the runes that churned and twisted with their tales.

Horrigan had put the whole incident out of his mind, feeling it was never good to dwell on things you cannot change. For as long as he could remember, he never had a family to call his own and he just kept telling himself he did not long or desire a family anyway. Besides, he always thought the warriors were all the family he ever needed. But seeing the beloved teddy on the floor suddenly made him aware of how alone he was. He desperately wanted to find the owner of that forgotten little teddy bear. He stuffed the bear into his pocket.

Quietly he made his way back down the creaking stairs, wincing at every squeak, as loud as cracks of lightning in the silent house. He entered the kitchen. The table was laid for dinner, and the plates filled with half-eaten food. Horrigan pulled his lips at the sight of beans and broccoli. He touched the vegetables. *Cold*, he thought and moved over to the fireplace to rake the coals. The upper coals were cold and coated in white ash but the bottom coals were still warm to the touch. Whatever happened must have happened within the last day.

A slight movement outside the kitchen window caught his eye and he moved swiftly to slip behind the door. It swung open slowly with a soft creak.

"Horrigan," a voice whispered softly. It was Nequam; they had arranged to meet at this last house. Horrigan released his pent-up breath in a low whoosh and pushed the door behind Nequam closed with a resounding click.

Nequam whirled on his heels and crouched into a fighting position, his fists covering his face.

"It's me," Horrigan said and patted him on the shoulder. "Did you find anything?" He watched Nequam carefully. The youngster had said he was going to make his way to his parents' house.

"Not a thing. Every house is the same. I went to my parents' house. Nothing there either. I wanted to stay to look for clues, which I am sure they would have left for me if they could but I have this strange feeling that we are running out of time." He waved his hand at the dinner table. "They left without even eating."

"Something very frightening must have scared these people to drop what they were doing and leave," Horrigan said.

"Or ... maybe they were taken prisoner," Nequam finished. "But I found no signs of injury, no blood, no struggle ... it's like they got up and left whatever they were doing without any questions or arguments."

Horrigan was silent as he gazed around the room one last time.

Nequam shook his head. "Where are they? Where could they have gone ... are they even alive?" The questions hung in the air as he stared at the table; he bit his lip and rubbed the short stubble of his Mohawk cut again.

"We will find out what happened, Nequam. We will not leave here until we have found the villagers or found what happened to them."

"Yes," whispered Nequam with downcast eyes, then he straightened his shoulders and said, "I knew ... *I know* the family that lives in this house; they would have welcomed us and would have gladly shared food with us."

Nequam quickly found two chocolate brown pillowcases; he and Horrigan filled the cases with food that would be able to keep in the cave.

"Let us go. I also have that feeling we should not be here at nightfall. We can come back tomorrow – do a proper search for clues at your parents' house," Horrigan said as he slung the makeshift bag over his shoulder.

They slid back into the alleyway and darted from cottage to cottage, trying to conceal their presence within the darkened door frames. Soon they reached the last house that stood at the fringe of the forest. After a quick glance around they raced, hunched over, to the trees and mingled with the shadows.

Horrigan moved swiftly, retracing his steps back deeper into the forest. Without saying a word, Nequam followed.

10

Nyx stood outside the cave mouth, half hidden in the shadow of a boulder as she watched Horrigan and Nequam move between the trees towards the village. Within minutes they had merged into the darkness of the forest. Silently Nyx watched and waited for any movement betraying anyone following Horrigan and Nequam. Once convinced the two were safely away on their part of the mission, she gave a curt nod. With her dust shimmering in her hand she moved in the opposite direction. She stayed low as she blended with the ferns and the trees. She skirted around the little lake that was so smooth it seemed covered in ice. Reflections of the trees lightly shimmered on the surface. Nyx was careful to keep in sight the waterfall that hid the cave. *Okay, the first perimeter is safe. Time to widen the distance and move in a circular direction to ensure the second one is safe.*

She could just make out the flickering sun through the leaves of the trees that towered above her. Nyx paused very often, listening for sounds such as breathing, footfalls or any movements in the forest that did not belong. There was nothing.

It was late; twilight was but a breath away.

Again she paused at a large tree with deep grooves raked down the thick trunk. The grooves were dark brown to almost black and it seemed a very old tree. Yellow and white mushrooms ballooned around the trunk and dark green moss covered the bulging roots like a comforting blanket.

Something is not right, she thought as she leaned towards the tree and placed her hand against the bark.

Nyx was one of the few warriors who had learnt the different tree dialects. She could talk to any tree and found it extremely useful and entertaining, especially when they retold stories about how Jeff's best friend Rhed had tried to outrun the trees in Drakmere. The poor kid broke his ankle, which the trees healed with their tree magic and the result was that Rhed and the trees became best of friends almost akin to family.

She bowed her head as she listened to the faint humming of the tree and tried to feel the tree's energy. This forest was not unlike the forest in Drakmere or that around Little Falls. It had a magical quality to it. Normally trees were very chatty and vocal but *this* tree was very silent. Her eyes opened wide. *This tree is trying to keep a secret – the forest is hiding something!*

She patted the tree gently and a thin trail of dust wisped out of her palm and slid slowly around the trunk like a silver glittery ribbon. Nyx felt the dust infuse with the tree and then it sighed and the hum got a little louder. The tree was silent as if reluctant to trust her and give up its secrets.

She smiled and whispered, "I wish you no harm, great tree. I am a Sandustian warrior and I sense there are ill tidings within this forest."

Then she felt the tree move under her hand and words as soft as a whisper floated through her mind, so soft she could hardly hear them. *Hidden in the forest, find them.*

Nyx's eyebrows pulled in as she scanned the forest around her. *The forest is hiding someone ... the villagers*? She nodded to the tree and her dust trailed back into her hand.

Nyx moved deeper into the forest, stepping over knotted roots and creeping under fallen trunks, pausing every now and then to listen to the sounds of the forest.

It was almost dark when she heard the faintest whimper. She stopped and listened with her head tilted to the side, trying to decide where the sound came from. *That was a child!* She thought. Nyx moved slowly to the left and parted ferns around her. She placed each foot carefully so that she did not break any twigs or crackle any fallen leaves. *A hiding child would be very afraid. I can't just hop out of nowhere with a bright hello – I'd give them a heart attack and send them scattering into the bush. The forest is hiding them for a reason,* Nyx thought and her lips pressed tightly in a line.

She crept along the top of a very large fallen trunk, and then she saw them.

Huddled together, trying to blend into the darkness of a hollow beneath the fallen trunk that Nyx was crawling along, were six children. Large frightened eyes darted around at the night sounds. Nyx backed down the way she came; she did not want to scare the children into running away from her.

She slipped off the trunk and was about to move closer when she heard a twig breaking and something stomping a little way behind her. It sounded like someone was deliberately crashing through the forest to scare those hidden into a frenzied flight.

A large cloaked figure came ploughing through the forest on a direct path towards the children. Nyx could tell he was also searching by the heavy sway of his head as he brushed ferns and shrubs aside without bothering to keep silent.

Nyx held her breath as she crept closer to the children. Her glowing purple eyes were fixed on the cloaked man who was almost on top of them. From the angle he was charging from, he would see the children for sure. *Flaming comets!* she thought.

She had no choice. She had to act now. She pushed the ferns apart so that the children could see her. She put one hand in front of her, as a sign that she meant no harm and for the children to stay and the other she held to her lips in an effort to tell the children to stay quiet. Her dust streamed from her in front of the children and formed a large wall.

The children were staring at Nyx with wide eyes as if not sure if she was friend or foe. Nyx winked and grinned. She tapped her finger to her lips – *stay quiet.*

The cloaked man stopped mere steps away from the huddling children but he could not see them through the dust wall.

Nyx wrinkled her nose and silently gagged. *Wow he stinks, almost like a dreamon ... DREAMON here?* she thought with wide eyes, then quickly dipped her head so that the dreamon would not see the purple shine of her eyes.

The hooded man turned around as he scanned the trees and shadows, then he moved on.

Nyx waited until he was out of earshot before she whispered, "Do not be afraid. I am here to help you. My name is Nyx."

A girl whispered back, "I am Zazkia. We are from the village. He will be back with others; they are all over the forest. We have been lucky not to be caught until now." For a little girl, she seemed very grown up as she huddled there with her arms over the little ones. Her dimples and the shine in her eyes made her look cheeky.

Nyx nodded with a smile. "How many are here?

"I have five with me," Zazkia said as she smoothed a child's hair in a comforting gesture.

"What about the other children? Are they also hiding in the forest like you?"

Zazkia nodded. "But we don't know where."

"It's okay, we will find them." Nyx craned her neck to see if there were any dreamons lurking about. She dipped as she saw one in the distance, also crashing through the forest like a giant. Nyx sat back on her heels, her forehead crinkled in thought.

The forest was littered with smelly dreamons. She couldn't get them all to the cave on her own – it was just too far. She couldn't leave them alone and get help either. She would have to wait for Horrigan to come looking for her.

She turned to Zazkia, and whispered, "I am going to see if I can find the others."

When Zazkia's eyes widened, Nyx quickly added, "I will not go far, and my magical dust will hide you – those monsters will not be able to see you, but you must stay behind the wall and be very quiet. I will give an owl hoot like 'hoo-hoo,' then you will know that it's me. I will be back soon ... okay?"

Nyx waited while Zazkia whispered to the little ones, "We must stay quiet under the magical wall – the bad men will not see us. Nyx is going to try and find the others."

Nyx winked at the little ones and was rewarded with tired little lopsided smiles. The smiles did not reach their dull eyes as they were exhausted, scared and had probably been hiding in this forest for a few days already, moving from hiding place to hiding place.

Nyx crept away from the children. Her heart was heavy as she could sense the children were relieved at her presence and then afraid at her departure. Her dust wall stayed in place as a protective barrier.

Nyx spent the next hour moving from tree to tree, staying in the shadows of the branches and hiding amongst leaves. She was almost caught but the trees caused a distraction when a branch clattered into another. The sudden noise made the brute stomp into another direction. Nyx swung nimbly into another tree and out of sight. *I thank you old forest for that most welcome distraction,* she thought quietly.

She was about to give up when she finally saw another group of children lying flat on the ground hidden among long ferns. They were directly below her and she wouldn't have seen them had she not been moving from tree to tree via the connecting branches.

Nyx scanned the area and then gave an owl call: "Hoo-hoo ... hoo-hoo." She waited.

A boy's head lifted slowly out of the ferns.

The tree that Nyx was standing in rustled its leaves. The boy looked up and saw Nyx. His head shot back down. It was obvious he did not know who or what she was. Nyx jumped neatly and quietly into the ferns and placed her hand on his back as he was starting to squirm away towards the other children lying behind him.

"I am a friend; I am here to help you. Shoosh," she whispered. The warmth of her hand relaxed the box and he lay still. "I am Nyx, how many are here?"

"I am Quewin, I have five with me." The boy seemed about eight or nine years old. His hair was plastered flat on his forehead as if he had been running. Nyx could not tell what colour his clothes were because they were so dirty from crawling along in the mud and on the sandy forest floor. He had a splash of freckles on his nose and cheeks.

"Okay Quewin, I am going to check where those smelly dreamons are, then we're going to move quietly to where Zazkia's group is hiding ... okay?"

Quewin nodded and whispered with a hopeful, "You found Zazkia?"

Nyx nodded before she rose and darted towards the nearest tree. She leaned against the tree and peered around scanning the area. The forest was swarming with cloaked figures that crossed and forged back and forth.

There are too many of the ugly smelly brutes, she thought. *I can't take them all at once. I will have to find a safe place to hide and then take one or two kids out at a time. Horrigan! Come on – I need you.*

She studied a path that led to a safe hollow possibly big enough for the children to crawl into. She moved back to Quewin.

"There are too many around for all of us to go at once, but there's a tree hollow not far from here. We hide there and I will take one at a time. Okay?" As Nyx spoke she looked into Quewin's dark brown eyes and then lifted her head inches above the ferns to scan the area for the enemy.

"I know that hollow. We were there yesterday. They almost found us. They know that one and keep going back there in case we go back," Quewin said.

"But you did not have me yesterday. They won't find you this time,"

Nyx said with a firm nod. "Come on. Let's go."

Quewin beckoned to the little ones. Nyx took a boy about four years old onto her back; she lifted another small girl into her arm. Her right hand was free with her dust swirling in her palm … she was as ready as she could be under the circumstances. "Hold on tight," she whispered and smiled when she was rewarded with a death grip of little hands that almost cut off her air supply.

Quewin also took a child on his back, and held hands with the other two.

Nyx shook her head. Quewin was quite small in stature and yet he still carried a child on his back. *A brave little warrior.*

They inched their way towards the tree hollow. Twice they had to stop as a cloaked figure stalked past. The forest tried to help them mask their passage by rustling leaves and creating branch cracking noises that led the dreamons away from the hidden group. Nyx touched the bark of a passing tree to convey her gratitude.

They reached the hollow and Quewin and three of the children crawled inside. Nyx shot dust over the opening, concealing the kids so that the opening looked vacant.

"There is a magical seal so no one can see you, but you have to stay quiet because they will be able to hear you. I will be back for you. Okay?" Nyx could not bear to look at the little faces staring up at her. She turned and quickly moved into the forest with the small girl in her one arm holding on tight around her neck. The boy was hunched onto her back, his face hidden by her braided hair.

She tried to go as directly as she could without having to put down either of the children. The children were silent; she could hardly hear them breathe. It took a while as she had to stop now and then to avoid the cloaked figures. *Flaming comets, you can smell them a mile away*, she thought as she held her breath when one passed close by.

"Hoo-hoo, hoo-hoo." She gave the owl hoot so that the kids would not get a fright when she opened the wall of dust and was relieved to find the Zazkia group still safe behind the dust wall.

Zazkia fussed over the little ones, wiping their hair out of their faces, giving each one kisses on the foreheads. Nyx saw the kids were still wide awake, but seemed more relaxed and some even gave her a little smile and one little boy gave her a two-fingered peace sign.

Nyx smiled. "I have to go and get the others … nice and quiet like before."

Zazkia nodded and smiled.

Nyx crept away and headed back to the hollow.

11

Phoebe watched as the warriors and Nequam went around the corner. The cave was silent. She turned to Watroc and clapped her hands, which echoed loudly in the cave.

"Okay, let's get to work. We need to see how big this place is, and then we can make our way to the underwater lake to see if the water is drinkable … do you think it has fish? Is there an exit – I've seen enough movies to know that we must always have an exit plan." She paused and looked at Watroc who was staring at her with his tooth jutting out over his lip. "What?" Phoebe asked with her hands in the air.

"You are bossy, but I like it." Watroc snorted.

He roared green flames high into the ceiling, casting an eerie green glow around the cavern.

"Oh wow – this must be the biggest cave I have ever been in," Phoebe whispered as she stared above and around her. There were long shelves to the one side that almost looked like giant steps carved into the stone walls. The green light bounced off the rock columns that stretched down from the ceiling. "Those are called stalactites – the ones that hang down." She pointed to the columns that reached up towards the stalactites. "Those are called stalagmites; I read it in a book once. See how they try and touch each other – like fingers of lost loved ones." Phoebe's voice faded as she stared at stone-like structures that turned the cavern into a stone garden with Watroc's green light bouncing off the ceiling and walls. The cave dipped deeper into the darkness.

Phoebe shivered and rubbed her arms. "As pretty as it is – I still don't like caves too much; they always have a damp earthy smell … and sometimes evil witches live in them," she mumbled as she moved closer to Watroc as they headed down the tunnel. Her soft melodic voice echoed and bounced around the walls.

"How do you know we're heading in the right direction? Maybe we should have taken the other tunnel," Phoebe said she walked next to Watroc who kept shooting puffs of flames along the tunnel to light the way.

"A water dragon always knows where water is," Watroc replied.

They turned a corner and a smooth lake stretched out before them. "Look at that!" Phoebe exclaimed as she dropped to her knees and peered into the water. "I have never seen such a startling blue and it's so clear I can see the rocks on the bottom." She dipped her fingers and whirled the water around. "It's icy. I'm not swimming in that."

Watroc waded into the water and dived beneath the surface creating ripples like miniature waves along the lake shore. Phoebe laughed as his tail made a mighty splash.

"Wait for me," she yelled as she hopped from one foot to the other on the bank. There was no sign of Watroc. Suddenly bubbles popped to the surface and with a cascade of water Watroc's head appeared directly in front of her. He extended his tail for her to use as a bridge and she clambered over his tail and back until she was sitting in the dip of his neck in between his huge spikes. "This is so cool!" She laughed out loud.

Watroc glided on the surface. His body heat kept Phoebe warm as her feet dangled in the water. As they drifted around the lake he shot flames into different areas especially dark corners so that they could see the sides of the cavern. It was beautiful with different shapes and sizes of stone almost as if it were telling the story of the history of the cave. The ceiling remained pitch black. Now and then Phoebe saw a ripple in the water as a small fish swam away.

"There!" she said, pointing to the left.

Watroc turned in that direction and they came across a gentle stream that filtered away from the lake. It bubbled over pebbles and rocks down a large tunnel.

The stream became too small to swim so Phoebe hopped down and they followed the little stream on foot. Within minutes, they saw a round disk of bright white light.

"That's our exit; let's see where it comes out. How far do you think we are from the entrance?" she asked as she navigated from rock to rock over the stream until they reached the opening that was lined with large boulders. Phoebe was careful as she climbed over the slippery moss-covered stone. The colour of the water changed from bright blue to a creamy green as it snaked through the boulders and swept towards the forest and dwindled away in-between the trees.

The forest was dark green with large looming trees. Tall ferns encased the tree bases like fur collars. Birds sang and chirped happily as they flitted from branch to branch. It was exactly like the forest back home.

Watroc stayed just inside the darkness of the cave while Phoebe ventured out into the sunlight, shielding her eyes with her hand.

"Do not go too far, Phoebe. We do not know what is out there," Watroc said as he lay down with his head on his front legs. His green spiked tail dragged boulders out of the way as he curled it to his side. He watched Phoebe through narrowed slits.

"You're a dragon. Can it get any safer?" Phoebe asked with a smile and shrug. Her jeans were wet and dark blue from the knees down and she had tied her pink jacket around her waist with the arms folded in front. Her brown curly hair bounced as she hopped over to another boulder, windmilling her arms to keep balance.

Watroc lifted his head with a snort and sniffed the air. "There is a nasty smell in the air. Something evil lurks in this forest." He gazed into the forest and growled.

Phoebe jumped when she heard a rock dislodge behind her and pressed against a boulder.

A man in a large dark red cloak with his face hidden in a cowl stood with his back to her. She dropped to her knees and stretched her eyes as if she could not believe that he had not seen or heard her.

Great, what do I do now? I am too far away to get back to Watroc.

She bit on her knuckles to stop the scream as a thought drifted through her mind.

I will come and get you – stay quiet.

"Watroc? Watroc can talk to me telepathically? Breathe Phoebe, breathe," she muttered. *Watroc?* she thought.

Stay where you are, I am coming.

NO NOOOO, she yelled in her head. *They cannot know that we are here. It will put the others in danger!* She squeezed her eyes tightly shut as she thought furiously, trying to get her message across.

Phoebe peeped over a moss-covered boulder; the man was facing away from her. He was checking something in his hands.

I don't care. They are warriors, they can look after themselves, Watroc growled.

WATROC! Phoebe screamed in her head.

Okay, stop screaming! It hurts! Stay hidden, I will think of something, Watroc thought back.

Steam trailed out of his nostrils and drifted out of the cave. It crept along the ground, slipping between the rocks and boulders. Watroc started to hum softly.

I summon from the depths, to the mist of time,
I seek to hide that, which is mine,
Mystical clouds the fog will bring
Conceal the dragon that lurks within

Phoebe watched with wide eyes as a mysterious mist snaked around the bases of the boulders and rose into the air. It was like a horror movie with the fog appearing within moments, deadly and waiting to attack. She lifted her hands up but she couldn't see her fingers.

Watroc, what is going on – I can't see anything because a creepy mist is all over? Phoebe thought. "This is so weird; I am talking to a dragon with my mind," she muttered breathlessly.

It is my mist – it's not creepy. The strangers cannot see anything either. I am going to light a pathway which only you and I will be able to see. Start making you way back to me Phoebe. No one will be able to see you but they will be able to hear you, so walk quietly, Watroc thought.

An eerie green light infused with the mist. It was as if someone had dropped a dose of green dye into the smoky haze. Within seconds everything was green. A light lit up in front of Phoebe. She inhaled deeply and then slowly stood up from behind the boulder. She blinked rapidly but her vision did not improve. Her eyes darted left and right but she couldn't see where the man in the drapey cloak was. The odd light moved a little forward and Phoebe followed. She held her arms out as she tried to keep her balance; she was careful where she placed her feet as the ground was very uneven with pebbles. The moss and algae made stones slippery. She took one more step towards the light. She focused on her footing. *How far still ... did I go that far away from the cave exit?*

Just then her foot slipped and a pebble dislodged, knocking into other pebbles that tumbled with sharp cracks. To Phoebe it sounded like a thunderbolt. Her breath caught in her throat and she froze. *Oh crap. Watroc?*

She wrinkled her nose as the rotten smell of a putrid drain hit her in the face. She smelt the man before she heard him and suddenly he was right there next to her. Phoebe instinctively ducked as she felt the air whoosh above her as an arm whipped in the space where her head had been just seconds before. As she opened her mouth to scream, the mist brightened as if a light bulb had been switched on. There was a scream and a loud crunch. She looked up from her crouching position and saw Watroc looming above them.

Legs kicked wildly from Watroc's jaws. There was another loud crunch and then the suddenly limp legs disappeared in the dragon's mouth.

Phoebe saw Watroc's eyes widen, then close as if in pain. Then he shook his head from side to side as if he was having a seizure. The golden greenish glow of the mist made Watroc's mother of pearl scales glitter and his spikes sparkle.

"Watroc? Are you okay?" Phoebe whispered. She flapped her hands in front of her, unsure how to help because it looked like the dragon was battling to swallow. Maybe he was choking.

At the sound of her frantic voice, Watroc became still and then muttered, "It's not fair. It's just not fair."

Phoebe put her hand out and the air rushed out of her as she released all the air she was holding when she felt his smooth scales under her finger tips. "Watroc. Did you just *eat* him?" she whispered.

"Well you wanted to remain hidden so that he could not tell anyone about us. Let's go back, we must tell the others that there are dreamons in the forest."

Phoebe quietly made her way back to the entrance. There was no need for the light as the heat that radiated from Watroc gave a clear path of which way to go. The minute she entered the cave the mist started to dissipate.

They were well inside the cave and making their way along the ledge that hugged the lake when Phoebe spoke again. "You can talk to me with your thoughts ... how?"

"A dragon who has a link friend can talk to them but *only* when the need is great."

"Oh, so just in emergencies ... that's useful. I can talk to a dragon with my mind ... how cool is that!" Phoebe said and she shook her head in disbelief. "You were supposed to stay in the cave. What if there was another and he saw you?" she scolded the dragon and gave him her sternest frown.

"I know, but the dreamon was about to grab you." Watroc's voice was gruff and he did not sound sorry at all.

"A dreamon here? Are you sure? I could not really tell what it was because he was hidden in a cloak … could he have been a villager. Maybe you ate a villager!" Phoebe stopped walking at the thought.

"Dreamons taste good but they stink."

"I can't believe you just ate a stinky dreamon. That's so gross – yuck. He did stink." Phoebe stuck her tongue out. "I thought you were going to have a seizure. You said it's not fair … what isn't fair?"

Watroc roared into the ceiling. "Azghar and Calidus always get plenty of dreamons to eat, and I only get one tiny one with thin little legs. I want a big fat juicy one."

Phoebe grinned. Watroc was always hungry, ready to eat anything. "So what do they taste like?"

Watroc stopped and stared ahead as if he were thinking. "Not sure ... sticky, sweet ... like those black sweets you once gave me."

Phoebe's forehead wrinkled as she tried to remember what black, sweet, sticky sweets she had given to Watroc. "You mean liquorice?"

Watroc nodded. His spikes grazed the cavern wall and fine stones and sand trickled behind them. "Yes. Liquorice! Yum. I love liquorice-tasting dreamons! Next time I will let you try one … but just a little one because I am hungry. I will eat the fat ones."

"Ugh. Delightful," Phoebe muttered.

They reached the entrance of the cave. Phoebe looked around. "I think you must try and contact Azghar or Calidus to let them know what is happening here, but do it quietly okay?" Phoebe said with her finger in front of her mouth.

No one was back at the cave yet. Watroc blew a thin jet of flame at a stalagmite until it lit up like giant candle. The light flickered all the way to the ceiling and walls. Watroc chose a few around the cavern to light up and soon it was dimly lit with a beautiful mixture of gold from the stone and green from Watroc's fire.

"How did you get that alight?" Phoebe asked as he lit another one with a hiss.

"Dragon magic," Watroc said.

Phoebe watched the lights flicker as she paced back and forth. She wandered over to the curtain of water that cascaded down in front of the entrance. She wrung her hands. It was already dark and Nyx was still out there. She should have been back hours ago.

A little while later, she saw a flickering shadow near the hanging vines and leapt to her feet. "Someone is coming," she hissed.

Horrigan and Nequam came around the corner and dropped their pillowcases filled with food on the ledge. Horrigan nodded at the dimly lit cavern. "Nice touch – could not see any light from the outside."

Nequam dropped to his knees in front of the bags of food. "The entire village is empty; we saw nothing except for signs of a hasty departure or capture. It is as if they just got up and left."

Horrigan looked around and asked where Nyx was.

"Not back yet and she should have been back hours ago. She said she wasn't going far, just a quick scout of the perimeter," Phoebe said with wide eyes. "AND we saw a dreamon near the forest," she added breathlessly.

"A dreamon, are you sure?" Horrigan asked with raised eyebrows.

"Yes. There is an evil presence lurking within this forest," Watroc said. He was using his nail to scratch his tooth like a toothpick.

"Please tell me he did not see you," Nequam said with his hands on his hips.

"He did, but it doesn't matter because Watroc ate him," Phoebe said.

Nequam looked up at Watroc who was still busy picking at his long teeth with a talon, then moved to stand on the other side of Horrigan.

"Nyx should have been back already – something is wrong. We need to go and look for her," Phoebe said.

"I will go," Horrigan said and stood up in a fluid motion.

"I'll come too. I know these forests like the back of my hand – even at night," Nequam said and moved towards the thunderous waterfall curtain.

Horrigan strode back to the entrance with Nequam right behind him, and then they were gone.

12

Jeff stared at the mountain that towered in front of him. The sweat ran down his back and his hair felt like it was plastered to his head. He wiped his hair off his forehead with the back of his hand. He glanced back at the forest he had just left. This could have been the exact same forest as the one in Drakmere. It had the same mysterious feel and trees and the plants were super strange looking.

The plants were vivid shades of green and blue and seemed to pulsate when they detected movement. Jeff brushed against an odd looking lime-green flower that could have passed for a normal daisy when it suddenly started moving as if thumping to a beat. Big yellow dots popped open on the green petals and oozed orange liquid. Jeff wrinkled his nose – the yellow dots looked suspiciously like pimples.

The trees seemed silent but Jeff was sure they were watching him. He spun around every now and then determined to catch them in the act. He was very wary of strange trees since his encounter in Drakwood forest, where the trees decided to turn his best friend, Rhed, into a tree and he had to find the cure. He would just keep a healthy distance – *thank you very much.*

He saw no animals he could identify and any movement that caught his eye seemed like just a brush of wind before it was gone. It was as though everything was trying to stay out of sight – very weird.

He planted his hands on his knees as he tried to catch his breath. He had been going at a steady pace trying to reach the mountain before sunset.

He did not understand how the protection worked but also could not rule out that it was just a once-off and that the wuunacks would happily eat him tonight. Maybe extended periods of distance from Calidus would make his "inner fire," as Khrow called it, diminish. He looked up at the blue sky, dotted with wisps of cloud that seemed to be racing each other in the wind.

The sun appeared to be just more than halfway across the sky, so Jeff judged it to be just after noon. He needed to gather wood to make a fire that night, and then he could see if he could find a cave of sorts.

But how was he going to find this seer guy?

Hello ... are you there? He asked in his head. He shook his head when he had no reply. *Maybe he only answers at night.*

He looked back at the forest he had just emerged from. He missed Madgwick and Khrow but hoped they would not come after him. *Guys, don't follow me. Just trust me a little. I will come back for you.*

He gathered some twigs and thin strips of wood into a bundle. He had checked the bag earlier to find some bread and cheese and a skin of water. There was also a flint, a very long rope and some odd-smelling lime green leaves.

Okay – I suppose that is all he really could give at a moment's notice and only Madgwick would know what those leaves are good for.

Jeff stared at the grey mountain towering above him and frowned as he considered the way up. There was lots of growth and shrubbery on the steep slope, so that part looked easy enough. There was a section of sheer rock face which he was going to avoid: mountain climbing was not his thing. Just before the mountain curved out of his sight he noticed what looked like a black hole or indent – maybe a cave or somewhere he could protect himself. He would try and reach that, stay alive tonight and then reach the top tomorrow.

I am talking about staying alive throughout the night, he thought. *Great.*

He separated the firewood into two piles: one stacked and ready to light at the bottom of the mountain. He bound the other with rope, then tied the other end of the rope to his waist. If the cave was good enough to sleep in he could haul the wood up and light a fire. If he had to make a hasty descent then he would have a fire at the base.

Jeff took a deep breath and started to climb. It was harder than expected but he was making good progress. Soon he was wiping the sweat away from his eyes with his sleeve; luckily he had a lot of extra sleeve to use. It seemed like it was taking forever and he tried not to look down to see how far he had come. The sun scorching his back felt like it was intensified by a magnify glass. He reached the first part of the rock face and scuttled sideways to reach the other side. His rope dangled behind him and the wood had not been lifted off the ground as yet. His fingers started to slip from the sweat. Frantically he clasped at the jutting rocks. His calves started to cramp from moving from rock outcrops on his toes. Soon the firewood was dangling beneath him. The load weighed him down. Just when he thought he could not go any further, his fingers reached over the edge.

Over the ledge he pulled himself, looking down and beyond. The forest was a plush green carpet with the trees gently swaying in the breeze. He gazed into the direction of where he thought the castle was but saw nothing. He hauled the firewood over the ledge and then he turned around to investigate the cave.

Of course if there is something that will eat me in there then I am done for. There's nowhere to go except back down ... and it's a long way down.

Jeff peered inside the cave, and shook his head; it looked like a pit of darkness just waiting to swallow him up.

Crap – more shadows – just what I need.

He stayed close to the wall; he could not help the feeling that he was going to be cornered so he kept looking behind him at the sunlit entrance.

"I don't like this one bit," he said out loud.

"Well ... if you don't like it – then imagine how he feels," a nasal voice said out of the darkness.

Jeff scrambled backwards and automatically dropped into the first fighting stance that he had learnt at warrior school. He brought his hands up, palms facing down. He bit his lip and tried to feel for the dust's energy. He could make out faint warmth and a tingling in his palms but the dust did not appear.

"Who's there?" he asked in a hoarse whisper, exhausted from his climb.

A thin man dressed in a chocolate brown cloak with a deep red sash tied around his waist stepped out of the darkness. His face broke into a huge smile as he said in a chirpy voice, "Oh you clever boy – you figured out how to find him all by yourself. He was convinced he was going to have to guide you through the night. It wouldn't have been a problem; he is quite good with night guidance. His name is Soop, and he is the one who spoke to you, and the one you have been searching for." The man's teeth shone white as he grinned broadly.

Jeff tried to smile back at the open friendliness that seemed a little too forced.

"Uh … hi … I am Jeff. Where is he, the seer?" Jeff was not sure what to say to this old man as he stared at him. His head was almost bald but for the few strands of long grey hair that had been combed over his head as if in an attempt to hide the baldness. His grin looked odd because it seemed as if he had too many teeth for his mouth.

"Well – of course you are Jeff. He knew that already. He is *I*. It is easier to refer to myself in the third person since I have the *third eye*." The man tapped his forehead with his finger tip.

Jeff turned around and looked at the cave. He was not sure what to say now that he was here. This guy was very friendly and this third person talk was freaking him out a little.

He is too friendly. The other guy at the castle seemed more real and he did give very good advice – only trust Khrow and Madgwick, he thought.

"He is so pleased to see you brought extra wood for a fire. Don't think you need it for protection, but the wuunacks can be a bit uncomfortable, so let's get it ready to light and then we can talk. There is food here as well in case you are hungry. We might as well get comfortable as the night descends upon us," Soop said and gave Jeff a huge flashy smile. Again Jeff noticed how the old man's white teeth almost glowed in the shadows.

Jeff ignored Soop for a while; it gave him a chance to think about the whole situation. He was pleased to find another pile of firewood that had been placed in the cave at some point. Soon a fire stack was ready. There was no point in lighting it too early as the firewood had to last the night. The sun was low on the horizon and would be setting soon. The clouds started to have a pinkish glow about them. Jeff narrowed his eyes as he tried to see further, trying to find the castle that held Madgwick and Khrow captive.

"What are you trying to see?" Soop asked as he stared at Jeff's face.

"I am trying to see where the castle is. I came a long way and most of it was through the forest so I am not sure which direction it is in."

Soop stared out of the cave then he leaned towards Jeff as he pointed. "It's that way – over there. Just over that hill. That's why you can't see it."

Soop laid out some dinner, which consisted of fruits and nuts and some white gooey stuff, but it tasted rather good.

"Well, he is so pleased you were brave enough to make the journey to the mountain. He was not sure you would make it before the night settled in," Soop said in between bites.

"Can you answer some of my questions?" Jeff asked in-between mouthfuls. He was quite hungry.

"If he can answer then he will. Ask away." Soop leaned back against the side wall of the cave.

Jeff stared at the man sitting grinning opposite him. *I have heard that voice before ... but where?*

The sun hung low over the forest but there was still some time before it would melt into the horizon.

"Okay … where are we – what is this place?" Jeff asked.

"That one is easy – this is a world called Khadruz, and he already knows your next question. How come you are here with only one or two of your fellow warriors?" Soop answered with a smile.

Jeff sat straighter with the words *fellow warriors*. "That did cross my mind."

"This is a place in-between two worlds, but only to those with ties to their previous lives. They will remain here until they either leave this world or learn to let go of their ties – whatever they are. However, leaving is absolutely impossible. That is until *you* arrived. That is why he called for you to find him. He knows of a portal that will provide an exit. It's a long path but we can manage it if we leave at first light," Soop said with a slow nod.

"What do you mean until I arrived? How does that help?" Jeff asked with a frown.

"You, my dear boy, must have some essence like dragon fire in your blood or something like that, how or why, he does not know as there is nothing remarkable about you – rather dull. Be that as it may, that is why you are able to repel the wuunacks. Only a dragon can open the portal *but* if someone has dragon blood then that may be enough to do the trick."

Jeff looked out of the cave at the forest that stretched out below; the sky was starting to darken. He grimaced at the insult. He did not like this man.

"I think it's time to light the fire. He can see you have made the fire wrong. He will teach you how to make a fire. He has done it many times before and has perfected the art of lighting a fire," Soop said and bent over with the flint. He gave Jeff a smile.

Jeff stared at Soop's teeth.

Within moments the fire was blazing and the cave was filled with an orange glow.

"How far is this portal?" Jeff asked.

"Far enough. It's the other side of this mountain, through the valley and into a gorge. About a day's travel, so we will not waste any time. The quicker we get there the quicker we can leave this place."

"What about my warrior friends, Madgwick and Khrow – I will need to send them a message to meet us there," Jeff said thoughtfully.

Soop sat and nodded as if his head were on a spring. Then he said, "Sometimes we have to do things we don't like or want to do but it is necessary for our survival. The two warriors will stay here and be happy. He has foreseen this for he is a *seer* and what he sees comes true. They will not be going with us."

Jeff had to be careful not to be too agreeable or Soop would see through him. He had to find out the location and maybe that meant that he had to go with Soop for now.

I will find the location and then find a way to get to Madgwick and Khrow. For now, take it easy and play his game, Jeff thought as he studied Soop.

"Madgwick and Khrow would never leave without me and I can't leave without them," Jeff said carefully.

Soop stared at Jeff. "It will be hard but if we wait for your friends then others might find out about the exit and there would be a riot on our hands. Best we leave without anyone being the wiser about us going. Your friends will think the wuunacks got you in the end and it will be kinder for them to stay and accept their fate," Soop said.

"Well, you think it's best for them to stay where they are … but I still think I should somehow let them know," Jeff mumbled.

"He does think it's for the best – their memories of you will be of great comfort to them as they live their remainder of their days here."

The seer added more wood to the fire, which blazed brightly. The shadows wisped and flittered as the light played on the cavern walls.

Jeff leaned against the wall behind the fire and stared out in the direction of where he thought the castle was. *We will see about that,* he thought and smiled to himself in the darkness.

13

"Here they come, can you hear them?" Soop asked in a soft whisper.

Jeff tilted his head. "That faint whistling, cracking sound?"

"Yes that's the sound. They will be here shortly – stand between us as he is quite eager to see if you are still immune to them." Soop flapped his hands at Jeff.

So now I am your human shield – thanks a lot. Coward. Might as well find out if I am still covered or not, Jeff thought and clenched his jaw. He stood and faced the darkness, ignoring Soop's shuffling as he pushed against the back wall.

Shiny black creatures crept over the cliff ledge and tumbled towards the cave entrance. In the dark the clicking sounds sounded like gunshots. There were so many it seemed like a black tidal wave cascading over the edge. Jeff waited as long as he could before he softly whispered, "Calidus" – he did not want Soop to hear. The creatures recoiled, climbing over each other to scatter away from him.

Jeff pressed his lips together to hide his smile. *Right ... let's try a little closer.*

He kept silent until he felt the shiny creatures scraping with their claws against his shoes. *Calidus* he thought. The creatures recoiled again; some fell off the ledge into the darkness below.

"Ha. They moved away again – something about you makes them shy away. He knew it! What is it – do you know? Is it dragon blood?" Soop was so excited he almost tripped over the fire.

Without turning his back on the darkness Jeff moved backwards to stand behind the fire and then stared out the cave. He could not make out what these creatures were – there were so many they looked like a shiny black blanket moving along the floor. The clicking and the whistling were deafening, echoing in the cave.

"What are they?" Jeff asked Soop without looking away.

"Wuunacks … no one really knows what they are or how they got to be here. But they come and go in a cycle that lasts a few decades at a time … it won't be long before they are gone again … where to? Nobody knows."

Jeff glanced at Soop as he spoke and frowned when he saw Soop's lips pull up in a smirk. *What secret is he keeping?*

The night was long and Jeff did not want to sleep, so he sat facing the fire. He dozed off a few times and nodded awake with a fright. Each time he jerked awake, Soop was sitting in the same place: watching him – his white eyes staring at him, unblinking.

The firewood just made it until morning when the first rays of sunshine trickled over the horizon. The clicking sounds receded down the mountainside and into the forest. Soon they were gone completely.

"Right. Let's go. We can eat something later," Soop said as he stood with a stretch. He acted as if he'd had the most restful sleep.

Jeff groaned as he stood up. He was stiff from his mad rush through the forest and the strenuous climb up the mountain. Everything hurt.

"What's the matter … didn't you sleep?" Soop asked as he stretched his arms over his head. He put his hands on his hips and twisted his back left and right.

"Someone had to keep the fire going and I didn't see you add any logs," Jeff retorted.

"Oh … he slept beautifully – he has mastered the art of sleeping with his eyes open. He will teach you how to do it. He is absolutely perfect at it. No one does it better than he does – he could open a helpline for sleeping with eyes open," Soop said.

Sleeps with his eyes open – he flipping freaked me out all night, Jeff thought with a frown.

With his bag on his back and the rope looped around his shoulder and back, Jeff led the way back down the mountain. He thought it would have been easier to go down than up but it was harder and there seemed to be a lot more loose rocks today. He had to look for his footholds and every time he searched the distance to the ground seemed to sway in front of him.

"It will help if you don't look down so much," Soop offered in a chatty voice.

"I have to look down if I want to find a place to grip," Jeff muttered.

Soop seemed to have no trouble in the descent and it seemed like he had some practice at it. "He is very good at mountain climbing. He can climb any mountain like an expert. He can ..."

"Teach me ... yes I know." Jeff muttered in time with Soop's nasal voice.

"So ... Jeff ... how did you really know how to find him – did someone point out the way? He is not very popular at the castle. Don't know why because all he really wanted to do is assist them in making their lives better."

"Ah ... no one really said anything about you. I just figured that I would search for higher ground, hence the mountain. It was pure luck that I found you." Jeff was vague. The man who gave him the bag food had given good advice – trust only Madgwick and Khrow.

Once they reached the ground they set off towards the forest but in a different direction than Jeff came from.

After a few hours, Jeff asked. "Are you sure we're still going the right way? Because I think we passed this rock before. I remember that purple moss, because it's weird."

"Oh he is quite sure we are on the right path. He is very good with paths and has actually created a detailed map of this entire region. There is not a path he does not know and has not walked upon."

Jeff rolled his eyes when they stopped at a fork. "Can you ask *him* – which way – left or right?"

Soop turned around with a small shuffle. There was silence.

Jeff turned to look at Soop as he was taking rather long to decide.

"Well ... he ... uh he needs to think ..." he started.

Jeff sat down on a rock and put his elbows on his knees. "It's time for a break anyway. So you are not sure about which path to take? How long ago did *he* walk along this one?" Jeff asked innocently and raised his eyebrows.

"Not very long ago but he walked so fast because he thought someone was following. He can spot an imposter a mile away but it took a few turns here and there to get rid of the intruder who was probably trying to find the portal. So maybe that tainted his memory a bit. He has an excellent memory. He would be very happy to impart his wisdom with you to improve your memory skills."

"Why don't you want to share the location with anyone?" Jeff asked.

Soop spun around and stared at Jeff. "Who said he doesn't want to show anyone the location?"

"Uh ... you just said that someone was following you trying to find the location of the portal," Jeff said with a wave of his hand as if this was obvious.

"Ah yes, he is a little suspicious. But then he has every reason to be. They forced him out of the castle sanctuary without a second thought as to what would happen to him at all."

"Why would they force you out?" Jeff asked.

"Apparently they did not like him at all. All he wanted to do was improve on just a few things, not too much. Just their living conditions, their farming techniques and food supplies, their medicine, their mental health, their entertainment. Their idea of entertainment is open to interpretation! And then you know what? They rejected every suggestion he made. Did they appreciate him? No. They called him names and even said that he was the reason the wuunacks arrived in the first place. Like really – he is good but he is not *that* good that he can summon the wuunacks," Soop said with a click of his tongue. He stood with his hands on his hips and his single strand of grey hair that covered his baldness fell to the side.

"So how *have* you survived the wuunacks all this time?" Jeff asked as he tossed a small rock into the bushes and watched as bright blue birds scattered into the trees chirping noisily.

"Why do you want to know? Are you a spy?" Soop dropped his head as he studied Jeff.

"Well, they kicked me out too," Jeff said with a shrug. "So are you going to tell me?" He pushed, careful not to make any eye contact so it looked like he was just talking casually.

"No. He does not think he will tell. You ask too many questions. And they could have kicked you out for the sole intention of finding out his secrets. He is not stupid. He knows how spies work." Soop sniffed.

Jeff stared at Soop without blinking. "Right. So *you* telling me *in my head* to come find you, was a plan devised by *them*. I get it." Jeff shook his head.

Soop was quiet. "Maybe you are right. Not many people are proven right with him so don't get used to it as it won't happen very often. He is normally right in all matters," Soop said with pursed lips.

"So why did you want me to find you?"

"You somehow repelled the wuunacks, which means there is something different about you. To open the portal I need essence of dragon blood. He doesn't know *how* but you may have some dragon blood in you," Soop said.

He needs my blood, but how exactly does he intend to get it? I don't like this. Jeff stared at his shoes, which had started to fray at the seams.

"So you think that my blood will open the door, so I am like a sacrifice?" Jeff asked bluntly and stared at Soop without blinking, a trick he had learned from the Sandustian warrior Rig when he needed to get straight answers.

"Well ... sometimes sacrifices must be made, but he doubts it will kill you. He didn't foresee your death and he sees everything, as you already know." Soop glanced around as he spoke.

"Right. So you said. Let's go. Is there a cave or something that we can stay in tonight? We still need to make a fire." Jeff pulled his bag over shoulder and hopped up.

Soop was annoying but so far Jeff had not been able to tell if he had been lying or not. *He does not see everything because then he would have seen that Madgwick and Khrow will be going through the portal with me or nobody will be going through at all*, he thought as he followed Soop through the forest.

Jeff stretched as he exited the cave they had taken refuge in. The sun peeked through the trees and danced on the forest floor. He stared at the boulders near the stream and frowned, he had seen that stone formation before when he left the castle on route to the mountain – he had sat and rested on the flat one. Jeff shook his head, Soop had deliberately led them through the forest for an entire day just to make the journey seem longer than it actually was. He hid his smile as he realised that he was much closer to where Madgwick and Khrow was and he would be able to reach them very quickly.

Soop gazed at a hidden path that dwindled into the forest. "We are not too far now. See what he just did? He knows how to distract someone from their thoughts. You will never find this path again. All directional information has been wiped from your memory. You won't even be able to find your way back." Soop grinned. His large white teeth almost glared at Jeff.

Jeff stared at Soop with his mouth hanging open. *Is he for real? So far it's relatively straightforward: over the mountain, back down in a straight line, over the little stream of bright yellow pebbles, along the little path while keeping the purple moss boulders on your left, a little way along the stream before crossing at the flat stones and then along this topsy-turvy path. Past the rock that looks like a duck. Not my first time in a forest, dude. Anyway I have made marks to help me later. Not stupid,* Jeff thought, shrugged and lifted his hands in a surrender motion. "You are right. I can't remember a single thing. I am totally lost. Which way should we go?"

Soop smirked and then led the way down the left path. He had a skip in his step as if he was very thrilled that someone agreed with him without an argument.

Jeff grinned as he walked behind him. He still didn't trust the old man, but besides being super annoying, he had not posed a threat – other than a non-fatal sacrifice involving Jeff's blood.

They came around a boulder. Jeff was pushing away hip-high green ferns. He looked up and gasped when he saw a bright blue waterfall, white water cascading and crashing over the top. Not a sound could be heard. It was eerie.

"Why is it so quiet?" Jeff asked aloud but his voice came out as a whisper.

"It's the magic of the falls, something to do with dreams," Soop whispered back.

Jeff stared at the waterfall as they made their way to a dark swirling blue pool at the base of the falls.

"Come on, there is a path at the back."

The sun was low on the horizon when Jeff and Soop slipped behind the waterfall and disappeared from sight.

14

Khrow gave Srat a backhand across the face. The man would have flown back thirty yards except Khrow held onto his shirt with the other hand. "Oh no, you don't – you are not going anywhere. You are staying right here where I can hit you again and again until you tell me what you have done with Jeff." Khrow slapped him again. The man's head nodded like a dashboard doll dancing to a tune.

"We didn't do anything with him. I swear." Srat groaned.

"Right! I can see Jeff is standing right here next to me. Speak up, Jeff. I can't hear you. What? What? Oh wait … he isn't here is he. Where *is* he?" Khrow lifted the man till his toes were barely scraping on the floor. Khrow swung his arm and dished out another backhand. Srat's head snapped backwards and he groaned. His face was blood red with streaks of purple across his cheeks. He passed out and Khrow threw him to the side like a bag of potatoes. He turned around and lunged for the next man.

They were locked up in that underground room for almost a day and a half and when they were finally released – Jeff was gone and no one was talking about what happened to the youngster.

"Don't kill them, Khrow – one of them has to talk," Madgwick said mildly as he carved notches into a stick with a thin piece of metal. He looked bored but the anger was bubbling inside like a volcano eagerly waiting for an eruption.

Khrow was truly terrifying: very tall and muscular, and his black skin glistened with sweat as his muscles bulged and flexed.

Four of the men lay scattered on the floor unconscious around them as Khrow went from one to the next. Khrow pointed his finger and rasped, "Do not move!" when they tried to shuffle and scramble to the side. Some of them whimpered as they hid their heads under their arms.

The table under the lemon tree had been flung aside and some of the wooden chairs lay in splinters. Khrow had destroyed the wooden furniture to calm down before he grabbed the first villager.

Madgwick sat behind the group to make sure they did not move away from the designated spot Khrow had ordered them to sit in.

"What is the big deal … he was just a kid? He was not one of us," one of the men yelled out and flinched as both warriors turned in sync and stared him down.

"Do you think I risked my life to ensure the kid's safety because he is a *nobody* – he was not one of you – he is part of ME. He is *my* family. MY FAMILY. I want to know what you have done and if you don't start talking, I will personally throw you out of the castle gates this evening – every single one of you. Do not think I won't do it. Fireballs! I will even enjoy hearing you scream." Khrow shouted so loudly that a vein in his neck bulged as if about to burst.

Khrow lifted the man he was holding by his shirt into the air and pulled his arm back for another slap.

"We set him outside the gate yesterday!" the man screamed holding his arms up to cover his face.

"You did WHAT?" Khrow roared and slapped the man. His legs dangled like twisted cord. He threw the limp body of the unconscious man to the ground in a heap and then lunged for the next one.

"Where did he go?" he roared. His eyes were large and fierce and spittle flew over the man he was holding up with one arm.

"We don't know but we told him he will endanger all our lives … your lives too if he did not leave. We saved us and *you*." A man screamed hysterically while his legs were climbing stairs in the air.

"There was something off about him – he heard the voice of that madman," another man yelled before cowering under his arms.

Khrow threw the man to the floor and stared at them as they lay crumpled on the ground, groaning in agony.

He looked at Madgwick, who was holding his head with both hands as if his head was going to split apart.

"We have to go after him," Madgwick whispered and stared into Khrow's crazed eyes.

"He has already been a night out there – alone." Khrow's voice sounded hoarse.

"We have to find him Khrow. It's Jeff … out there. Alone," Madgwick said.

Khrow turned and strode to the closed gates. "ARGGGGGGGHHHH!" He screamed and banged on the doors until it seemed as if the hinges were going to pop loose. He stood with his stands pressed against the gate as if he were waiting for some kind of answer.

Those still conscious stayed quiet not daring to speak and draw attention back to themselves.

Madgwick waited for him to calm down. Now would not be a good time to interrupt Khrow. He was a very dangerous warrior and even more so when he was angry. He might not have had his dust, but he was still lethal. The men here had no idea who they were dealing with.

Finally he turned back towards the men staring at him with big eyes. He gazed around at the castle walls but saw nothing. In front of Madgwick he came to a stop, rubbing his hands over his shiny bald head. "Madgwick – we must let Jeff run his course. We have to wait here. There is something about him that kept the wuunacks at bay."

Madgwick opened his mouth to argue but Khrow waved him down.

"We must trust him, Madgwick – he will come back to us when he can, if he can."

The few men who could still stand started pushing to their knees but sank back down when Khrow glared at them and lifted a finger as if they were naughty boys.

"No – you will all stay out here. You will experience the same discomfort as Jeff does. If he is out in the open then so will you be. Any of you try to move and I will break your legs. DO NOT tempt me, DO NOT make me look for you and DO NOT make me say this again."

As he walked off he growled, which made the men shudder and sink to their knees on the ground – no one was moving. The men of Dunargh sat huddled in the courtyard. They were too afraid of Khrow to move.

***

A while later, Madgwick stood on the castle wall, almost in the exact spot Jeff had stood. He gripped the wall as he stared out over the forests and at the tall snow-capped mountain that stretched into the sky. His jaw bounced as he clenched and unclenched his teeth. *Where are you Jeff, are you safe?*

He heard a movement behind him. The man who had helped Jeff with food had shuffled over and said in a very low voice, "I gave him food and told him where to find the seer. If he is a smart kid then he will find seer and find the exit of this place. He will come back once he knows the location. I told him not to trust anyone. Best thing you can do right now is to wait it out and not become candy for the wuunacks," the man said gruffly.

Khrow stood next to Madgwick. "He will be okay," Khrow muttered. "I have been trying to reach him but for some reason he is not hearing me. He is a smart boy and he has been through a lot – he knows what he must do."

"What if he never comes back? What if he is lying in a ditch somewhere hurt or dead?" Madgwick asked and stared into Khrow's face.

"Then I will destroy this entire compound and burn it to the ground," Khrow said and clenched his jaw.

"What do we do in the meantime?" Madgwick asked as he slapped the stone surface.

"The only thing we can do – prepare like I did when I realised someone was coming to this dimension. We must prepare wood stacks. We must build a few in every direction so that when we know where Jeff is we can move towards him. It's the only protection we will have."

Madgwick nodded as Khrow spoke. "Yes, at least I feel like I am doing something constructive instead of waiting around. It's a good plan. We must be able to reach each stack with ease."

"I think tomorrow at first light we will head in different directions and try and make as many as we can. We must be back here before twilight," Khrow muttered.

Madgwick turned and stared at the huddled men in the courtyard.

"Did they move? I hope so. I really want to kill one of those villagers down there." Khrow ground his fist into his palm as he pulled his lips back.

Madgwick and Khrow spent the night on top of the castle tower so that they could see the land around the castle; they took turns to keep watch in case there was any sign of Jeff.

When the sun started to peek over the horizon, they gathered some water and walked towards the castle gate.

Khrow pointed at the men who lay sleeping. "Will Jeff have breakfast – yes? No? WE DON'T KNOW. So you will not either. You will stay where you are ..." Khrow thundered at the wide-eyed men.

"But Khrow, you are being unreasonable ..." one man was brave enough to mumble although he kept his head bent low to avoid Khrow's glare.

Khrow stopped and strode to tower over the man sitting on the floor. His voice was deep and menacing as he growled. "It was unreasonable to banish a boy from the safety of this castle with no help. It was unreasonable to lock us up the WHOLE FIREBALL DAY to stop us from finding our brother. You took the action, this is the consequence. Suck it up."

He glared at everyone, catching their eye. "Know this. You move – you die."

Khrow and Madgwick walked out of the castle gates.

15

Jeff sucked in the damp air as he stepped behind the waterfall. The contrast was breath-taking from the silent cascading water over the ledge behind him to the tranquil pool that lay in the middle of this little cave. Jeff stepped closer to the pool, hardly daring to blink in case he missed something. It was like a dream. The pool was midnight blue and as smooth as glass; pinprick lights twinkled and sparkled on the surface like glitter. He gazed at the flickering lights then noticed his hands and arms sparkled with tiny blue dots and realised it was a reflection. He turned around and stared at the wall behind him. Shiny blue stones embedded in the wall dazzled and glittered. As he moved he lifted his hands, the lights were dancing over his skin, he felt like he was part of the wall. Jeff knelt at the pool and was about to touch the eerie blue water when Soop yelled.

"Don't touch it!"

Jeff jerked his hand back and sat on his haunches. He could not take his eyes off the glinting spots on the water.

"It's mesmerising, feels like part of a dream and you want to touch it so badly that it takes immense willpower to avoid slipping your fingers through the silky water. Many have fallen into the spell of these bewitching pools. A mere drop of that water and you will be cast into a trance or dream – he doesn't know which but it's powerful. Also … if the water is disturbed then it releases the wuunacks from their nocturnal pattern until the water settles again into its dream state aligned with the moon – just a day or so. He has foreseen this to be true," Soop warned and tapped his head with his finger.

Soop shuffled around the pool, hopping from stone to stone until he was on the far side of the pool. Hidden in the corner was a small wooden door with broad metal straps that crisscrossed over the wooden panels. Jeff saw a round gold-bronze disk in the middle of the door, almost like a keyhole but without the hole for the key.

"This is it, the exit out of here," Soop said as he smoothed his grey strand of hair over his head. His teeth glittered with tiny blue dots when he grinned. "It has been foretold that dragon essence will open the door. Let's try it now, bring your arm." Soop pulled out a thin metal object that looked like a very crudely homemade knife.

"So the portal has been in this cave all along and no one has ever found it?" Jeff asked as he studied the door. He stayed on the far side of the pool.

Soop flapped his hands impatiently. "Well, he can't say for sure that no one has ever found the door. This pool is of ancient magic and has been here a very long time. And he supposes most of the visitors were lured into the water. The door can only open if certain criteria have been met. But he has read … or rather *seen* that dragons can open any door or portal. He obviously does not know for sure if you have dragon essence. That fact will be revealed before long, because he sees everything. Anyway it is foretold that the one that repels the wuunacks has the essence to open the door. That must be *you* and it must mean *this* door." Soop beckoned for Jeff to join him with his hand.

Jeff nodded and folded his arms across his chest but did not move. "So where does it come out?" He knew enough about portals to know that the other end may not be a desirable exit for survival. Entry to the world called Torturra was an instant death sentence if you did not have the correct protection.

Soop sniffed. "What do you mean? Somewhere – who knows?"

"Wait. You don't *know*? You expect to open it without *knowing* where it leads? I am not going through *any* portal unless I know where it comes out," Jeff said calmly and gazed around the room again.

Soop sighed and sat on smooth rock near the water's edge and stared at Jeff without saying anything for what felt like a long time.

No way. You are not going to try and intimidate me, Jeff thought as he stared back at Soop, trying not to blink.

"Be careful boy – he only needs your dragon essence … he does not actually need *you*," Soop said softly.

Jeff felt the hairs rise on the back of his neck at the threat. "Right. That's good to know. I need some fresh air. I will be right back." He turned on his heel and made his way back to the curtain of water cascading down.

"Oh, come on Jeff, don't be so sensitive. He was just talking nonsense out loud. He knows all about talking nonsense because he is the best at it. He can teach anyone to talk nonsense all the time. Don't go," Soop said loudly in his nasal voice. Soop pinched his nose with his forefinger and thumb as if he suddenly had a headache.

Jeff pressed his lips together and turned around before the wall of water. "Since you're *the* best at visions, work on a vision that indicates where the door comes out if you want me to help you open *that* door." Jeff pointed at the little hidden door in the corner of the cave.

Soop threw his hands in the air. "Oh don't be so dramatic, you are really very bad at it. He will give you a few pointers on how to be successful at drama. He *knows* that you want your friends to join you but they can't. They are not really your friends so he thinks he needs to help you deal with that issue right now." With his foot, he nudged a pebble into the pool with a resounding PLONK that echoed through the cavern. "Oops," he said and grinned broadly. The tiny pin lights danced on his large white teeth.

The change was instant. Jeff's mouth dropped open as the smooth surface of the pool shattered like glass and the ripples ran through the water to lap on the stones. The room suddenly lit up as the reflections caused a chaos of lights across the walls. It seemed as if the pinpricks that were so tranquil were zig-zagging in all directions as if suddenly launched into warp speed.

He looked up at Soop but could not get the words out. "What did you just do! Why? Why would you do that?" he stuttered and rubbed his face with both hands.

"Well – now the wuunacks are running free, the warriors will be eaten and you are free from any burden or obligation to 'save' them. You are welcome," Soop said as he turned to study the disk on the door as if his actions were normal.

Jeff clamped his mouth shut, spun on his heel and pushed through the water curtain; the chill of the water was so refreshing it cleared his mind. The whole cave with the twinkling lights seemed like a dream. He knew what to do; he had no time to spare.

Soop shouted. "Jeff. Come back. He is sorry – but your friends can't come along. Okay, go and take a break and deal with your anger but don't be too long because the sooner we get the door open the sooner we can leave. Okay: take a few minutes – take five minutes. He knows you are angry with him but don't go too far because you will never find this place again. You know he is the only one with a fool-proof sense of direction. You will get lost! He has not taught you anything about directional guidance yet. Jeff. Jeff? JEEEFFF!"

Jeff heard the shouting from within the cave but ignored it. The water dripped off his cream shirt, cool and refreshing as if he'd just had an ice cold shower. He rubbed his hair and took careful note of landmarks, outcrops, trees and anything to help him find his way back to this very point.

There was no time to waste. On the way to the waterfall, he had been very careful to remain behind Soop to make discreet marks here and there. It was easy to let Soop take the lead because of the old man's self-proclaimed expert navigational skills. Now as he backtracked on the path, he found the marks he had obscurely left and smiled grimly. *So far so good.*

He hurried along the forest path. Soop's pitiful yelling started to fade.

Khrow, Khrow, he thought every few minutes as he half-walked half-jogged through the forest.

16

Khrow lifted his head and gazed into the trees that huddled together creating an eerie shroud of darkness. He lifted his chin and sniffed as if there was a distinct odour in the air that could confirm the uneasiness he felt … something was amiss. When he heard a faint scream in the distance he frowned. He turned in a circle to listen.

Then came the sound of someone or something crashing through the forest. He darted to the side as a herd of black and white striped creatures with red spiralled horns raced past him. They did not even acknowledge his presence. This mass movement was really weird as until now he had hardly seen any creatures at all besides the wuunacks.

The wuunacks attacked at night but he had been told there was a time where there were no wuunacks and the inhabitants of Dunargh lived peacefully and happy. On the odd occasion, the wuunacks had attacked in daylight but that only lasted for a day or so before they moved back to their night-time feasts. No one knew what exactly set them off to attack during the day but it made the folk fearful, suspicious of strangers and distrustful of anything out of the ordinary.

"KHROW," a voice cried out in the distance.

Khrow spun around and sprang into the dense bushes in the direction of where the shout came from. It was Madgwick. He jumped over boulders and fallen trunks, almost slipping on the soft green moss that blanketed the tree stumps.

Then he saw the warrior wading and hopping through the ferns, trying to move as fast as possible.

"We need to get back right now. I heard the alarm for the urgent retreat to Dunargh."

"They are closing the gates! If they lock us out we are in trouble!" He dropped the logs he was carrying and sprang through the forest as he joined Madgwick in his mad dash for the castle. They ran like dreamons were chasing them. Ferns whipped at their thighs, they sprang over fallen tree trunks and leapt over boulders. Madgwick slipped but before he could stumble and crash to the floor, his arm was gripped by Khrow, whose momentum kept Madgwick on his feet and shoved him forward. Khrow was considerably older than Madgwick and had decades of warrior experience ahead of him. Back in Sandustian, no one messed with Khrow. Kojo, Horrigan, Rig and Khrow had progressed through the warrior ranks at the same time. All four were formidable warriors – with or without dust.

Madgwick had not been surprised to see Khrow had inadvertently spread his authority over Dunargh. He was an intimidating warrior even if he no longer had magical dust. Madgwick nodded as he understood what it felt to be bonded to magic that was suddenly not there anymore. He struggled with that hollow feeling inside himself. It was like the heat was gone – replaced by a cold chill.

The two warriors ran out of the forest and down the long yellow gravel road towards the castle. They were about half way to the castle when they heard the dull THUD of the doors closing.

"Open the doors!" Khrow yelled breathlessly as they came to the door.

As they stood outside the gates, the sounds of scrambling could be heard within.

Madgwick stared at the large wooden gates with narrowed eyes. "Hate to state the obvious but I don't think that they are going to open up for us," he muttered and curled his hands into fists.

"Open these gates or I will break them down and then I will start on each one of you," Khrow shouted. He rammed his shoulder into the door but it did not budge.

"Now the gates will definitely not open," Madgwick said with a shake of his head.

Faces peered over the wall and stared down at them. "We can't do that. Just leave now. You are with that mad boy. Go. We do not want you here. You are bad luck."

"THEY ARE COMING!" someone screamed from within.

Another shouted. "SILENCE. SAY NOTHING!"

"There is something odd happening here," Madgwick said. He turned around to watch their backs. The men were not happy when he and Jeff arrived but this hostility was on a complete other level."

The old man, who had told Khrow and Madgwick that he had given Jeff some food and pointed him towards the mountain, came around the side of the castle. He had not returned in time before the gates were shut.

"Khrow – you have to run, before it's too late." The old man tried to hurry towards them.

"SILENCE," someone screamed from above.

"They are cowards. The wuunacks have been released from their night constraints. Run Khrow – RUN!" he shouted.

"They are coming. Look. They are coming," another screamed.

Khrow and Madgwick whirled around and gazed in the direction the man on the top of the wall was pointing. They could not see anything.

"Open these gates," Madgwick yelled and pounded on the door with his fists.

The old man stood with his back to the gate and clasped his hands and bowed his head. He had a small smile on his cracked lips.

Khrow grabbed Madgwick's arm. "Thunderbolts. We are on our own – let's go, Madgwick."

He pulled Madgwick away, but Madgwick was still staring at the wall and at the faces peering down at them. Some were laughing openly at their dilemma.

Khrow grabbed the old man by the arm and said, "Come, get on my back, I will carry you. We need to go."

"Go? No. It has been a long day and I am tired. I look forward to my sleep – I choose this. Go – don't look back." The old man smiled at Khrow.

Madgwick tugged on Khrow's arm and dragged him away.

Khrow took a few steps backwards as he stared at the man and then shook his head, but it was clear the old man had made his decision when he sat down on a stone.

The two warriors sprinted for the forest towards the fire stacks they had spent the day building. They arrived at the first stack and Khrow hastily fashioned strips to make slings to carry as much wood as they could. "Let's move as close as we can to the mountain, as far as we know, that's the direction that Jeff went in. Let's go!" Khrow growled.

They passed four stacks before the clicking and whistling sounds of the wuunacks could be heard. Khrow threw his wood down with a clatter. "We have no choice; we will not make the next stack. This is where we must make a stand."

Khrow and Madgwick tossed wood in a circle to form a hedge-like wall around the fire stack. The chattering and clicking sounded so loud they expected the wuunacks to make an appearance at any second.

"Light it," Khrow ordered as he stared at the forest. The monsters flooded out of the dense bush and stopped at the border of the fire circle, moving around the fire, looking for an entry like a wheel.

Madgwick watched as the creatures crawled and crept over each other like snakes in a pit. Their black shiny shells seemed to glisten in the sunlight that filtered through the trees. They looked like gigantic dung beetles with tiny pincers that opened and closed – looking for something to grab. The trees had become became very still as if trying to stay out of the picture. Not a bird could be seen or heard. The forest was empty except for the wuunacks and their lunch: Madgwick and Khrow.

"We are in trouble," Madgwick said as he walked around the hedge-wall to make sure it was tight and lit.

"Hah – we have had worse than this," Khrow muttered.

"That sounds like something Rig once said when we were surrounded by shimmers. At least you could see them and their rows upon rows of teeth," Madgwick said.

"Yeah ... they were nasty to fight but these don't look so bad – they look like beetles ... big black beetles. I think it will be a day or two, then they will return to their nightly adventures," Khrow said as he stared at the beetles that started churning around the fire.

"What do you mean?" Madgwick asked.

"It has happened before that the wuunacks suddenly attacked in sunlight but it only lasted a day or two before they went back to their nightly ritual. But no one could explain why?"

"But how?"

"That's a question for another time. Right now we have other issues."

Khrow and Madgwick waved the fire at the wuunacks to keep them away from the circle.

"Do not light the stack – we must use the wood to keep the circle of fire intact," Khrow said.

Neither made mention of what would happen when they ran out of wood, which was going to happen eventually.

17

Horrigan stopped just outside the cave and glanced around as if to gather his bearings. Nequam stood next to him. Without a word they moved into the forest.

"Watroc is right; there is a strange presence here," Horrigan whispered as he sniffed the air. "Nasty smell." He wrinkled his nose.

They moved in-between the tree trunks, melding and blending in with the forest, all the time listening and watching, but there was no sound or movement.

Suddenly Horrigan sank to one knee and stared into the gloom, his purple eyes glowed brightly.

"What is it?" Nequam whispered as he hunched down and glanced around the forest.

"That is Sandustian dust – dust from Nyx." Horrigan breathed and pointed towards a tree in the distance.

A very small shimmering light buzzed around close to the ground around a tree, then it darted under a large leaf. It looked like silvery fairy light.

"That? No way, it's a firefly. We have a lot of them here." Nequam breathed as he watched the little light zip around.

Horrigan held his hand out and a pinch of dust trailed out of his hand, with a nod from Horrigan it dashed off to find the darting dust in the forest.

They waited still crouched by the tree; both were looking in opposite directions to make sure they stayed hidden. It was a few seconds before

Horrigan's dust came floating back to them, accompanied by the first sprinkle of dust.

"Hello, little dust, will you show me where she is?" Horrigan whispered to the hovering dust.

It shot off into the darkness, then stopped as if to wait for them to catch up. Quietly they moved through the trees, over boulders, under fallen trunks and waded through waist high ferns. Twice they had to stop and blend into the darkness when they saw a hooded figure cross the path ahead of them.

The dust floated to the darkness of a large tree and then winked out of sight.

"There she is," Horrigan muttered and moved slowly forward.

"Hey Horri." Nyx whispered casually as if she knew all along that Horrigan would come and find her. She leaned against a tree as she peered around the trunk again as if scanning the forest.

"Very clever ... using your dust to show us the way. What is wrong? Why have you not gone back to the cave?" Horrigan asked as he too scanned the forest for any movement.

Nequam went down on his haunches with his back to them, watching for dreamons.

"I found a forest full of children from the village – hiding. The poor dears are tired and scared. I had to stay and help them. I knew you would come looking for me."

At that, Nequam swung around and hissed, "The children from the village ... all of them?"

"Not all of them, unless you only have twelve kids in the village. I have four kids hidden not far from here, and I have another group of eight that I've hidden inside a tree with dust protecting them, that way." She pointed with her finger. "I was on my way back to get another two when I saw a dreamon. Then I heard you and decided to wait. Come on," Nyx muttered softly.

"Lead the way, Nyx and do not call me Horri," Horrigan growled.

Carefully and quietly they sneaked, crawled and moved through the forest. Now and then they took to the trees and moved like shadows from branch to branch. Nyx dropped quietly to the ground and moved towards a large tree. Horrigan and Nequam followed her lead.

"It's me." She whispered and dust flew into her hands, revealing a large crack within the trunk. Within the crack were little white faces staring out at them.

"Fireballs," Horrigan exclaimed breathlessly as he peered inside the hollow.

Nequam shoved Horrigan aside and leaned in; there was a soft cry as the children recognised one of their own. "Shooosh ... shooosh," Nequam calmed them down. "Quiet now."

Nyx and Horrigan scanned the area and then nodded to Nequam, "Bring them out," Nyx said.

Horrigan was quiet as the children came out and stood huddled around them. The children stared at his brightly glowing purple eyes.

Nyx bent down in front of a little boy of about five. He clambered onto her back and held onto her thick braid like a rope. "Quewin, walk behind me," Nyx whispered softly into the boy's ear.

Nequam picked up a girl and deposited her onto Horrigan's board back. She wrapped her little hands around his leather straps that crisscrossed his back. Horrigan looked a bit awkward but he nodded and was ready to go. Nequam knelt down and soon he too had a child on his back. They were so small they could not take the chance they would not make a noise or run if they got scared. This was the quickest way to get them all travelling at once.

Nyx led the way, with Quewin tucked in between Nyx and Nequam – Horrigan brought up the rear. It seemed to take forever but they soon reached the first group. Horrigan and Nyx stood guard while the children hugged Nequam. He calmed them down and made them sit quietly on the floor.

"There must be more children out there," Nequam said quietly. "In the event of danger, the children have been taught to depart in groups of six; the oldest one would lead the way and watch over them until help came."

"We need to get this group to safety, at the same time look for the others," Horrigan said with a nod to Nyx.

"Those were my thoughts exactly, but how?" Nyx asked.

"Nequam, you start taking the children to the cave." Horrigan held up his hand when Nequam opened his mouth. "It must be *you* because you know exactly where the cave is. We will look for more children and bring them here, and before you argue – *we* have to do that because we can hide them with our dust."

Nequam closed his mouth with a snap. "Okay, yes. That makes sense."

Quewin held his hand up as if asking for permission to speak. Horrigan looked at him with raised eyebrows.

"I can stay here and keep the children quiet when you find them," he offered.

Nyx nodded, "Okay, that's a plan then. Let's move out."

Into the darkness Nyx and Horrigan disappeared.

18

Nequam chose a small child and Zazkia to take on the first trip to the cave. Zazkia would provide comfort for the children in the cave, especially if there was a big green scaly hungry dragon in their midst.

It took Nequam almost an hour to make it back to the cave; he had to take a detour to avoid the dreamons who were sticking to the paths in the forest. They made a huge racket and it almost seemed on purpose to scare children out of hiding. Nequam sagged against a tree and released his pent up breath with a whoosh when he finally saw the entrance of the cave close by. He ushered Zazkia through the entrance into the golden-green lit cavern.

Phoebe leapt up and rushed over with her hands flapping in the air. Zazkia was a bit shy but Phoebe ignored her shyness and brought the girl closer to the stone fire to warm up.

Nequam placed the younger child next to Zazkia and they held their hands out to the green fiery glow. Both children were staring at Watroc who stared back at them unblinking.

"Food?" Watroc asked with a hopeful note in his deep voice.

"No." Phoebe and Nequam answered at the same time.

"Where did they come from?" Phoebe asked in a hushed voice.

"Nyx found them! That's why she didn't come back."

"How many are there?" Phoebe exclaimed.

"Nyx found twelve. Horrigan and Nyx are looking for more."

"I must go back, took me forever to bring these two here because I had to avoid dreamons searching the forests. There's another ten I must bring to the cave. I don't know how many Nyx and Horrigan will still find."

Watroc stretched his neck towards the ceiling and roared, "TEN – that is going to take FOREVER. I am hungry!"

The children hunched down as the flames hit the ceiling and bounced around the walls like a puppet show.

Phoebe looked over at Watroc and placed her hands on her hips. "You are going to have to do something or just wait, cos those kids are out there and we need to bring them to safety." She pointed her finger at the waterfall curtain. "Watroc … imagine if *I* was out there … would you eat first before you did something?"

Watroc closed his eyes and shook his wings as if he needed some air. "ARRRGGHHHH. Okay, I will do something because I AM HUNGRY!"

Nequam looked from Watroc to Phoebe back to Watroc. "Do what?"

"Something," Phoebe nodded. The gold specks in her eyes looked like stars as they sparkled and her braces gleamed in the green glow of the cavern.

"What is he going to do?" Nequam asked.

"Dragon magic," Phoebe said shortly.

"I need a stone." Watroc reached over to a boulder and with a flick of his talon, cracked it in half. A piece about as big as Phoebe's hand flew into the air before it landed on the sandy cave floor with a soft thud. Nequam fetched it and placed it in front of the dragon while Phoebe helped the two kids onto a ledge so that they were out of the way.

"It is dragon magic but we don't need you getting caught in a spell by accident and turned into a miniature green dragon now, do we?" Phoebe winked at the kids.

Watroc stared at the broken rock with narrowed eyes. A thin stream of green fire shot out of his nostrils like a blow torch. The fire was so intense it had streaks of blue within the green. Soon the stone was bright green as if it had a lamp inserted inside. Watroc started to hum.

With dragon's hum and dragon's roar,
A circle of fire I wish to draw
With flame and fury I fling my might
To bewitch this passage of magical flight
Be wary those with evil ways
Deny temptation, avert your gaze!
For should you seize that which is mine
A dragon's rage is what you will find.

Watroc blew a thin string of fire on the sandy floor around the glowing stone until the green flame formed a large circle. When the ends of the circle connected, a wall of green flame rose so high it almost scorched the cavern ceiling. With a whoosh it was gone, leaving a thin lime green line in the sand, neon and liquid-looking. Smoke tendrils curled and danced from the edges of the fire circle.

"There, I have done something," Watroc said with a huff. A round smoke ball puffed out of his nostril. "Draw a circle with this stone; it will be a safe passage and transport the little things from that circle to this circle. Take it – it is not hot."

"Oh wow – that is awesome, Watroc," Phoebe exclaimed. "How long will it last, how much time do we have?" Phoebe's eyebrows were raised as she shot the questions out.

"There you go again … lots of questions – I LIKE IT. It lasts as long as it lasts. You can send one at a time or all at once because the passage is big enough. I will close the circle once everyone is through and when the other warriors are back.

Nequam reached out to the stone and then jerked his hand back as if anticipating that it was too hot to touch.

Phoebe rolled her eyes, picked the stone up and held it out to Nequam, "Now is not the time to be stupid. Take the stone and say thank you!"

Nequam stared at the glowing green stone in his hand; he lifted his hand to Watroc but was unable to say anything other than give a firm nod.

Watroc snorted and turned away. Two circles of smoke shot into the air from both his nostrils and the two kids still sitting on the ledge giggled.

Nequam moved swiftly through the forest, leaping over stumps and crawling around dreamons that strode along the forest paths. He was in a hurry to get back to the children. The stone glowed so brightly that he tucked the stone under his shirt to dim the shine. In the distance he saw dreamons as they crossed his path but he was so silent that they had no idea that he was moving among them. Moving from shadow to shadow Nequam steadily made his way through the forest.

"It's Nequam," he whispered when he approached the hollow beneath the trunk. He leaned in and saw Quewin with the sleepy children. The boy gave him a thumbs-up sign and a tired smile.

Nequam held up the glowing stone. "Thanks to a dragon, you are going to be travelling in style. Wake them up. You are all leaving right now."

Nequam moved to a small space next to the fallen trunk. Another tumbledown tree trunk blocked the one side and large leafy green ferns the other. It was a bit risky as they could still be seen but it was the only place that had enough space.

Nequam drew a circle in the sand with the rock. Right away the outline filled with a green glow like liquid fire filling a tube. He didn't like being in the open like this but he had no choice, and he couldn't waste any time. He hastily beckoned to the little ones who were yawning and rubbing their eyes.

"Do not be afraid, this will take you to Zazkia and my friends Phoebe and Watroc, the dragon. He is big and looks scary but he is on our side, so a friendly dragon."

With wide eyes that seemed to glow from the green circle, the children held hands and stepped towards it. Nequam could see their lips quivering from fear. As they stepped into the circle, a whoosh of fire leapt up and they were gone. Quewin was the only one left; he stood staring at where the kids had just disappeared in a flash of green flame.

"I can stay here and help the others through," Quewin said as he stared at the green circle. The flames had vanished as quickly as they rose into the air.

"Do you know how many groups made it into the forest?" Nequam asked, bending down so that he was on eye level with Quewin, his hand on his shoulder.

"All of us made it into the forest, but I am not sure how many are still hidden as we heard screams when those beasts dragged a few away," Quewin said with shining eyes.

"Okay – I can really help with finding the others. So yes, stay here, but Quewin, if the dreamons find you, jump into the circle and leave. I will be back as soon as I can."

Nequam waited until Quewin was hidden behind the dust blanket and then bounded into the forest. He knew this forest, it was like his second home and he knew exactly where the pockets of children, if they were still free, would be hiding. Thanks to Watroc's magical passage, he could now help the warriors find the village children.

19

Horrigan stopped and hunched down. The leaves crackled softly beneath Nyx's boots as she crept up behind him. With two fingers he pointed ahead at the dreamons that crossed their path.

Nyx peered through the waist high ferns and whispered, "There is no getting past them Horri, we will have to go around."

Horrigan dropped his head. "Horrigan, the name is *Horrigan*," he muttered. Still on his haunches, he shuffled backwards and followed Nyx as she sneaked around the trees to the left. They had been searching the forest for an hour with no success. If the children were out here, then they were well hidden.

We would look as threatening as the dreamons so the kids are not likely to jump out and wave their arms to gain our attention, Horrigan thought and wiped the sweat from his forehead. "This is hopeless. We will never find them. I think we should head back and ask Quewin or Zazkia for the location of the other hiding places," he whispered over Nyx's shoulder.

Then he noticed a movement. Someone was moving swiftly towards them, blending into the trees and shadows. Horrigan touched Nyx on the shoulder and pointed in the direction of the silent traveller. "That must be Nequam: moves too silently to be a dreamon." He breathed.

"Is everything okay? How many children did you manage to get to the cave?" hissed Nyx when Nequam hunkered down beside them.

Nequam's head whipped around as if searching for dreamons as he softly spoke. "Everything is just perfect. Watroc made a magical passage to transport everyone safely to the cave."

"A travel passage. That dragon has powerful magic," Horrigan muttered.

"His magic is really impressive. All the kids except Quewin have gone from the hollow to the cave in one step. Quewin will send the kids through as we bring them."

"Well, that's a problem because we cannot find them," Nyx said.

"That's because you don't know where to look. Each group has a predetermined hiding place and I know where each one is. Follow me," Nequam whispered.

The warriors followed Nequam as he moved like a shadow from tree to tree, under fallen trunks, and crept along logs that balanced over streams. They moved swiftly because Nequam knew exactly where to go.

"We have been here before," grumbled Horrigan. Nyx nodded in agreement.

Nequam shrugged and then moved closer into a dense fern patch before he dropped to his knees and covered his mouth with cupped hands. He made an owl call with a soft "hoo-hoo-hoo." He waited and then repeated the call: "hoo-hoo-hoo."

Horrigan tilted his head as he listened to the night sounds. Other than the rustle of the leaves overhead, it was silent. Then he heard a hollow knocking sound, *KNOCK KNOCK KNOCK* like two blocks of wood tapping against each other, almost like a call from a frog.

Nequam held up his hands again … "Hoo-hoo." He turned to Horrigan and whispered, "They are here."

Horrigan could not make out Nequam's face in the darkness of the night but he knew he was smiling. They had found the kids. Well, at least one group.

Nyx, who was watching for dreamons, gave the thumbs-up that the coast was clear, and they followed Nequam into the waist-high leafy plants.

Horrigan peered around. There was no way anyone was hiding in here. They would have seen them.

Nequam touched Horrigan's arm and pulled him down to his knees.

Horrigan instinctively reached back and pulled Nyx down too. Then he saw Nequam had disappeared down into a hole on the side of a large flat rock. *I could have walked over this rock a hundred times and not know that there is a hiding place here. Very clever!* Horrigan thought and shook his head as he too slithered through the opening on his stomach.

Nequam hugged one of the kids and ruffled the hair of another. "Shoosh, shoosh. We must stay silent." He hushed them into silence, holding a finger to his lips.

"Great job, Nequam," Nyx whispered as she patted a little girl on her back in a reassuring way. She looked at Horrigan. "What's the best way to get them back to Quewin?"

Nequam looked at the two warriors. "It seems like a long way but that's because we have been going all night and when I found you, you were quite a long way off. Quewin is actually very close by."

"I will take them; my dust protecting Quewin will be my compass. You two find the next group."

Horrigan held his hand up. Two separate little pockets of silver dust buzzed around like two fireflies playing a game of catch with each other. "I like how your dust showed me how to find you earlier. Let's use that to our advantage. Let's leave a pinch with each other and a pinch with Nequam so that we can always find each other."

Nequam frowned at the two balls of silver glittering dust darting around his head like flies. "Moonballs," he muttered.

Horrigan stared into the trees above. He held out his hand to Nyx for a high five. "I have an idea that you are just going to love – and we get to take all the kids at once."

"Oooooh, I love good ideas, what is it?" Nyx asked as she high-fived Horrigan without any sound.

"A zopline. Jeff explained the concept to me."

"Jeff said it was a *zip*line. I was there when he told you about it."

"No – it's definitely a zopline." Horrigan sniffed.

"I am sure it was a zipline but nevermind, it sounds great. Let's do it," Nyx said and her purple eyes shone brightly.

"We create a line from tree to tree, all the way to the hollow. Each child is connected in a swing chair type of contraption and then they float along the line from one tree to another until we get to the hollow. It will be silent and also high above the dreamons – they won't even know that we are there."

Nyx threw her dust into the air. The shimmering dust slithered from tree to tree, creating a washing line effect high in-between the branches. Hanging swing chairs formed and hovered in front of the warriors.

Nequam lifted the first child into the second chair and nodded with approval when the dust tightened around the kid, holding the little one in place. Nequam pressed his finger to his lips. "Shoosh … you have to be very quiet – we are going to go like this to Quewin, then you're going to travel via *magic* to Zazkia … okay?" Soon Nequam had all six children secured in the glittering chairs. Their eyes were large but it was a mixture of fear and excitement.

Nyx settled into the first chair. The dust line with all the hanging chairs rose slowly into the air and connected to the line. Nyx held her one finger to her lips and counted down from three with the other hand. When she reached one, the chairs started to move slowly along the line to towards the next tree.

Horrigan watched for dreamons as Nyx made off with the children in tow. Within seconds they had silently vanished into the gloom of darkness above them.

When they reached the first tree, Nyx looked back at all the kids and held up her thumb with raised eyebrows as if to ask – *all okay?*

Some returned the thumbs up sign and one little boy gave her a peace sign. She grinned and gave a firm nod. The chairs moved down the line to the next tree, this time going just a little faster. Nyx turned and again held her finger to her lips and pointed down. Below a hooded figure stumbled around but they were moving so silently he had no reason to look up. Nyx's dust dissolved behind them and raced ahead to continue the line. More than once they saw a dreamon crashing through the forest below but Nyx did not say anything as the children were very quiet: they understood the importance of their silence. So they travelled from tree to tree, a little faster than when they started but not so fast that anyone would get scared. The dust made a little circle around a tree and they all swung around it like a rollercoaster. The kids held their hands in front of their mouths to stifle the giggles. All too soon their zipline ended and the chairs started on the downward trajectory. The chairs moved straight through the dust curtain, surprising Quewin. Nyx was the first one off the chairs so she was able to catch the kids as they came through. The dust flew back into her hands as the chairs and line dissolved.

"That was fun!" she whispered then she turned to Quewin. "Hi Quewin, where's this circle Nequam spoke about? Let's get them out of here quickly."

Quewin poked his head through the dust curtain and peered around for dreamons. He crawled under the trunk lying across the forest floor to a small open space where a circle of green fire still smouldered on the forest floor. He beckoned to the kids and they moved closer to him.

"Hold hands, that's right. This will take you directly to Zazkia. Don't be afraid of the dragon, he is a good dragon. All together now, step into the circle. Go." Quewin whispered his instructions quickly. He exhaled when the green flames shot up and the kids were gone.

He turned back to Nyx and then his eyes opened up wide. A dreamon stood right behind her on the fallen trunk. His cloak had parted down the front to reveal red lines moving along his torso like worms crawling under the skin.

Nyx winkled her nose. The air smelt like rotten stinky fish. She saw Quewin's eyes widen and instantly dropped into a warrior stance with one knee barely touching the floor.

Her dust swung around like a whip in her hands. It whipped up and twisted around the torso of the dreamon as he reached down to grab her. With a yank of her wrist, the dreamon tumbled right over Nyx and landed head first in the middle of the ring of green fire. With a whoosh of green flame he was gone.

"Shooting comets! Watroc, you better be paying attention as to who and what is coming through your passage," Nyx muttered. She was about to jump into the fire circle to follow the dreamon when the deep voice of Watroc wafted through the circle.

"A dreamon? NICE!!! I am *so* hungry."

Nyx stopped in mid stride … she grinned at Quewin. "I think Watroc is taking care of that one." She paused and stared at the fire for a moment. "The dreamons will be drawn here by the fire, so I think you should go through the tunnel. If we get here and you are gone, we won't know for sure if you have gone through the passage or been taken prisoner. I would feel better if you went through now. Okay? Just tell Watroc the fire circle is unattended and he must watch for dreamons. He will love that!"

Nyx watched as Quewin stepped into the circle. She narrowed her eyes as the flames whooshed up and then the boy had vanished. Leaving Horrigan's little dust ball and a part of her dust to dart around the fire like the forest fireflies, she disappeared into the forest.

20

Nequam and Horrigan moved to the next hiding place and found it empty. They did a quick search in the forest but there was no one but dreamons around. They moved to the next one. Six kids were huddled together waiting for a rescue. Nequam had just finished hushing the children and telling the plan when Nyx arrived with a wide smile. Her eyes shone bright purple.

"Worked like a charm," Nyx said breathlessly. "A dreamon made an appearance and flew into the passage."

Horrigan and Nequam gasped. Horrigan put his hand on his chest as if to silence his beating heart.

"Watroc took care of the uninvited traveller. I sent Quewin through the passage too, just in case another dreamon is drawn to the fire while we are not there."

"Good thinking." Horrigan said. "Are we ready to take the next bunch?"

"I'll take them," Nyx said and gave a little wave at the kids looking up at her. Soon Nyx and the group were settled in the hanging chairs and whooshing away on the glittering line strung between trees.

The night passed slowly, Horrigan and Nequam moving from hiding place to hiding place, and Nyx took the found kids to the circle of fire via zipline.

When they had secured the last batch of kids and watched them whizz away, they did another sweep of any other potential hiding places.

Nyx returned shortly and reported that it looked like another dreamon had gone through the passage as half a cloak was found next the glowing green embers.

Nequam turned to Horrigan with hands on his hips. "I don't think we will find any more. We have gone through all the hiding places, and this was the last one."

"We head back to the cave?" Horrigan rubbed his head. "I don't want to leave anyone else out here."

"I think we must go back and find out what happened to everyone," Nequam said.

"Let's spread out as we make our way back. That way the chance of finding anyone is greater. We will meet back at the cave," Nyx said.

Horrigan nodded and they split into three directions, spreading out to conduct a final search.

Horrigan had moved through the forest for about an hour when he paused and tilted his head, hearing something. He leaned against the trunk and dropped to his knees and waited. *There! There it is again. It sounds like a cry, but strange, not from a child. Might as well be ... sounds angry as well as scared. Thunderbolt!* Horrigan snarled and clenched his fists. He moved towards the sound, rose up behind a log and saw a dreamon leaning menacingly towards a little black creature pushed back against a tree root.

"I am going to take you to Uzas: he likes strange new things to play with. He will teach you some manners. Now come here or you will not like the condition you will be delivered in. I said come here!" the dreamon said with snarl and lunged for the creature.

The little creature pulled his ears flat against his head and growled. Horrigan could see all its pointed white front teeth. Its back arched against the root. Jaws snapped at the fingers stretching out and the dreamon snatched his hand back with a yell.

Horrigan raised his eyebrows at the vicious sound. What a huge growl from such a little thing. Impressive.

The dreamon lifted his fist and shook it at the little beast. "Try and take my fingers again and you will not like what I will do to you."

The creature crouched back and growled again.

Horrigan rose to his full height, his eyes gleaming deep purple. He flexed his arms and cracked his knuckles loudly. "I do not think it wants to go with you ... maybe because you stink. I could smell you a mile away. Just saying."

The dreamon whipped around. His cloak swung open and Horrigan could see the red veins that raced around like worms squirming over his torso. His hood fell back, revealing a bald head. His eyes were black and his lips were pulled in a sneer. The dreamon rolled his shoulders and then without a word, lunged at the warrior.

Horrigan made a small sidestep and caught the dreamon in a silver dust net that sprang from his open palm.

At the same time, the little creature leapt forward and bit the dreamon's calf, its sharp teeth sunk deep into the flesh. The dreamon reared back and screamed in pain.

Horrigan used this opportunity to swing his dust sword through the dreamon, causing him to dissolve in a puff. Horrigan looked down to see the small black creature sneezing from the sudden dissolving particles of dreamon.

He glanced around to see if there were any other monsters around. "That distraction was a brave warrior move," he said with a nod.

The little beast looked at him with wide chocolate brown eyes, its head tilted to the side as if trying to figure out what Horrigan was saying.

Horrigan tried to smile to reassure the little thing he was no danger to it. "You should go home now before other dreamons find you."

Horrigan gave a little wave and then moved softly back into the darkness. After a few moments, he heard a whine and turned around. The little creature had followed him but was hobbling and held his front paw in the air as if hurt.

Horrigan sank down be to on the same level, and stuck a hand out as a sign of friendship. The creature slowly moved forward and sniffed Horrigan. The tail started to wag very slowly as if it was not yet sure if Horrigan was a friend or foe. Horrigan smiled as he scratched behind the animal's ear. "You are hairy and soft, almost like ... Scott that lives with Jeff's family ... he is a dog. Are you a dog?"

The dog whined and pushed his tilted head into Horrigan's palm.

Horrigan rubbed his bald head as he stared at this black little dog. "I don't want to leave you here all injured with dreamons around. Do you want to come with me?" Horrigan held out his hands.

The dog seemed to understand that Horrigan was offering him safety and comfort. He moved into Horrigan's arms and relaxed as Horrigan's muscular arms closed around the little body. Horrigan blinked as he stood up. He held the dog close to his chest. The body was warm and soft and Horrigan felt a strange feeling course through his veins. *If there is a thing called instant love then this must be it. I think I can feel its heartbeat; it's in sync with mine! I will find his home and make sure he is safe before I leave here.*

Horrigan gently carried the dog as he weaved in-between the trees. After a few moments, he heard a snore and with a frown he looked down. The dog looked small, and its paws were dangling as if he felt very safe with Horrigan.

He is asleep! His tongue is sticking out! I think I have fallen in love. No one will hurt you ever again! Horrigan promised the sleeping dog. *Poor thing, he must have been very tired,* Horrigan thought as he softly stroked the black head.

21

Horrigan entered the cave and was met with echoing whispers. At a glance he saw the outlines of sleeping kids on large glittering dust mattresses with blankets and pillows fashioned by Nyx.

Nyx, Phoebe and Nequam were huddled around a glowing stalagmite and whispered; hands flew in all directions as they spoke in hushed tones. Watroc stood to the side and was staring transfixed at a strange green circle of fire. The dragon did not blink. Small puffs of smoke darted out of his nostrils every few seconds.

"Horrigan!" Nyx hurried up to him. "What took you so long? We were about to come looking for you."

Horrigan nodded down to the still sleeping dog in his arms. "I intercepted an ugly, smelly dreamon trying to bully this creature. I don't think it wanted to go with him."

"Oh ... he is so cute," Phoebe crooned softly as she peered at the sleeping bundle of fur.

"He is so tired that he just went straight to sleep. I'm not sure ... is it a dog?" Horrigan asked Phoebe in a whisper.

"Looks like a dog – I think he looks like a French bulldog." Phoebe stroked the dog's head with a finger.

"I will make sure he gets back to his home before I leave here," Horrigan said and pressed his lips together.

"Uh ... Horrigan, we don't have dogs in Bylleraz. He is not from here," Nequam said and shrugged.

"Then I wonder how he got here," Phoebe said. "Oh dear, what do we do now?"

Horrigan frowned and then smiled. "He will stay with me until we get back to Sandustian, then we will decide what to do."

"But ..." Nyx and Nequam started at the same time.

"I am *not* leaving him," Horrigan said and frowned at Nequam. Then he nodded towards the dragon. "What is Watroc doing?"

They all turned to stare at Watroc, who was still gazing unblinking into the fire circle.

"Dreamons have been popping through every now and then," Nyx explained and bit her lip.

"No!" Horrigan's head whipped from side to side, expecting to see dreamons lurking in the cavern shadows.

"Watroc ate them all," Phoebe said in a matter-of-fact voice as if this was a normal day-to-day occurrence. She scratched her head.

"The kids must be so traumatised." Horrigan breathed and squeezed his eyes shut as if he could not bear the thought of all the fear the kids must have experienced.

Phoebe sniffed then said, "Everyone was quite scared and a few kids yelled when the first dreamon popped out of the circle. He had not taken one step when Watroc came storming through the cave screaming *MINE LEAVE LEAVE* and then devoured the dreamon in one gulp. We all sat there with our mouths hanging open and I expected screams and crying. I mean, a dragon just brutally ate a dreamon with blood and guts splattering everywhere. After a few minutes of shocked silence, the kids started to laugh, one even said *cool*. They thought that a dragon eating a dreamon was the most spectacular thing they had *ever* seen ... they even *clapped*!"

Horrigan's jaw dropped and Nequam shook his head and stared at his boots.

"It was somewhat creepy," Phoebe admitted. "After that, a dreamon appearing was almost like a show; I don't know who was more excited, the kids or Watroc. He has been keeping them entertained until Nyx came back and sent them all to bed. A bloodthirsty bunch ..." Phoebe stared at the sleeping forms on the ledge.

Nyx turned to Watroc. "We are all back now, so you can close the transport passage."

Watroc shook his head. "What if more dreamons want to come through?"

"It's not safe, Watty. What if a whole lot of dreamons come through and no one is here to protect the kids?" Nyx said and flung her braid over her shoulder.

"I will stay here and keep watch and besides, I am still hungry. Do not call me Watty," Watroc grumbled and clawed the sand with his front nail.

"I am surprised you don't have tummy ache with all you have eaten," Phoebe muttered.

"Shut it down. We are not taking chances." Nyx's voice was firm.

"Ahh, don't worry – we'll find another way for you get some dreamons to eat," Phoebe soothed while she stroked his pearly green scales.

Watroc started to hum and within seconds the green fire died out, leaving a scorched circle in the sand.

Horrigan leaned against a wall with the dog still sleeping in his arms; he refused to put the little creature down.

Eventually Phoebe coaxed him to make a dust bed and place the still snoring dog on the bed. "He'll sleep better if he's more comfortable and you'll be able to rest too. We have some tough decisions to make tomorrow about what to do next."

Nyx nodded to Horrigan. "Right, I will take the first watch; I will wake you up in a few hours for your turn. Then you can wake Nequam for his watch." She strode over to the waterfall entrance.

Horrigan woke up with a start. Immediately he noticed the dog was gone. He looked around and saw that the kids, Nyx, Nequam and Watroc were also nowhere to be seen. Phoebe was sitting on the ledge singing softly to herself as she twirled her curly hair in between her fingers.

"Morning," Phoebe said brightly. "Before you ask, Nequam is scouting the forest. Nyx has taken the kids for a swim in the underground lake; it's also a good way to get them clean and fresh for the day. We will have breakfast when they get back. Nyx said we should leave you to catch up on sleep since you kept watch until early this morning." She smiled at Horrigan.

"Where is Dog?" Horrigan asked, gathering his glittering dust from the bed that the dog had slept in.

"Oh well, Watroc was hungry ..." Phoebe started.

"WHAT?! HE ATE DOG?" Horrigan roared as he leapt to his feet. The tattoo that stretched from his forehead all the way down to his chin seemed to stand out against his pale face. His hand clutch at his chest as if to keep his heart in place.

Phoebe stood up and waved her hands in front of her, as her mouth opened and closed like a fish's as she tried to get a word in. "No no, the dog is fine."

"DOG! WHERE IS DOG?" Horrigan yelled.

"THE DOG IS OKAY," Phoebe yelled, and then said in a softer soothing tone, "They went out to find something to eat."

"Together? Dog is alive?"

"Yes, they have become friends." Phoebe held her hand out in front of her to calm Horrigan down.

Just then Nequam came through the entry with the dog trotting at his heels. Watroc soared through the vines, pulling a few loose as he landed.

The dog raced to Horrigan and jumped into his arms, licking his face as if he had not seen him in years.

Horrigan laughed softly and stroked the dog's fur with his fingertips.

Phoebe laughed and leaned in for a few licks. "He won't break, you know."

Horrigan ruffled the dog's ears with a grin. "Hello Dog."

"So what's his name?" Phoebe asked, laughing, as she wiped the moisture off her face with the sleeve of her pink jacket tied around her waist.

"Dog," Horrigan said shortly.

"You can't call a dog just *Dog*," Phoebe said with a shake of her head.

"Of course I can, he is a dog, therefore called Dog," Horrigan said.

"He is not a dog," the dragon said as he shook his wings dry.

"Why can't I call him Dog? Dog is a dog," Horrigan said.

"It's like call calling me Girl because I am a girl," Phoebe said.

"I happen to like the name Girl very much, and I think it would suit you!"

"Okay, how about we call you Warrior because you are a warrior?" Phoebe said with her hands on her hips.

"Has a nice ring to it," Horrigan said with a sniff.

"Oh I give up!" Phoebe threw her hands in the air and turned away.

Nequam rolled his eyes and shook his head.

Watroc grunted and said. "You cannot call him Dog because he is not a dog."

Phoebe turned to Watroc. "He looks like a dog."

Watroc flopped onto the ground with a heavy thud and said, "He is a cyflith – and a cyflith is he. He told me his name is Belugg," Watroc said.

"What is a cyflith?" Horrigan and Nyx asked at the same time, studying the creature.

"A cyflith is related to the dragon family but we have not seen one in many decades – they disappeared a long time ago. Azghar is going to be thrilled to meet Belugg," Watroc said. He yawned and closed his eyes.

"So he is a dragon – so to speak?" Phoebe asked as she stared at Belugg.

"You can call him a dragon – he has the courage and soul of our kind," Watroc said.

"Belugg … what an odd sounding name," Horrigan remarked with raised eyebrows as he looked for the cyflith. It was sniffing around. "Belugg?" he called.

Belugg's head snapped up his ears pricked into spikes.

"Belugg!" Horrigan sat on the floor and played with the dragon-dog.

"He does not look like a dragon at all. Maybe Watroc has eaten too many dreamons," Nequam muttered to Phoebe.

The sounds of voices came drifting through the tunnels and Nyx and the children came chattering around the corner.

"We are washed and ready for a new day. I checked everyone out, no injuries other than a few scrapes, scratches and bruises. Nothing that will not heal in a few days."

There were cries of excitement as the children ran to Belugg and stroked him and laughed at the kisses and licks.

"Meet Belugg, he is a cyflith," Horrigan said with an affectionate smile.

"I am surprised Watty did not try to eat him ... considering that he is always so hungry," Nyx said with a smile at Watroc.

"Hmph ... have you seen his teeth? He will chew my whiskers right off!" Watroc snorted.

22

Nequam settled everyone down and handed out bread and other food taken from the village the previous day. Everyone sat and ate in silence.

"Right. Talk time," Nequam said. "Who can tell me what happened?"

Quewin stared at his hands as he spoke in a low voice. "We don't really know much. We heard the triple gong, which means Razz three ..."

Nequam interrupted as he explained about the different levels. "Bylleraz has different warning stages and we call them the Razz levels. From Razz one which is stay indoors to Razz three: Evacuate to the designated hiding spots." He waved at Quewin to continue.

Quewin nodded and said, "We moved with our groups as we have been trained. All around us we heard fighting and screaming." He paused and stared at the sand for a moment as if remembering the chaos.

Zazkia carried on: "Before my group entered the forest, I saw the cloaked monsters separating the elders from the villagers." She stopped with a shuddering exhale and hiccupped. "My dad saw me hesitate and signalled me to move into hiding. I saw how they hit him and dragged him away."

"None of the adults made it into the forest and I know that a few groups of kids were rounded up in the forest," Quewin finished.

Horrigan sat with eyes closed. His forefinger and thumb rubbed his chin while he stroked Belugg with the other hand. "They wanted everyone in the village including the kids ..."

"Why?" Phoebe asked.

"Maybe ... hostages?" Nyx said as she looked at Horrigan.

Horrigan nodded. "Yes ... leverage! They need the hostages as leverage to force the elders to do their bidding."

"So, Nequam, what would the elders of Bylleraz have that the dreamons want so badly?" Phoebe asked with raised eyebrows.

Nequam shook his head. "I don't know. Maybe it's something in the Razz chasm carved into the side of the mountain. We flew over there when we arrived – remember? No one but the elders can access the Razz chasm and the magic in there is so strong we couldn't enter even if we tried. They perform some kind magic in the chasm but it is forbidden to speak of it."

Phoebe turned to Watroc. "Do you know what they do in the chasm?"

"Yes." Watroc's answer was short. "But ask me not. The secret is guarded by our Dragon Oath. I cannot reveal the secret." He sighed and lowered his head to Phoebe. "I cannot even speak of it to you, my dragon link." Watroc's massive green eyes blinked slowly at Phoebe.

Nequam slapped his thigh. "Oh great ... it will help us figure it out. So spit it out."

Nyx shook her head at Nequam. "Do not ask a dragon to reveal a secret that was sealed by a Dragon Oath."

"The dragon will be more inclined to eat you for just *asking* about it," Horrigan said with a frown at Nequam.

Phoebe stretched so that she could reach Watroc's flank and smoothed her hand over his pearly green scales. "That's okay, Watty. An oath is an oath. It would be meaningless if no one stuck to their promises."

"We can't leave. We need to find out what the dreamons are up to ... please," Nequam said as his eyes darted from warrior to warrior.

"Leave? Of course we cannot leave. We are warriors ... guardians ... and not just of Sandustian but of many realms and worlds," Horrigan said and his lip pulled up as if the idea of leaving was absurd.

"What should we do?" Nyx asked, looking from one to the other.

"Can you contact Azghar or Calidus for help?" Horrigan asked Watroc.

"I will send a message to Azghar and Calidus, if they are within reach then they will hear it." Watroc said. He put his head back on the ground and closed his eyes.

Phoebe snapped her fingers so loudly everyone looked up. "I have it! One of us has to go undercover to see what they're up to."

"I will do it," Nyx and Horrigan said simultaneously and started to argue about who it should be.

"One of us has to stay and protect these kids. The dreamons are still looking for them," Horrigan said and Nyx nodded in agreement.

"What about me?" Nequam asked.

"They already know you, both this form and your dreamon form," Horrigan said with a shake of his head.

"So ... I am a shape shifter ... I will take on another form," Nequam argued.

"Is everyone a shape shifter here?" Nyx wanted to know.

"It's just me – it's a long story which I will tell you another time," Nequam said quietly. "But I can do this."

"No you cannot. There is a particular brand of magic within the Bylleraz hall that blocks all other magic except for dragon magic. Your true identity will be revealed – you will not be able to shape shift inside," Watroc said softly without opening his eyes.

They all hung their heads as they thought about other possibilities.

"What about me?" Phoebe asked. Silence ... "Hello, I can do this, you know." Phoebe pouted.

Horrigan shook his head. "We know you can but we need you here in case the dreamons find our cave. You will react quickly and will get everyone to safety."

Phoebe frowned as everyone nodded quickly ... too quickly.

Horrigan stood up ... "So it's between Nyx and me."

"Or me," Watroc said.

There was silence and then Horrigan, Nyx and Nequam burst out laughing. Nequam fell over backwards and Horrigan's shoulders pumped up and down with mirth. Nyx covered her mouth with her hand as she laughed.

"What is so funny … you think a dragon cannot go undercover?" Watroc's voice rose over the laughter. He rose to his paws and moved away from the laughter that echoed within the cavern. He disappeared through the waterfall with a whoosh.

Phoebe stood up. "There is no reason why Watroc could not go undercover – he would be as good as any of you, in fact better because at least be able to *use* his magic." Phoebe stalked off after Watroc.

"I wonder if we hurt his feelings." Nyx bit her lip.

Horrigan rubbed his stomach as if his laughing fit gave him a cramp. "I will go and speak to him. Nyx and I will decide who goes undercover tonight. I will also tell Phoebe that although it's a good idea … Watroc cannot go undercover."

He strode off toward the entrance next to the waterfall.

23

Horrigan parted the vines and smelt the presence of the dreamons before he heard or saw them. He dropped to a knee and peered around.

The dreamons were too close for comfort. "We should have kept watch!" he muttered and slapped his fist into his palm. In the distance Watroc roared, then came the sound of jaws snapping, like lightning cracks.

That was not normal. *Sounds like he is in trouble!* Horrigan rushed back to the cave and skidded to a stop barely past the entrance. "Nyx, Nequam. Dreamons," he hissed.

Nyx and Nequam rose in a fluid motion and raced to his side. There was no need for discussion. Phoebe was standing at the entrance waiting for Watroc to return.

"Phoebe. Stay here but at any sign of trouble, or if Belugg starts to growl, then lead the kids to the other exit and head up the river away from the village. We will catch up to you. Belugg, guard Phoebe!" Horrigan barked.

Horrigan flashed Phoebe a grin when Belugg came to stand in front of her. His tail stopped wagging in mid wag as if he understood the gravity of the situation. Horrigan turned on his heel and led the way away from the cave. They entered the forest at a run heading towards the racket that Watroc was creating.

Horrigan raised his hand in a fist to indicate they needed to stop. He crouched down and leopard-crawled through the bushes to the edge of the forest. Nyx fell into place on his left and Nequam on his right. They pushed ferns out of the way as they tried to see Watroc.

Watroc was surrounded by a host of dreamons, draped in heavy cloaks that swayed in the breeze. The dragon swung his head from side to side and roared as if under duress. His wings were clamped tightly to his side and his tail whipped from left to right as the spiked fork gorged the earth and knocked a small tree down. Barnacles from his wings flew and knocked against trees with sharp taps.

"Oh boy, he does not look like a happy dragon," Nyx muttered and bit her fingernail.

"Or he has a bad earache." Nequam breathed and lifted his head to try to count the dreamons surrounding the beast.

"He is fighting a spell from that dreamon!" Horrigan said softly pointing in the direction of a dreamon with a deep red cloak.

A dreamon stood within the circle with his arms stretched wide as if inviting Watroc to a hug. The dreamon's deep red cloak draped to the ground and a hood covered his face. The only visible features were his hands high above his head as if pleading with the heavens. The hands looked grey and skeletal with chopstick-like fingers.

Watroc roared and smoke flew from his nostrils. He snapped at the surrounding host, caught a dreamon standing just within range of his massive jaws and with a single crunch the screaming dreamon was gone. A jerking leg hung out of Watroc's mouth. Watroc closed his eyes as he chomped and chewed as if the dreamon was bubble gum.

The dreamons scattered. Then the dragon tossed his head and roared into the air, green steam and fire pulsing into the air.

"We have to help him," Nyx whispered. Her knuckles where white as she gripped the bark beneath her hands.

Then Uzas, the self-proclaimed leader of the dreamons, spoke in a thin weezy voice. His tone was soft but everyone could hear. "With my power, I summon you to join me, oh mighty dragon. You will obey my commands. You will enslave those who stand against me and enforce my will. You will be mine to direct and command at every turn and every whim. I hereby bind you with my power!" A red haze swirled around the dreamon and spread towards Watroc.

The dreamons closest to Uzas groaned and sank to their knees as the power from Uzas radiated to those around him. Some could not withstand his power and lay on the ground in an unconscious heap under their cloaks.

Horrigan growled and bared his teeth when he saw the red smoky mist swirl into the air. The red mist surrounded the dragon and Watroc started to snort and sneeze, blowing short funnels of flames from his nostrils with each snort.

"NO! Fight it. Watroc. Do not succumb to his magic. Fight. Fight." Horrigan punched his fist into the ground, making bark and moss jump into the air.

Watroc's roar became even more violent and he swung his head to and fro. With a vicious roar, green fire shot into the air like a beam of light. The beam shot through the clouds into the sky, vanishing through a small black hole. His tail swung back and forth and the spike at the end of his tail ripped the ground around him. His jaws snapped at the dreamons who dared to step closer, and again the dragon caught a dreamon and flicked the screaming creature into this mouth. Watroc tossed his head back to flip the dangling leg into his mouth. His feet stomped the ground making the standing dreamons lose their balance. The dragon turned and twisted as if in pain. Then the red dust evaporated and Watroc was still … his head drooped as he eyed Uzas. Watroc huffed and snorted but only puffs of smoke bellowed from his nostrils. It seemed like the fight had gone out of him.

"We must help him." Nyx held her hand over her mouth as she watched the dragon's mind being enslaved by the dreamon leader.

Horrigan spoke: "We will find another way to free him from whatever spell Uzas has over him. But right now, we cannot risk being seen. We are the only ones keeping those kids out of the dreamons' clutches. We carry on with our plan of going undercover until we find a way to save the village folk and Watroc," he said firmly. His eyebrows bunched and his eyes gleamed purple.

He watched as Uzas dropped his hand and approached Watroc.

"I always wanted a dragon … *always*! This make my power complete. Those who do not obey will be *eaten*. I LOVE IT." Uzas clapped his hands.

Horrigan's lip pulled up at the way Uzas moved so close to Watroc that he could touch the dragon's nose. "Eat him, come on Watroc, eat him," Horrigan whispered.

"Come, beautiful dragon. Come!" Uzas moved away towards the path that led back to the village.

Horrigan groaned as Watroc blinked a few times then turned and waddled behind Uzas.

Watroc took a few steps then stopped; he turned his head and stared directly at where Horrigan, Nyx and Nequam were hiding. He blinked a few times as if he could not see them. The dreamons passed by making a wide berth as he was still a dangerous dragon the size of a three-floor building.

"Come back to us Watroc!" Nyx whispered urgently as if the dragon could hear her.

Watroc snorted and turned to stare at the direction where the cave was hidden. He snorted once more and a large smoke ring puffed from his nostrils and danced into the air as it floated up. The dragon then turned away and followed the dreamons away from the warriors.

Horrigan and Nequam pulled away from the bushes, leaned against a tree and stared into the forest. "This is a mighty blow; it will not be easy to tell Phoebe that Watroc is lost to us. We really need that pesky witch Angie right now," Horrigan muttered.

Nyx lay where she was, watching Watroc as he wandered away. She pushed to her elbows and was about to turn away when a movement stilled her. Watroc followed the line of dreamons. When he snapped his jaws and the dreamon in directly in front of him was gone. Watroc had *just* eaten the last dreamon in the line: unnoticed.

Nyx pressed her lips together as she squeezed her eyes closed.

24

Phoebe watched as the warriors and Nequam dashed out of the cave. She turned to the kids huddled together. They stared at her with big eyes.

"Sit quietly and be alert. We're not going to be caught unawares so I'm going to keep watch. Quewin, Zazkia, if you hear me call 'hoo-hoo' or if I come running, then get everyone up and run to that tunnel that leads towards the lake. Wait for me before you go out into the forest. Got it?" Phoebe pointed to the tunnel and nodded to ensure they knew exactly what tunnel to head down.

She slipped out of the entrance and climbed a few boulders to the right that led to a flat rock that jutted out like an overhang. She lay on the rock and scanned the river bed and forest below. Belugg wiggled on his belly until he lay next to her; he dropped his head on his paws as he too stared out in the same direction. His ears were pricked and alert.

"There's Watroc! Oh crap. Look – he's totally surrounded by dreamons," Phoebe muttered to Belugg as she gazed with narrow eyes at the scene below.

She craned her neck as she searched the forest for any sign of the warriors; there was a slight flicker of movement in-between the trees but it was so fast she was not certain – perhaps it was the warriors and Nequam racing through the forest? "Come on, hurry up. Hurry up." He probably didn't need any help, but it would be better if they were closer in case he did. She breathed and tapped her fingers on the rock as if that would make them move faster.

Phoebe gazed at Watroc. Near him, a dreamon stood in a long darkish cloak, his hands held out as if he was trying to communicate with the dragon. Watroc swayed from side to side. Phoebe's eyes narrowed as she watched.

"Why is he just swaying and blowing out steam? I've seen him in action and he could easily take them all out. So what is he doing? Wait … don't tell me! He's going to do it!" she muttered to the silent Belugg. Phoebe shook her head and rubbed her cheeks.

"Oh dear, that dreamon is trying to put a spell on him with that red mist … like *that's* going to work!" Phoebe laughed softly.

Watroc swayed and growled when suddenly he reared up and roared into the sky. The intense flame turned the puffy white clouds green and the flame was intertwined with red and yellow ribbon-like streaks. A green beam of flame shot higher and there was a splitting crack as it hit the air barrier. A small black hole appeared, allowing the beam to sneak through before the hole closed in a second. The clouds faded back to white and bubbled along as if nothing had happened.

"Wonder what that display was for?" Phoebe muttered. "A little dramatic, Watty … don't overdo it … nice and easy. Don't eat too many or you'll be busted." She watched Watroc eat two more dreamons, playing with Belugg's soft ears as she lay there watching the scene below.

Down below, she saw Watroc look up at where she was lying. Slowly she lifted her arm slightly and waved. Only Watroc with his dragon vision would see her. Then she smiled as he sent a smoke ring into the air before he turned and followed the line of dreamons.

"Wait for it … wait for it … there! Look Belugg, he ate another. Couldn't resist." Phoebe laughed quietly. She stayed on the rock for a few more minutes until she could no longer see Watroc. She scanned the area for any danger but the dreamons were nowhere close to their hideout. She and Belugg crawled backwards away from the edge and returned to the cave to wait for the warriors.

Soon the warriors came back to the cave. They were very quiet and no one met Phoebe's eyes. Horrigan's eyes looked red and watery.

"What's wrong?" Phoebe asked with a frown.

Horrigan opened his mouth to speak, cleared his throat then began, "Phoebe, this is hard to say but Watroc is lost to us. He was magically enslaved by the leader of dreamons. But I promise we will find a way to free him. I promise." Horrigan's voice sounded hoarse.

Nequam and Nyx nodded at the same time as if they were agreeing to the promise just made by Horrigan. Nequam stared at the ceiling.

"What are you talking about? Watroc is not *enslaved*." Phoebe looked from one to another and shook her head; her brown curls flew over her shoulders.

"Fee … we saw the whole thing … he …" Nyx could not carry on and closed her eyes.

"I saw everything too. Belugg and I were on the rock edge outside watching. Ohhhhhh … you think he was caught in that spell or whatever that dreamon was doing with that red stuff – ohhhhh nooooo – not at all." Phoebe shook her head and smiled. "Watroc is officially *undercover*."

"Undercover?" Nyx asked.

"He cannot go undercover – he is too big, how would he remain unseen?" Nequam asked and promptly sat down as if he could not support his legs any longer.

Horrigan and Nyx stared at Phoebe; their blinking eyes were wide as they struggled to understand.

Nyx put her hands to her forehead as if she could not quite grasp Phoebe's words.

"Look. Obviously you guys have not seen a lot of crime movies because undercover does not mean being *unseen* … it means making sure *they* are *convinced* that you are on their side when you are not. I think Watroc pulled it off beautifully. It was a little dramatic when he ate that second dreamon but he does have a weakness for them." Phoebe sat on the ledge and twirled her hair.

"Uh Phoebe, I do not think that Watroc ..." Nyx started.

"Are you sure? That magic from the dreamon looked quite powerful." Horrigan interrupted.

"He is *fine*. He sent me a smoke ring – that was our signal that he's okay. Honestly, I would have thought you warriors would know more about dragon magic. You can't just *enslave* a dragon like Watroc. I just hope he does not eat too many dreamons while he is scouting the halls. It could make him sick."

"Did you plan this without telling us?" Horrigan asked with a frown.

"No, but I think that Watroc took advantage of an unexpected opportunity that just arose by chance."

"He will never pull it off," Nequam said as he crossed his arms.

Phoebe rolled her eyes.

"So Watroc went undercover ..." Nyx said with a frown.

"Well I suppose, he going to be able to come and go as he pleases, I mean ... which dreamon is going to say no to a dragon," Horrigan said with a smile as he bent down to stroke Belugg's head and ruffle his ears.

"Exactly, he can be in the thick of things and do whatever he wants," Phoebe said with a smile. Her chocolate brown eyes twinkled.

25

"Well! I just don't see what the problem is. It's very trendy. It glows!" Angie sniffed as she stood staring at her sofa tied onto Azghar's back. The olive green had large yellow diamond shapes splashed all over.

"It's ugly and it looks old with all that white stuff coming out." Azghar growled as he titled his head to the side as if he were trying to see the monstrosity on his back. The midnight blue scales moved like shimmering diamonds as the dragon moved.

"It is certainly *not* old. The stuffing comes out on purpose because it gives the chair *flair* and *character*."

"The only thing that would add *flair* is a *flare*. A bright flame would do the trick," Azghar muttered.

"What do you think, Trezz?" Angie whirled around. Her red streaky hair flew around her shoulders. Her arms were crossed over her green waistcoat and her red skirt hung to the floor. A black cloak draped over her shoulders and swung around her feet. Her green eyes flashed as she glared at Trezz.

"I am not getting into the middle of this discussion." Trezz shook his head. He had a healthy respect for the blue air dragon. And the witch was dangerously crazy. He was not taking sides.

"Well easy for you to say. No one complains about your smoky look. I still think a few drops of essence will do the trick. I can do that with a simple spell."

"Do not touch my black smoke – I like it." Trezz inhaled and clenched his teeth.

"I like it too – has a devious twist to it." Azghar nodded.

"It is very intimidating and all that blah blah blah but a dash of purple will make all the difference. You can still *scare* everyone with purple dust," Angie said in a sing-song voice as she tried to catch a tentacle of black smoke that wisped around her head.

"I don't scare – I terrify." Trezz narrowed his eyes at her.

"Lovely, you are certainly going to make a lot of friends with that attitude," Angie snapped.

"A Nytezard does not need to make friends," Trezz said and frowned at the witch.

"That's just too bad because you *already* have friends. Just saying."

"No I do not," Trezz said.

"Never argue with Angie, it's not a healthy habit. Nytezard or not, a frog you will become," Azghar said with a sniff and a puff of blue smoke flew out of his nostrils.

"I will take heed. We have travelled through a mysterious weird swamp and over hills and through meadows. We are no closer to finding Rig and Calidus. If the dragon leaves a smoke trail then I can follow that to find him." Trezz said with raised eyebrows.

Angie dropped her head and sighed as if she could not believe what she was hearing. She waved her hand as if conducting a song. "Try and keep up. We are searching for *why* and *where*. Not Rig and Calidus," Angie said and rolled her eyes at Azghar.

Trezz narrowed his eyes at Angie.

"We're heading to the home of the magical power that forged the path Calidus agreed to. He will tell us where Calidus went. I believe Calidus did not intend to take Rig with him."

"How will we find it?" Trezz asked.

"The one with this power resides in a place that is most dangerous. None are invited, no one is welcomed. It's hidden from the most prying

151

eyes. And those who have wandered into this magical domain are often never seen again. You can follow the breeze to the whisperer if you hear your name drifting on the wind. The only other way is to follow a magical trail that is only seen by dragon eyes. It's tedious but it's the only way," Azghar said as they moved along the stream.

Trezz inhaled and stared at the blue sky. He frowned as he saw a swirl in the clouds. "What is that?" He pointed into the sky.

Angie, Azghar and Trezz stared at the rapidly swirling clouds as if someone was stirring them in a pot. The clouds were distorted like there was a tornado happening right on that spot. Then a pinprick black hole appeared. The black dot seemed to bulge out and then burst with a loud crack.

A green beam of light shot through the hole. It looked like a laser and shot out several feet into the sky before the beam shut down and the black dot vanished. The clouds still swirled like water going through the drain. The air itself seemed to be circulating. The sky changed colours with streaks of green.

Trezz slapped his hands to his ears as an ear-splitting shriek boomed through the air. "What is that?" he yelled.

"It's a message that can only be sent from dragon to dragon," Azghar said as he stared at the sky. The clouds formed symbols and runes in bright shades of green.

"All that green – it's Watroc. He is alerting us to a situation. I need to talk to him about his colours. They are looking a little bland," Angie said.

"What situation?" Trezz asked.

Angie glared at Trezz. "How in flying comets am I supposed to know that if we have not heard the message yet?"

"If it's dragon to dragon then how come you can hear it? Trezz asked with a frown.

"Because I *made* the buttercups. Trezz. The moon was low on the horizon and I MADE THEM. That's why!"

"That's the best answer you can ask for," Azghar said, satisfied.

At the same time, frowning deeply, Trezz said, "That does not make any sense. At all." He shook his head, mystified.

"Let's see," Azghar continued, ignoring Trezz, "What is wrong with Watroc. Let me see. The message reads: Bylleraz-gone-hungry-dreamons-bitter-jelly-fastest," the dragon read the message out loud.

Again, Trezz said, "That does not make any sense!"

"Tsk, of course it does. It's as clear as day – Watroc has moved to Bylleraz. He has gone crazy. Everyone is hungry. The dreamons are very bitter about something and Phoebe likes jelly. The fishes are the fastest. See?" Angie pointed a finger in the air as she made each point.

Trezz stared at Angie while Azghar shook his head as he studied the spectacular hues.

"Watroc needs assistance in Bylleraz. That is all that is important. We must respond. A message like this is not done in jest," Azghar said.

"Warriors and Phoebe went to Bylleraz – they left the day before we arrived back in Sandustian. They don't even know about Jeff and Madgwick," Angie said with a sniff.

"Are you going to respond and let him know that we are coming?" Trezz asked.

"No, he will hear us coming," Azghar said.

Angie turned to Harley, who was turning on his bristles. "Oh you are clever – yes, I think a message to the rune door in Sandustian will do the trick. They also need to know that there is a problem in Bylleraz."

Trezz raised his eyebrows.

"You have a lot to learn. The chamber door has magical runes that foretell the past present and future. The keeper of the runes will see the message and ensure the elders are aware of the message from Watroc."

"What about Rig and Calidus?" Trezz asked.

"There is a tomorrow for Rig and Calidus. Today we will attend to the ones who need us," Azghar said.

"WAIT. Wait. I need to strap Harley down on the sofa," Angie yelled.

Azghar shook his body and stood still so that Angie and Harley were strapped down on the ugly green sofa.

"Come, Nytezard. We need to travel with haste and through realms and passages that only a dragon may traverse. Bind yourself to my spine with your smoke but do not float away or you will be lost in the nothingness." Azghar dropped his head so that Trezz could clamber onto his neck.

"Angie. I hate that sofa, but it is better than the pink one," Azghar sighed.

"I know – right?" Angie grinned broadly; through her goggles, her green eyes were magnified to double the size.

26

Jeff hurried along the little trail. He looked left and right as he mentally ticked off his markers on the jog. He needed to make sure he would be able to find his way back once he found the warriors. The sky was an odd green and it seemed ominous. He didn't like it at all. Maybe his imagination was working overtime but it looked creepy as if the end of this world was near. He started to run.

He sloshed through the river near the stones they had carefully navigated over earlier and clambered over the embankment. He was wet and full of mud but he did not care – he knew time was of the essence if he had any hope of reaching Khrow and Madgwick before the wuunacks got to them in the castle. He reached the top of the ravine and quickly glanced both ways to locate his marker. He moved a little left and shoved ferns out of the way to find the hidden path. He was about to plunge down into a steep descent when a movement on the other side of the ravine caught his eye. Near the edge of the forest were Khrow and Madgwick.

Their circular fire blazed brightly and a crawling mass of wuunacks churned and twisted around the fire. Khrow and Madgwick stood with a flaming stack behind them and swung their torches at the beetle-like wuunacks to keep them away from the fire ring. Even though they moved rapidly and the fire glowed brightly, the fires seemed to be burning out.

"KHROW! MADGWICK!" Jeff shouted and waved his arms above his head as if directing a parking plane.

He jumped up and down, trying to catch their attention. "KHROW!

MAAADGWICK!"

Madgwick looked up and waved his fiery branch over his head. "JEFF!" He nudged Khrow to look up.

Khrow whirled around. "RUN, SAVE YOURSELF JEFF. THAT IS AN OOOORDER!" he yelled.

The wuunacks were slowly gaining entrance through and over the fire wall. The warriors had fought bravely but they were doomed – there was no way out, no escape.

"I'm coming! I can repel them," Jeff said as he again hurried past the ferns in search of the narrow path down the ravine. He found it and was about to jump down in a long slide when he was tackled from behind.

Jeff grunted as he landed flat on the ground with his arms stretched out. Moss flew into his mouth. He flipped over and kicked out at the same time trying to defend himself from this unknown attacker.

"OW!" howled Soop. Jeff had kicked him in the shoulder.

"What the heck? Get off me!" Jeff yelled as he pushed to his feet and scrambled backwards.

"You cannot save them. This is their path to fulfil their destiny, to be at one with the wuunacks," Soop said as he hobbled away, rubbing his shoulder. "Did you have to kick him so hard?" His single strand of hair hung down the side of his face and he rolled his shoulder to ease the pain.

Jeff's green eyes flashed as he yelled, "I am NOT LEAVING THEM TO DIE."

"Jeff, it's their fate … and yours to go take *him* through that portal. Now stop this nonsense and let's get back to the door. He has foreseen this – it happens. They stay here and die and you go through the door."

Jeff turned back to the warriors who were still trying to keep the wuunacks from entering the fire circle. Khrow kicked a wuunack that managed to get through right over the fire. If one got through it was just a matter of time before more did.

"You'd better try and see a different outcome, because if *they* don't go through the portal then *I* don't go through. If *I* don't go – then *you* don't go! Foresee that!" Jeff clenched his fists. He pressed his lips together to stop from screaming. His heart was thumping and it felt like a vein in his forehead was about to pop.

Soop rolled his eyes and shook his head as if he could not believe this was happening. He squeezed his eyes shut and pinched the bridge of his nose with his thumb and forefinger in concentration. "Okay okay – he has just received a new vision … we *all* go through the portal. You can go ahead and save them," he said with a heavy exaggerated sigh and held his hands up in surrender.

Jeff turned and headed for the path … again.

"What are you doing? You cannot get there in time – what … you're going to run down the ravine at the speed of light and chase the wuunacks away? There's hundreds of them – save them from up here and hurry up. They are about to lose their fire," Soop said and shook his head.

"HOW? HOW DO I SAVE THEM FROM HERE!" Jeff yelled at the old man.

Soop grabbed Jeff's arm and spun him around so that Jeff was staring into his eyes. "Exactly – you cannot save them. Just turn around and walk away," Soop said quietly.

What about my dust? A fleeting thought crossed his mind. "I can send my dust," he said out loud.

"Dust? As in throw sand into the air? Yes. By all means – let's do that."

Jeff ignored Soop; he clenched his fists and closed his eyes. He tried to block out the shouting of Khrow and Madgwick far below him and concentrated on his dust … on Khrow's dust. He felt his energy swell and the dust build within him as he gathered the force to the surface and held it there to gain momentum.

PROTECT AND SAVE YOUR WARRIOR. GO DUST GO, he screamed in his head. He tried to project the urgency to the dust.

Jeff shoved his hands in front of him and felt the dust and energy swirling around him. It poured out of his hands with such a force that he staggered back. He watched in awe as the silvery glittering dust swirled above him like a tornado. His shirt flapped from the wind. The dust had pinpricks of light that increased in size as it spun around. Jeff had to narrow his eyes from the white sparks. Anxiously he watched as the dust floated into the air, turning and churning like a glittering tornado when it seemed to reach the blue of the sky. It swarmed towards Khrow below.

The dust connected with the wuunacks with a bright white explosion which radiated a pulsating blue light.

Madgwick covered his head with his arms as he was flung to the ground from the radiating light. The shockwaves disintegrated the wuunacks and their black residue swept into the forest like a sand storm. The wuunacks outside the initial blast radius were swept away from the ring of wood as if in a tsunami.

With the bright light extinguished, the wuunacks started to scurry back towards their prey – the warriors.

Jeff waved his arms in a circle and pushed his hands forward – the dust formed a barrier between the warriors and the wuunacks. The barrier had a few sparks that incinerated the wuunacks on touch.

"I have never seen this kind of magic before – I think you and I are headed for a great future together. Maybe you can even give me some of that stuff," Soop murmured.

Jeff gazed at the dust that flung the wuunacks away. He waved his hands but it almost felt like the dust was doing his own thing to keep Khrow and Madgwick safe.

The magic dust formed a circle around the warriors and they moved within its confines towards the steep incline.

"Go Madgwick – this will keep them at bay for a while," Khrow instructed.

Madgwick did not hesitate – he leapt up the trail and scrambled as quickly as he could towards Jeff.

Jeff jumped up and down to keep visible so that Madgwick would stay on the right path. It was not long before he could stretch out a hand and pull Madgwick up.

"You made it," Jeff said as hugged the warrior.

Jeff and Madgwick looked back down the trail. They could not see Khrow but saw dust swirling around. Jeff heard the scattering of loose rocks as they were dislodged by Khrow's scrambling ascent.

Jeff and Madgwick reached down and hauled Khrow over the lip of the trail. Khrow grabbed Jeff by the shoulders and pulled him into a bear hug.

"You found us and saved us – you came back," Khrow said quietly.

Jeff did not know how to answer so he just blinked and said nothing.

Madgwick slapped Khrow on the back. "Did you see the sparks?"

"That was a new development," Khrow said.

Khrow turned to stare at Soop.

Jeff slapped his head. "Oh sorry. Khrow-Madgwick … this is Soop. Soop is the one that spoke to me. Soop, this is Khrow and Madgwick."

"So these are the warriors for whom you are willing to risk everything, including your life. Disappointing yet interesting," Soop said, twisting his lip and frowning at the warriors. He smoothed the hair strand back over his bald head.

Madgwick pulled Jeff into a bear hug again.

"Soup." Khrow nodded.

"It's Soop," the old man corrected.

Khrow gave Madgwick a side glance and said, "That is what I said … Soup. Let's move out. Those wuunacks will be after us in no time. The dust will stay and give us a head start before it re-joins Jeff."

"There is a portal but it's quite a distance away. We'd better get moving." Jeff led the group into the forest with a jog. He grinned, feeling light hearted. He was with the warriors and he knew where the portal was – they just had to reach it before the wuunacks got to them.

Soop brought up the rear and could be heard muttering, "Soop, it's not a difficult name to pronounce. SOOP. He sees that he has his work cut out for him to educate these warriors on how to pronounce names. Luckily for them, he is an expert teacher. He will drum it into their skulls. He is sure that they are probably pronouncing their own names incorrectly … what a disaster."

"He?" Khrow asked with raised eyebrows.

Jeff rolled his eyes and hurried forward.

27

As they ran, the silver dust streaked back to Jeff. He pointed out the markers that led the way back to the waterfall.

"Tsk-tsk," Soop muttered and shook his head at each marker. "He could have shown you how to make perfect markers, Jeff. These are a little crude if you don't mind him saying so … he hap …"

"Happens to be the best trail marker you will ever meet," Jeff finished Soop's sentence.

Madgwick gave a soft laugh and even Khrow had a grim smile on his face. They did not slow the pace.

"Why do you refer to yourself in the third person? It's a little weird," Madgwick asked.

"He has the *third* eye. No respect," Soop muttered as he scrambled to keep up.

Khrow turned around at intervals to peer down the trail for signs of the wuunacks. So far they were alone on the trail but the wuunacks would not give up so easily. In the distance they could hear whistling and clicking. Eventually they would catch up.

They were wet, muddy and gasping for breath by the time Khrow yelled that they needed to run – the wuunacks gaining.

Jeff stepped to the side and let Madgwick and Soop pass him. "The markers on the right hand side!" Jeff yelled.

As Khrow ran past he grabbed his arm and pulled him along. "Keep going, Jeff," Khrow growled.

161

Jeff yanked his arm out of Khrow's grasp. "No. I can repel them – keep them off us until we get to the waterfall – I'll be right behind you," Jeff said breathlessly. His eyes widened when Khrow released him and moved ahead.

Jeff saw Khrow glance over his shoulder every now and then to check he was still keeping up with the mad dash through the forest.

Before he saw them, Jeff heard the wuunacks. When they sounded like they were just behind him, he spun around on his heel and made a stand. He heard the others crash through the forest.

Jeff swallowed as he saw a black wave of wuunacks streaming under a fallen tree trunk. "Calidus," he said firmly and watched the wuunacks came to a stop and shuffle backwards as if the words caused them pain.

"Jeff," Khrow whispered in his ear.

Jeff jumped at the low whisper but then felt his heart start to pound. He expected Khrow to keep running but now all that was standing between the warrior and the wuunacks was him. If he slipped up, Khrow was in danger.

"Okay, you got them to stop – now use your dust to form a wall then turn and run. Focus now. Tell the dust exactly want you want it to do – think it. Trust it," Khrow whispered in his ear.

Jeff focused on the dust and brought it up to the surface in his palms until he felt his hands itch from the heat. *A barrier – form a barrier,* he thought.

The dust shot out of his hands like a jet spray from a fireman's hydrant and formed a silver glittering wall. Jeff stared at the dust as it had never been so strong or responsive. *It feels Khrow's energy and presence,* he thought.

Jeff and Khrow dashed after the others and slipped through the waterfall. The dust flew back into Jeff's hands and he immediately formed another barrier, sealing them behind the waterfall.

Khrow and Madgwick stopped and gazed around the room. It was clear that the sudden silence of the cavern surprised the warriors. They stood with their mouths open as they absorbed the stones encasing a tranquil midnight blue pool. The twinkling lights seemed to distort as the ripples of water lapped against the stones. They turned around and stared at the blue stones embedded in the wall behind the pool.

Jeff nudged the warriors to break them out of the trance effect that the room had.

"Do not touch the water," Soop said with a sniff.

Jeff glared at Soop, and then beckoned to the warriors to follow his path on the stones around the pool.

They gathered around the wooden door with black steel casings holding the wood together.

"So this is the portal, the exit," Madgwick said as he ran his hand over the smooth grain of the wood and over the gold-bronze disk.

"Do you know where it leads to?" Khrow asked as he also ran his hands over the smooth wood finish.

Jeff looked at Soop with raised eyebrows.

"Well of course he has not foreseen the exact exit point. He is a very good seer but it's not a – ahem … it's not an exact science," Soop said with a shake of his head as if this was common knowledge to everyone in the room.

"Great. Well, we don't have much of a choice. We will deal with whatever it is when we get there," Madgwick said with a nod.

"What if the exit opens up in a hostile world like Torturra?" Khrow asked.

"He thinks he would have seen that," Soop said with his hands on his hips and glared at Khrow.

"I think that *he* does not even know where that is," Khrow said as he stared at Soop without blinking.

"Well … he knows a lot more than you think. He knows that *you* cannot go through the portal." Soop gave a sharp there-you-go nod.

"What? Do not start that with me again. He is going through!" Jeff said.

"No Jeff. He can't. It is written there – engraved in the stone. You can't read that language but he is fluent in all languages so only he can read it."

"I am getting a little tired of all the *he* and *him* talk!" Madgwick muttered and clenched his fists.

Jeff glared at Soop, then bent over the stone to see the crude carvings. He shook his head. "What are you talking about – it's plain to read ... here listen." Jeff read the words out aloud.

Hidden in a magical place.
Traces of essence it will embrace.
For one who can repel the dark.
Friend or foe a flight embark,
Passage granted for magic entwined,
Journey for one heart enshrined.
But be wary and take heed.

Soop turned his back on the door and spread out his hands. "He can tell you exactly what this means and he knows it to be true as he has already seen it happen. Seer and all that." He held up his hand and counted on his fingers: "You, Jeff, can repel the dark and thus can open the door – you can take him through but only him – it says 'one heart enshrined.'" Soop shook his head as if he was thrilled about his deduction of the cryptic message.

Jeff frowned and stared at Soop. *This does not make any sense.*

"Take Madgwick and go. Leave Soup and me," Khrow said. He turned away to face the waterfall and bowed his head as if in thought.

"Fireballs. No – you have been here long enough. Jeff, just take Khrow and get out." Madgwick slapped his fist into his palm.

"No, he needs to take him, and leave you two behind. And it's Soop, not Soup," Soop said with a nod and a wide toothy grin.

Jeff said nothing as he read the words again. He frowned and said softly, "I have essence embraced. So I can go through. But with magic dust I could also go through – am I reading this correctly?" Jeff asked, posing the question to everyone.

"Correct. So make a choice and be quick because the wuunacks will be able to overcome your barrier once night falls. That's when they are the strongest. Madgwick will fit in quickly and Khrow is already used to being here. He won't mind. Will you?" Soop whined and smiled at Khrow's back.

Madgwick stepped forward and rubbed his clenched fist as if he wanted to give Soop something to whine about.

Khrow held his arm out to stop Madgwick from thumping Soop. "Wait Madgwick! Jeff – open that door and let's get this going. I need you and Madgwick to get out of here. I will be fine. I have seen you and that is the best I could have ever hoped for," Khrow said softly.

"Oh blah blah blah …" Soop said and rolled his eyes.

Jeff shook his head and turned to Soop. "I have already told you – if they do not go through the portal then we don't go. Final."

"Oh great. Then everyone will be stuck here – marvellous," Soop muttered.

Khrow stood with his hands on his hips as he glared at Jeff. "I command you to open that thunder-bolting door. Take Madgwick and go. I command it." Khrow sounded very fierce.

"Wait a minute. I am thinking. I have this weird feeling that I am missing something – missing something big," Jeff replied and turned his back on them.

Madgwick pulled Khrow away and they moved to the side, whispering furiously. "I will stay with you," he whispered loudly.

Jeff glanced at the warriors over his shoulder and then frowned at the door. Leaving either of them behind was not an option. There had to be something he could do – something he must do. He kept thinking of Ruogh. Hang on a minute, this verse was cryptic and maybe they were making it too difficult, so … Jeff read and reread the words. The he knew exactly what to do. *This is what Ruogh meant when he said I can save them all – this is it*, he thought with a small smile.

Soop was watching him closely as if he knew Jeff was trying to figure a way out. "He knows this is a tough choice and that you will feel like a part of you will be missing but we must move on. If needs be then he will stop you from making the wrong choice. Leave the warriors behind or he will ensure they do not survive the wuunacks … take him through the door now and he will guarantee their safety," Soop said in his nasal voice.

"I will lose a lot more than just a part of me if I don't do everything I can to save those two warriors. And *you* do not have the power to stop me," Jeff said firmly.

Soop straightened up and took a step back as if no one had ever spoken to him like that before. His mouth opened and closed but no words came out.

28

Jeff stared at Khrow's back; Madgwick was whispering and using his hands as if trying to convince Khrow of something. *I will do what I need to do without telling them or they will just try and stop me. This is the only way.* Jeff nodded as if a decision had been made.

Jeff balled his fists. He knew that once he started the dust would do the rest because he could feel the connection between the dust and Khrow – they were one. Even if they were not in the same bodily unit, they were still one. It felt right to return the dust – it was never his to start with.

He closed his eyes and focused on the dust, drawing the energy up from within, trying to gather it all in one huge ball but not releasing it. He felt the familiar heat pool for the last time in his hands. When the dust was swirling and coursing through his body, Jeff thought loudly in his head: *RETURN TO YOUR WARRIOR KHROW – I WILL IT. I COMMAND IT. RETURN TO YOUR WARRIOR KHROW.* The words seemed to ignite a storm within him and he felt as if an electric bolt was going through him.

"Jeff, what are you doing?" he vaguely heard Madgwick cry in the background.

"JEFF! What is he doing?" Khrow cried.

"STOP HIM," Soop yelled and tried to grab Jeff but he was flung away by the dust as if it was having no interruptions of this event.

But it was too late to stop him. The dust was activated and it was excited to be returning to its warrior. It swirled around Jeff as it exited his fingertips, his ears, his nose and eyes. He felt his feet lift off the floor. It glittered and glowed around Jeff and it felt magical and peaceful as it swirled and danced around him. The dust suddenly stopped as if someone had pushed an emergency stop button and then poured towards Khrow. It hit Khrow like a battering ram, lifting the warrior into the air, his arms and legs stretched out. The dust poured into Khrow's open mouth. A blue light shone out of him, from his outstretched fingers, his feet, his eyes and ears. It seemed like the warrior was going to implode when suddenly the shine was gone. The light vanished and Khrow dropped to his knees, his arms outstretched in a typical warrior fighting position. His head was bowed. Then his head snapped up and he stared ahead of him. His eyes gleamed with a deep purple shine.

"YES!" Jeff tried to shout but it came out as a whisper. He felt drained but it had worked because warriors *with* dust all had purple eyes, and Khrow's eyes glowed brightly.

The barrier wall collapsed when the dust left Jeff and the wuunacks started to scurry towards their prey.

Khrow spun on his heel and waved his hand – the dust formed a new barrier between them and the wuunacks. It slammed against the wuunacks with a powerful BANG. The dust carried sparks that incinerated the wuunacks on touch. The barrier was so strong it pulsated as if it had a heartbeat.

Khrow turned and with a leap he was standing in front of Jeff. "What did you do Jeff?" he almost whispered.

"What I had to do. You have the magic now." Jeff shrugged and sagged against the wall.

"But the sacrifice to give up the dust ..." Khrow murmured and he pulled Jeff off the wall and supported his weight.

"It was no more of a sacrifice than the one you made when you sent it to me – it was never mine." Jeff smiled.

Soop was the only one who was angry and pointed at Jeff. "Take it back NOW. You read the words on the stone!" Soop yelled and stamped his foot.

Jeff nodded "I did. It does not say it has to be me that has to have magic. I am already covered." Jeff gave Soop a fake smile that dropped the moment he looked away. "Let's open this portal and get out of here."

Soop muttered in the background but no one was listening to him.

"YOU MUST GIVE IT BACK!" Soop screamed at the top of his lungs. The spittle flew from his mouth. His hands were shaking.

"He can't give it back – it's done. What is wrong with you? You can still go as well." Jeff said with wide eyes.

"What is going on – what is your problem?" Khrow asked with narrowed eyes which glowed brightly and made him even more intimidating.

"It has ruined his plans – Khrow has to stay here," Soop said.

"Excuse me?" Madgwick said.

Soop pointed at Khrow. "He needs to stay or Soop does not go. You have to make the choice!" he crossed his arms and gave a firm nod.

Jeff stared up at the ceiling, "Uh this is a tough one … uhhhh – okay. Soop, you stay. We're going. Let's go, guys." Jeff turned back to the wooden door.

"How can you choose him over him, he helped you. He *spoke* to you – in your *thoughts*. He gave you food and sent you to the mountain. He showed you this door. He will not accept this from you. You owe him."

"What? The old man at the castle gave me food," Jeff snapped.

"*He* told the old man to do it. *He* made sure they kicked you out so that you had no option but to come to me. *He* made sure they closed the gates on your two loser friends here so that the wuunacks could feast on them."

"The wuunacks killed that old man!" Khrow yelled.

"It was his time – he chose to stay outside the gates," Soop yelled back at Khrow.

"Wait a minute – you planned to disrupt the water so that the wuunacks got released during the daytime putting everyone in danger?" Jeff said and shoved his hair off his forehead.

"Only until sunrise tomorrow, then they go back to night creatures. Your *special* warriors would have been eaten by then." Soop sneered with a side look at Khrow and Madgwick.

Khrow growled and Madgwick started thumping his fist into his palm.

"He knew that without them in the picture – he would get your blood," Soop said.

"But the old man also told me not to trust you. So I don't," Jeff said quietly.

"That was just an act – okay? Now let's stop this madness so that you and he can go. FINE. The two losers can keep their magic. It will make life a lot more interesting for them here. But they stay," Soop demanded.

"You are not taking a single drop of blood from Jeff," Madgwick said quietly.

"I don't understand. Why you are so determined that the warriors must stay, according to the verse I can take myself and another, and Khrow has the magic and can take one." Jeff said with his hands in the air.

"No ... it's not all the verse says – mud covers the last bit!" Soop said.

Jeff moved closer to the stone and wiped beneath the last sentence. "Khrow can your dust give me some light?"

With the stone illuminated with a blue shine, Jeff could see. "Oh right. There is something else here." He read said aloud.

Hidden in a magical place.
Traces of essence it will embrace.
For one who can repel the dark.
Friend or foe a flight embark,
Passage granted for magic entwined,
Journey for one heart enshrined.
But be wary and take heed.
When the door is open and magic aligned

Two of the same must be declined.

"See? That's Khrow, he can also speak to your thoughts. He was horrified when he found out. He is the 'same'."

Jeff straightened up. "Khrow has the dust now. He is going. It's done. You tried to kill them. I am sorry but I don't owe you anything at all."

Soop stared at them, then strode to the water. "He will see those two warriors dead before they leave before Soop. He can overcome your stupid glitter wall with another rock into this pool – it feeds the power to the wuunacks. He has a bond with the wuunacks so they will never harm him. He wanted to take you, Jeff but really – he needs just your blood. You don't have to be alive for that; the wuunacks can eat you too. In fact you are just a snotty nosed brat. It will be better this way." Soop sneered and scooped up a rock to toss into the pool.

Khrow roared and grabbed Soop and in one action threw him into the barrier. With a sucking motion the dust crept over him until he was on the other side. Soop was standing with the wuunacks screaming to let him through.

"Right. We don't have a lot of time. When those wuunacks break through we are done for. Let's open that door so you can get out of here – you have to leave … if you can take Madgwick, then even better," Khrow said.

"We are *all* getting out of here – the verse says that I can take one – Madgwick, and the one with magic can go through – that's you. I am right. I am sure I am right," Jeff said with a nod.

29

They huddled around the wooden door. Madgwick and Khrow ran their hands over the smooth wood. Jeff peered over their shoulders trying to see what they were looking for.

"Are you sure you understood the verse correctly?" Madgwick asked as he studied the door.

"I think so – I can go through because of essence embraced and I can repel the dark. I can take friend or foe. The one with magic also has a passage. But Soop and Khrow can't go together because they both can speak to thoughts. That's why Soop was so adamant that Khrow could not go. See? I hope I am right but if not …"

"Well … if not – then we will find out and I would rather find out together," Khrow muttered.

"It just feels like a normal door. I don't detect any magic here," Madgwick said.

"Maybe I must do it," Jeff said as he glanced over his shoulder at Soop's endless yelling and cursing.

Soop was leaning against the dust barrier with his hands cupped around his face to try and see through the glittery wall. The wuunacks had started to ram the barrier with a loud BAM BAM BAM.

The faint screaming of Soop could be heard: "He willlll have his revennnnge if you do not open – he will killllll you and your familllllies – he will wipe out everyone! Let him throooooough."

"Hold that barrier, Khrow," Madgwick warned.

"I am trying, but we are still a little weak from being apart for so long. Our combined strength has to build." Khrow panted and he leaned forward in an effort to provide more strength.

"Build it faster, Khrow – those wuunacks are making a dent," Madgwick muttered.

"You try, Jeff … see if you can open it with *essence* and all that," Madgwick said and moved aside for Jeff to slip in.

Jeff took a deep breath and placed his hands on the door. He closed his eyes. "There's nothing. No vibration. Don't feel a thing." He groaned.

"Is this the right door? Maybe Soop is just some total moon job."

Jeff pressed his hands harder against the wood as if he could force a reaction – nothing. He was about to pull away when he thought he felt something. "Wait! I feel a twinge or a tingle."

Madgwick turned to stare at the door. "What? What do you feel?"

"It's just a tingling sensation in my fingers – but nothing more than that." He kept his hands on the door. "Maybe I need to offer it blood."

"Disgusting – don't do that. It's very rare that dragon magic will ask for blood. Madgwick has told me everything that happened with you and the fire dragon in Torturra. I don't know Calidus but I do know Azghar, the air dragon, and Azghar would never allow for blood to be spilt in order to complete a dragon spell," Khrow said as he glanced over his shoulder.

The battering of the wuunacks pounded the barrier harder and louder. And there seemed to be hundreds of them. The silver glittery wall was totally covered in black as they tried to cling to it. They were running out of time.

Jeff kept his hands on the door. *Calidus. What am I supposed to do here? Help me*, he thought furiously.

Jeff felt a strange calmness overcome him, like he was suddenly bathed in a warm mist. He tilted his head to the side as if he could hear Calidus calling his name.

Calidus! He called in his mind. *Where are you, Calidus?*

What toooook you soooo loooong ... open the door, Skinny. A slip of a thought entered his mind. It was so fleeting that Jeff almost missed it. Then it was gone.

"Calidus spoke to me – I am sure of it!" he gasped.

"What did he say?" Madgwick asked.

"It was so quick – I think he asked me what took me so long and that I must open the door." Jeff stood back and looked at the door.

"Are you sure it was Calidus and not our friend out there playing mind tricks on you?"

"Yeah – positive. It was Calidus." Jeff leaned back towards the door. He put his ear to the wood. There was a weird rustling sound within the wood. "Guys – I think I am hearing something here. Shoosh, shoosh." He waved their talking down with a flapping of his hand.

A faint voice came through the door that sounded like a whispering song.

A magic buried within the soul
Tied with magic to make one whole
A spark, a flame, dragon's roar
From one world to another, open this door
A ring of fire, this space to dazzle
Onward and outward friends to travel
Speak your name for the magic to ignite
Endure the flame to embark on this flight

Jeff spoke the words out loud to Madgwick and Khrow ... then repeated it again to make sure he got it right.

"That sounds like something Angie would have said," Madgwick said.

"I can't hold it any longer. Speak your name, Jeff," Khrow yelled.

"Jeff," he said out loud. Nothing happened. "JEFF," he said again. "Nothing is happening," he yelled.

The noise of the wuunacks was deafening. Khrow's barrier got closer and closer to where they were standing shoulder to shoulder.

"Think, Jeff. What other name could you have been called?" Madgwick yelled.

"Ahh man – no way," Jeff said loudly.

"What is it?" Khrow asked.

"Never mind. It's just a nickname Calidus has for me. Can't be that," Jeff answered shortly.

"TRY IT, JEFF – WE ARE OUT OF TIME," Khrow yelled.

"Skinny," Jeff mumbled, not really believing this would be the magic name that would open the door.

ZAP.

A round spot appeared in the middle of the bronze-gold disk and started to go red.

"That's it! Grab my hand. Get ready to withdraw your dust, Khrow," Madgwick yelled.

Khrow glanced over his shoulder and then with a flick of his wrist sent a string of silver dust towards them. The dust wound itself around Madgwick's and Jeff's wrists. They were connected.

"AGAIN, JEFF," Madgwick yelled.

"SKINNY," Jeff yelled and watched as the disk burn away, leaving a dark singe mark on the door. The mark started to grow rapidly as if a blow torch were on the other side burning a hole in the door.

A wind started to whip around them and between the wind and the wuunacks, it was almost impossible to hear each other. Their clothing flapped and Madgwick's hair stood straight into the air.

Within seconds the hole was about the size of a soccer ball. The flames snapped out like darting tongues, latching onto the edges of the door.

Jeff gazed at the fire. A thin strand of flame leapt out of the hole and wrapped around his wrist. He gasped but there was no heat. Calidus's magic still protected him from fire. The string of fire laced around his arm and curled around his chest. He started to feel a tug from the string of fire as it began to drag him towards the hole.

Madgwick, closest to the door, started to lift into the air.

"KHROW … COME ON!" Jeff screamed. He was terrified that the warrior would get left behind if the pull became stronger and he went through the door without him.

Jeff was bound to Madgwick with the fine string of silver dust and Madgwick was already heading towards the hole in the door. Jeff held his free hand out towards Khrow, who was still holding the barrier in place.

Madgwick was shouting for Khrow.

"KHROW, KHROW!" Jeff screamed and stretched out for the warrior.

The pull became stronger. Jeff was being dragged after Madgwick, who had already disappeared through the hole. At the last second, Khrow dropped the glitter barrier and lunged towards Jeff. Their hands gripped each other as Jeff went through the hole. The lick of silver dust wrapped around Jeff and Khrow's wrist and dragged him after Jeff like a gale force. As Khrow was being sucked through the hole, he stretched his free hand out and the remaining dust dived into his palm just before they slipped through the darkened door. Then the hole slammed shut.

Gone were Jeff, the warriors and Khrow's dust.

Soop dropped to the floor and screamed in fury. He threw his fists into the air and shook them as he screamed curses. The door stood as it was before as if nothing out of the ordinary had happened.

30

Jeff yelled as he tossed and turned. The red and orange streaks raced past as they flew through a fiery wormhole. The warriors, still connected to Jeff with Khrow's silver dust, grunted and cursed as they were flung against the walls of the narrow passage. The fiery string dragged Jeff through the funnel towards a small black dot in the distance. As they flew closer, the dot grew larger. It was hard to keep track of the dot because they were bouncing around and knocking into each other as they tumbled. All of a sudden the dot loomed in front of them and they flew through into a dark room and slammed onto a hard stone floor.

Groaning and panting they lay on the floor. No one said anything as the impact had knocked the breath out of them. It was a hard landing.

Jeff tentatively stretched his arms and legs to see if anything was broken. "I can't believe we made it. We are alive," Jeff groaned.

Madgwick flopped onto his back. "I can't believe nothing's broken."

Khrow lay staring at the stone ceiling. "I can't believe you are called Skinny ... of all the names ... why skinny?" he asked as he propped himself on an elbow to look at Jeff who was still lying on the floor.

"Never mind." Jeff groaned.

"Legs ... it's the legs," Madgwick muttered to Khrow, who immediately leaned to the side to peer at Jeff's legs.

"Really? That's what we're doing now?" Jeff asked with a frown.

Madgwick and Khrow started to laugh. They flopped onto their backs and just lay laughing until Jeff could not hold it any longer and started to laugh too. The three of them laughed until the tears rolled down their cheeks.

Finally Madgwick hiccupped and said, "It hurts to laugh."

"Yeah, but we are out. We are out," Khrow said softly. "I thought I was doomed to stay there until the wuunacks caught me. Not only am I out but I am reunited with my precious dust and that all because of you, Jeff."

"You saved us," Madgwick said.

"I kinda knew you weren't really dead … I mean I kept hearing your voice … it was you, right?" Jeff asked Khrow.

"Yeah, it was me. I could always communicate with someone in dire circumstances. That gift stopped when I ended up in Dunargh. I think you and I stayed connected because we were linked with the dust. I'm sorry about your sacrifice but I'm not sorry to have my dust back." Khrow pulled his lips in a grimace.

Jeff rubbed his stomach. He felt empty as he processed the vacant feeling the dust had left. "I would do it a hundred times over again just to have you and Madgwick back again," Jeff said softly.

Khrow sat on his haunches and looked around. He was healing a lot more quickly with his dust back. And his dust was obviously happy because it kept coming out and diving back into his hands. Khrow kept looking down and smiling at it.

Jeff watched Khrow's face and smiled. *The pain of losing the dust is totally worth it to have Khrow alive and see that smile.*

Madgwick pushed himself to his knees and brushed his hair off his forehead. "I wonder where we are?" he whispered.

Jeff staggered to his feet, his arms and legs heavy. "I think I have a million bruises everywhere." He groaned and looked around. "It looks like we're in a large room. Why would we end up here and where is *here*? It almost feels like nothing's been in this room for decades. That damp dusty smell."

Madgwick tilted his head. "Did you hear something?" he asked.

178

Khrow and Jeff stopped and listened. They looked around but it was hard to see anything in the dimness of the room.

Tick, tick

A soft tapping sound came again.

Tick, tick

"There! I hear a ticking noise. This does not sound good," Khrow said, he moved with his hands stretched out as he tried to find the walls.

"Sounds like something knocking on a surface," Madgwick said with a frown.

Tick, tick

Skinny

Jeff gasped as he heard the word flitting through his thoughts.

"What? What happened?" Madgwick asked.

"I heard Calidus. He is here," Jeff said as he turned in a circle as if to see if the fire dragon was coming through the walls.

Tick, tick

Skinny

Tick, tick

Skinny

Jeff moved to the side and in the darkness he found an almost invisible opening in the wall. "It seems louder this way. Come on." He beckoned with his hand.

TICK, TICK

The knock seemed louder as they moved along the passage.

"Skinny ..." The crooned word drifted down the hallway.

"I hear it too," Madgwick murmured.

"Should I call him?" Jeff whispered.

"No ... let's see if we can get closer before we alert anything or anyone to our presence," Khrow whispered back. He glanced behind them to make sure that nothing was creeping up on them as they moved along the dark stone passage.

TICK, TICK

"Skinny ..."

Jeff and the warriors crept along the corridor; Khrow's dust lit their way like a little candle: Bright enough that they could see but it was not so bright as to give away their presence. As they walked they found doors with round windows like portholes.

Jeff shuddered as the dust revealed a slimy mouth licking the porthole glass from the other side as if it could grind away the barrier with saliva.

"If that tongue is that big – how big are the teeth?" Jeff whispered as they slid along the wall, keeping their distance from the dripping glass window.

Another porthole seemed vacant when suddenly a flower resembling a white and yellow daisy bobbed harmlessly before it turned and landed on the glass with a splat of teeth and a sucking motion. Jeff jumped a step back and shook his head. There were some scary things down there.

TICK, TICK

"Skinny ..."

Jeff stopped in front of a door. A large eye was pressed up against the glass: a mix of green and sky blue, almost turquoise. In the middle of the eye was a flare of green flame. "He is here. That is Calidus!"

TICK, TICK

"Skinny ..." The word seemed to float through the door. The eye did not blink but gazed ahead as if in a trance.

Jeff reached up and knocked on the glass. RAP.

Khrow hissed, not wanting Jeff to announce their arrival so plainly.

The eye blinked slowly and then sprang open and darted around, searching.

"Skinny?"

"It's me, Calidus. I'm here!" Jeff leaned against the door trying to find a handle.

"It's them ... see, I told you. It's Jeff," Calidus turned to say to

180

someone behind him.

"Calidus, open the door," Jeff said.

"This door won't open for our magic. We have tried and tried. I have been waiting a long looong time. Skinny!" the dragon growled.

"I'm sorry – I was … well I don't know exactly where I was," Jeff started to explain and shrugged as if that would explain his helplessness.

"I know where you went. That is why I came here, to open the porthole when you got to the door."

"You opened the door?' Madgwick asked as he peered over Jeff's shoulder.

"The first door had to acknowledge his dragon essence with that funny tingle sensation. Only then could I open the second door to bring you *here*. Otherwise you would have ended up elsewhere. He took FOREVER."

"I came as fast as I could. I didn't know you were waiting for me. Come on – open the door and let us in," Jeff said with a frown.

"I can't. This door is shut with powerful magic. I am hungry, tired and he is driving me CRAZY."

"Who is?" Khrow asked as he too stood behind Jeff.

"That warrior. He is so angry at me because he thought I killed you. But I had a path to follow, a path that was forged with magic that even I could not stray from. You had to go to save them. It was the only way. Someone told me ... forget who," Calidus said and the eye blinked again.

"Can we see the warrior?" Khrow asked.

"No. I might eat him." Calidus did not move away from the door.

Khrow stared at Jeff and widened his eyes as if conveying a message.

"Oh right. Calidus – can *I* see the warrior please?" Jeff put his hand on the glass as if he was trying to touch the dragon.

Calidus growled, blinked and then moved back.

Rig's face appeared in the portal. "Jeff!" he said. He saw Madgwick standing behind Jeff. He put his hands on the glass as if he had to hold onto something. "Madgwick? You are alive?" he gasped.

Madgwick grinned and nodded, "Not just me – look!" He moved to the side so that Khrow could face the porthole.

Rig's eyes widened. "Khrow … please let this be true!"

"It's true, my brother," Khrow said in his deep voice and placed his hand on the glass, over Rig's hand.

Rig shook his head so that his ponytail hit the glass. He snapped over his shoulder. "*I know*! I will tell them! Okay, so we are in this place and it's sealed with powerful magic. Even my dust is dormant here. The only way to open this door is with the combined magic of all the dragons. You need to find Azghar and Watroc and yes …" he glanced over his shoulder again. "I *know*! I am trying to tell them! Angie. Calidus says that Angie *must* come as well. Flying comets – she is going to be so happy to see you alive." Rig nodded as he spoke.

"Please do not take too long," Rig continued, "because either this dragon is going to kill me or I am going to kill him. He is VERY …" Rig said with a slow shake of his head, his lips pressed together to show his seriousness.

"Are you safe here? Food?" Khrow asked.

"We are trapped in this room but not in any danger as far as I can tell. It's neither hot nor cold and we are *not* hungry – except for him. He is *always* hungry. He is driving me insane with his constant whining about food. Please hurry," Rig said with clenched teeth.

Rig flew out of view as Calidus shoved him aside. "I *am* hungry. Tell Azghar to bring dreamons, shimmers, screatures and some jellispickles for dessert … and shadowraiths but if he can't bring lemons to sprinkle on top then just leave the shadowraiths."

Jeff nodded with each request. "We will be as quick as we can but in the meantime do *not* eat Rig."

Rig pushed from under Calidus to get to the porthole again. "Tell them what you told me." He panted and he shoved the massive dragon to the side.

"Don't know what you're talking about."

Rig elbowed the dragon. "About the smell!"

Calidus shoved Rig out of the way and he suddenly dropped out of sight. "Oh yes. Be wary of evilness. Go down the corridor – take the forty-seventh door on the left ... or the fifty-seventh. I can't remember now, maybe it was the eighth – anyway one of those doors will take you closest to home. But be wary of evilness behind that door. I can smell it from here ... nasty. I think that is where Watroc is but he doesn't smell nasty," Calidus said, swinging his body as if keeping Rig at bay.

Khrow pushed against the glass pane as he yelled to Rig, "We will get you out of here – we will be back. I promise."

Rig yelled back. "Your promise is as precious as dust."

Calidus blew a tiny smoke ring that bounced against the glass.

Jeff placed his hand over the circle of smoke, and said, "I will be back, Calidus."

31

They stared at door forty-seven; little bronze numbers hovered above the wooden beam. The door looked the same as all the others in the dim corridor, a plain wooden door with metal bands crossing each other. Black bolts dotted the straps and a dirty round glass portal in the middle. Jeff peered into the porthole waiting for something creepy to appear.

"There's mist swirling inside there and it looks like finger smudges on the glass," he whispered. He frowned, leaned against the door and pressed his ear against the wood. "I can hear screeching ... I don't like the sound of this one."

Khrow and Madgwick took turns to listen before they moved to door fifty-seven.

Jeff leaned forward and touched the door. He wrinkled his nose. "There is an odd smell. I think it's this door he was talking about. Can you smell anything?"

Madgwick sniffed the air around the door, pulled a face and waved at the air. "I can – it smells disgusting, like a mixture of sewage and fish."

"I smell rotten cauliflower." Jeff wrinkled his nose.

Khrow shrugged his shoulders. "Okay – this is the one. Magic upon magic will sometimes do the trick if it's a simple lock. Doors like the one Rig and Calidus are behind are locked with powerful magic that can only be opened with a higher magic." His dust formed a round silver door knocker.

RAP RAP.

Jeff leaned back against the wall with Madgwick and Khrow; he held his breath as he waited for some stinking monster to leap out at them. Slowly and with a loud creak that made Jeff hunch, the door swung open. A blast of wind shot out of the door and swept down the corridor as if a ghost had escaped captivity. Madgwick and Khrow peered around the edge. It was a long, dark corridor with stone floors, smooth black stone walls and the ceiling so black it seemed as if it had snuck into the darkness.

Into the passage they stepped.

"This is simple enough – only one way to go," Khrow said as he tossed a drop of dust into the air to light their way. They limped and rolled their shoulders as they tried to relieve their aches and pains. After what seemed like a very long walk, they arrived at a normal wooden door which swung open of its own accord.

The three tiptoed into the room and gazed around.

"Looks like a large room. Let's stay quiet until we know what we are dealing with or where we are," Madgwick whispered.

The door closed with a creak and vanished.

"No going back now." Khrow muttered.

"This must have been a hall. That table is totally destroyed and those chairs are ruined. Look at the broken chandeliers. Don't stand under them, Jeff. They look like they are about to drop."

"I think I have been here before," Khrow said and rubbed his head.

Madgwick leaned to the side and then backwards to stretch his back as he gazed around.

Jeff moved slowly around the hall, lightly jumping over a heap of smashed wood that looked like remnants of chairs. "Uh guys … I found something but I don't think it's a good thing," he said and pointed to the corner.

Khrow and Madgwick moved as quickly as they could to where Jeff stood at a dirty blue curtain. The heavy cloth draped on the floor as if flung aside in a mighty battle. Half hidden under the folded drapes were parts of skeletal remains.

"That's nasty," Jeff said and wrinkled his nose.

"Judging by the destruction in the room, something ate that," Khrow said and looked around.

"We have to get out of here," Madgwick said at the same time and turned in the opposite direction of Khrow.

"There's a door. Let's go," Khrow said and they moved, half hobbling and running towards the massive two doors that stood slightly ajar.

"Uh ... those are big doors. Something huge came through those doors. Shouldn't we look for a window?" Jeff asked as they moved quickly towards their exit.

The doors swung open with a mighty crash, slamming into the walls with a jolt. Dust trickled down from the metal clasps and a black bolt the size of a tennis ball fell to the ground with a mighty THUD.

"It's too late. Stay behind me," Khrow said quietly.

Jeff heard a dull thump and low breathing just outside. The coarse breathing made Jeff's neck hair stand up.

"That sounds huge ... dragon-huge. Could it be Watroc?" Madgwick whispered.

They backed all the way to the middle of the room with Khrow standing in front, his hands stretched out, ready for a fight.

A thin green flame like the end of a blow torch scorched the doors. A massive big dragon head twisted around the corner with surprising speed.

It was a tight squeeze but the dragon shoved his way through entrance, causing the wood on either side of the doors to splinter and snap. A pair of legs dangled from his mouth. The dragon swung his head back and forth as he enjoyed his little snack ... with two swings both legs had vanished.

Jeff swallowed hard and cringed, hoping the dragon did not hear him.

The dragon sniffed the air and then with startling precision lunged forward, his head lowered as he caught the three in his piercing gaze.

"Oh how lovely. I am tired of my current diet – you will do nicely to wash down the bitter taste the last one left."

"Fireballs! It's Watroc and he is hungry," Madgwick whispered.

"Stay behind me, we feign going to the left but cut to the right and around. We are smaller. It will take this brute a second or two to turn around. We may make it. NOW!" Madgwick and Khrow lunged left and then dived to the right. They raced for the door.

With a few loud clicks of his talons on the stone floor, the dragon whipped around. His spiked tail swept beneath Jeff's leg and sent him tumbling into the air. Jeff rolled as he landed and then scrambled backwards trying to stay clear of the talons that tried to pierce him. The green scales looked like shimmering liquid flowing from one to the next.

Madgwick leapt over the dragon's tail and dived to his side, grunting as he landed on his elbow. He kicked against the dragon's side and slid away from the gem-encrusted, green-scaled body.

Khrow somersaulted over the dragon's tail but now he had Madgwick on the right and Jeff on the left. Either way he could not protect both. He shot his dust out to Madgwick who had just slid away from the dragon and gave him an extra tug to the side.

Madgwick slammed into the side of the hall. The bones clattered and rattled as Madgwick crashed into them. Khrow turned to Jeff but it was too late – the dragon's mouth was right above Jeff's head.

Saliva dripped onto Jeff's shoulders as he stared at the mighty tooth closest to him.

"Jeff!" Madgwick groaned.

"Watroc?" Jeff asked in hope that the dragon would recognise or remember him. His voice sounded feeble even to him. The hot drool dripped down his back.

The dragon lifted his head an inch, turned his head slightly as if to see Jeff more clearly. "How do you know my name, you tasty looking worm?" the dragon growled. Sparks flew from his nose. His piercing green eyes narrowed.

"Watroc! It's me, JEFF," he said and tried to hide his shaking because there was no guarantee the dragon would remember him. "We were together at Drakwood Forest … with Angie and Azghar!" he yelled.

He tried to edge backwards as trying to reason with a dragon whose teeth hovered right above did not seem like a good idea.

"I only remember oysters, but a worm like you will be tasty too." The dragon opened his jaw to reveal rows of pointed teeth all jammed into his mouth. "You smell a little off … I might have to get some seasoning for the others … let's see what you taste like."

Again, the dragon growled. Then he reared back in preparation for a lunge.

32

"PHOEBE!" Jeff yelled and windmilled his arms as he tried to move backwards from the dragon that was about to devour him.

The dragon dropped down … he swung his head back and forth, causing a draft of wind in the room. "Phoebe," Watroc growled.

"Phoebe is our friend! We are friends with Phoebe, and it would break her heart if you ate her friends. BEST FRIENDS," Madgwick shouted as he caught Watroc's hesitation and what could stop the dragon.

He gazed at Madgwick. "Yes. I remember you – you are Angie's tasty but lost friend. I can't eat Angie's friend now that he is back. She is much more than a witch and she will be angry with me. She is frightening."

Then he stared at Jeff. "YOU are linked to Calidus, the fire dragon – I will not eat you either."

He turned to glare at Khrow and green steam puffed out of his nostrils. "But I do not know you. Come here to be eaten." He opened his mouth as if he fully expected the warrior to willingly walk to his doom.

Khrow raised his eyebrows … he was not with the group when they went into Drakwood Forest to find the cure for Jeff's best friend Rhed. He shrugged. This could work or not. "I am friends with Azghar!" he stated firmly, crossed his arms and stood his ground.

"Hmph – I cannot eat you either." The dragon huffed … plumes of smoke trailed from his nostrils.

The floor shook as he suddenly dropped and slammed his head onto the floor. "I AM HUNGRY AND DREAMONS DON'T TASTE GOOD ALL

THE TIME. I WANT TO GO BACK TO PHOEBE," he wailed.

Jeff, Khrow and Madgwick glanced at each other with raised eyebrows. Jeff shrugged.

"Where is Phoebe? Watroc?" Jeff asked tentatively, wanting to soothe the dragon but not really knowing him well enough to go up to him with a there-there pat on the nose.

"She is in the cave waiting for me with those warriors and the ugly one. I do not like the ugly one." Watroc growled.

Khrow and Madgwick shuffled forward to join Jeff as they stood in front of Watroc. Now was the time for answers.

"Watroc …where are we?" Khrow asked softly.

"Bylleraz. We came because the ugly one wanted to bring my Phoebe here."

"Ahh. I remember. Nequam believes her real name is Lyric and that she is a lost girl from Bylleraz," Jeff said quickly when he saw the raised eyebrows of Khrow.

"And who are the warriors with Phoebe in the cave?" Madgwick asked.

"Stupid and Annoying." Watroc sniffed.

"Do you know their names?" Khrow's lips twitched at the names given by the dragon.

"Yes, S T U P I D and A N N O Y I N G. Oh, Belugg is also there. I like Belugg," Watroc said.

Khrow spread his hands out with a little wave as if he was trying to encourage more information. "Who is Belugg?"

"A cyflith. Azghar is going to be so happy to meet Belugg." Watroc hiccupped and a ring of green smoke puffed out of his nostrils.

"A cyflith? Cyfliths are a distant cousin to dragons. A name forgotten in time. Nice! I can't wait to meet Belugg either!" Khrow said with a smile.

"Can you take us to Phoebe?" Madgwick asked.

"No. I am undercover. I have to eat all the dreamons. That is what my job is – eat them all."

"Eat all the dreamons?" Madgwick asked and looked at Jeff as if Jeff could give an explanation.

"It's Watroc. Watroc eats ... everything." Jeff pulled his lips down and shook his head.

Khrow was quiet. "So if I am to understand this correctly. Bylleraz is under threat from dreamons. The two warriors, uh ... Stupid and Annoying, Phoebe and the ugly one, are waiting at a cave for you to eat all the dreamons," Khrow said.

"And Belugg," Watroc said.

"And Belugg," Khrow amended with a serious nod.

"And the children who clapped when I ate the dreamons. They could be young dragons," Watroc said with another hiccup.

"Children ... so the children of Bylleraz are with the warriors. Are there any other villagers from Bylleraz in the cave?"

"No. Dreamons took them away."

"Okay. Then we need to find out what is going on here. Here is what I think. The warriors arrived here with Phoebe. They found children and are keeping them safe in a cave. The villagers were taken away by dreamons. We need to find out where the elders and villagers are being held."

"We also need to let Stupid and Annoying know we are here – we can help," Madgwick said with a large smile.

"Right, one of us must get to Stupid and Annoy– the warriors and find out what they know. The other must stay here and scout for the villagers and for answers," Khrow said.

"I know where they are," Watroc said as he inspected a talon that had just scratched a tooth.

"Great. Let's find them and find out what is going on. Watroc ... can you take us to the elders?"

"You can take my place and be undercover – I will go back to Phoebe," Watroc said.

"Ummm … Watroc. It does not work that way," Madgwick started.

Watroc's eyes began to narrow and flame flashed in his yellow iris as he glared at Madgwick.

"Watroc, if we had to go undercover in your place we would have to be as big and as terrifying as you are." Jeff held his hands up as he tried to explain to a three-story dragon why he had to stay undercover. "They already know you. They will see that we are not the same as you."

"No – you are not. Little worm things." Watroc sniffed and a small puff of smoke trailed from his nostrils.

Khrow whirled around at the sound of voices and footsteps in the passage. If the dreamons came in now they would be caught for sure.

Faster than lightning, Watroc spun around and at the same time released a torrent of fire through the open arched door. So hot were the flames that the walls in the corridor caught alight. Screams echoed as the intruders ran away.

"I *told* them to stay away … unless I am hungry. Some of them taste very bitter and there's no garnish anywhere in sight," Watroc growled.

Jeff could not help it. He grinned. He glanced at Madgwick and both quickly masked their grins. It was never a good idea to laugh at a dragon especially a dragon as grumpy as Watroc.

Khrow delegated the tasks: He and Jeff would stay with Watroc. "I am not staying with that dragon on my own. He at least knows you," he told Jeff quietly.

Madgwick would find the warriors. "I can't wait to find out who Stupid and Annoying are," Madgwick said with a crooked grin.

They hurried to the door and peered out. "The monsters are everywhere. How are we going to get out without being seen?" Madgwick hissed.

Watroc lowered his head opened his jaw. "Get in." He winked.

"Are you mad – no way we are climbing into your jaw without a fight and a lot of screaming," Madgwick muttered.

"Get in. I will not eat Phoebe's friends. Stop wasting my time. I am sick of undercover work," Watroc growled.

Jeff shrugged and Khrow shook his head slowly.

Madgwick threw his hands into the air, "I can't believe I am doing this," he muttered.

The three warriors clambered over the sharp rows of teeth.

"I was once in Calidus's mouth. It smelt about the same," Jeff said with a wrinkled nose.

"It smells like something died in here," Madgwick groaned.

"It did," Khrow said.

They were thrown from side to side inside the dragon's mouth as the beast waddled out of the castle and into the grounds.

"Eeuuww, this is sooo gross," Jeff grumbled as his hand slid off a tooth and landed in a blob of slime. He lifted his hand but had nowhere to wipe the goo off.

They were gagging and heaving by the time the dragon stopped and lowered his head to the ground. He opened his jaw. The three tumbled out and knelt on all fours, sucking in fresh air. Jeff wiped his hands on the grass.

"Head down the path, along the river. There are green moss boulders and beyond is the back entrance of the cave – it's well hidden so look carefully. We will go back to the castle now."

Madgwick faced the direction the dragon had indicated. Watroc stretched forward and licked the warrior like a cat, making him jump to the right with a yelp.

"Just a lick … a very tasty lick. YUM." Watroc growled. He opened his mouth and with heavy sighs and soft cursing, Khrow and Jeff clambered back over the razor teeth. He turned around and headed back towards the castle.

Madgwick breathed deeply to fill his lungs with fresh air. He shook his head. Being in the company of dragons was a very dangerous undertaking.

33

"Phoebe, have you heard anything from Watroc?" Horrigan asked as he leaned against the cave wall.

"You have asked me that same question one hundred times today already – no. I have not heard or seen him," Phoebe replied crossly. She flung her hair over her shoulders.

"There are rooms that are a stronghold against any magic so he may not be able to get any signals out. Or maybe he is having so much fun he has decided to stay on the dark side. Sounds like him," Nequam offered as he chewed on a piece of bark. "Here, chew on this – it's really sweet." He handed some peeled bark to the kids.

"You don't know him at all. No wonder he doesn't like you – you're mean to him," Phoebe snapped at Nequam. The gold specks in her chocolate brown eyes flashed.

Horrigan ignored the banter and carried on as if they had not said anything at all. "The problem is that unless the moon globe in the Sandustian chamber alerts the elders of the troubles in Bylleraz, no one in Sandustian will know what is happening here. And our only ride out of this realm is now undercover and not communicating with us."

"The day we left Sandustian, Galagedra and the elders were still waiting for news about Madgwick, Rig and that crazy witch, Angie. And don't forget that Jeff was badly hurt and disappeared. He is still out there somewhere," Nyx said with her hands on her hips.

"Don't call the witch crazy – she just knows how to dance in the rain,"

Phoebe mumbled.

"They won't worry about us because this was supposed to be a low-key mission," Horrigan continued as if Phoebe had not spoken. He stared at the cave exit.

"Well … we can't just sit here. We have to do something constructive. Let's take stock: We have the kids in a safe area but the elders and villagers are still being held captive. We don't know where they are. We cannot talk with Watroc and we cannot communicate with anyone back in Sandustian." Nyx counted the points off on her hand.

"And we don't know why the dreamons are here," Phoebe added.

Horrigan was busy nodding when he suddenly whirled around and crouched down. "I heard dislodged stones – someone is coming." He hissed and held his hands up to the kids to stop the chattering.

***

Madgwick followed Watroc's directions and was soon navigating over the green moss boulders. He kept a low profile as there were patrols of dreamons about; now and then he had to submerge himself in pools of water which seemed safe, as dreamons did not like water. Finally he saw the darkened entry of the cave. With another look around, he hurried towards the entrance. He clambered over the small rounded rocks and paused in mid-step when a few gave way with a stony clutter. After a few minutes, he was satisfied that the dreamons had not heard anything and resumed his careful treading to head further into the cave.

The tunnel was dark and he could only just make out the two forms crouched in a fighting position … like warriors. They launched into the air in full attack. Silvery glittering dust shot out of their hands in the shape of weapons. Arrows flew towards Madgwick but he sidestepped with a side dive and a low roll.

Madgwick hissed. "It's me … Madgwick. It's me."

195

The warriors landed in front of him. Nyx's mouth was open and her eyes were wide. Horrigan pumped his chest with his fist and then with a small shake of his head he pulled Madgwick into a bear hug.

"For someone who was apparently being tortured, you are looking very healthy. I am glad to see you made it," Horrigan said. He kept Madgwick's hand firmly in his grip as if he didn't want to let go of the younger warrior.

"Horrigan," Madgwick said with a crooked smile.

"Oh hey, Madgy." The other warrior smiled. She stood in a wide stance and crossed her arms. Her calf-high boots seemed scruffy as if she had been walking through mud. Her brown waistcoat hooks were half undone and her long braid hung over her shoulder.

Oh it's you ... the annoying one. I should have guessed Madgwick thought but smiled back at Nyx.

Sitting around the fire, Madgwick told them a short version of what had happened and how they found Watroc.

"You were dead? As in DEAD. And Khrow is alive? But how?" Horrigan breathed but his features were lit up with a smile that could wrap all around his face. He had been very fond of Khrow and his death had taken a huge toll on him.

"You said Jeff is there too!" Phoebe said and lightly clapped her hands to not make any huge sounds.

"They are going to look for the elders. But we need to help them," Madgwick said.

"I do not think any other help will be coming our way as no one knows about the siege at Bylleraz," Horrigan said and traced the tattoo along his chin with a finger in thought.

Madgwick nodded. He walked around the kids who were playing stone games around a green fire that Watroc had left burning. A fire lit by a dragon was magical and would only be extinguished when the dragon commanded the flame out. The kids looked relaxed and happy after their rescue ordeal but the danger was not over.

"So this is Belugg!" Madgwick said as he gave the cyflith a tickle behind the ears. A forked tongue darted out and gave Madgwick a quick lick.

"These are not all the kids. The dreamons managed to catch some and marched them to the castle," Nyx said with a cluck of her tongue. She threw her cloak over two of the kids where were already sleeping on a ledge behind them.

"We need to get back to the castle and give Khrow backup. His dust has been restored so he is ready for the fight," Madgwick said and sat back down on a rock in front of Horrigan.

Horrigan opened his mouth as if to ask but Madgwick waved his hand. "Restored by Jeff but it's a long story for another time."

"Who stays and who goes?" Nyx asked with raised eyebrows.

"I'll go, I *know* I *know* – they already *know* me but I can stay out of sight until we have to fight. I know the layout and can find the hostages quicker." Nequam stood up and wiped his hands on his jeans.

Nyx turned to Phoebe and said, "We hate to leave you, Fee, but I think this is an emergency situation. An extra couple of warriors could tilt the scales in freeing the hostages."

Madgwick nodded. "I agree but Phoebe needs to come with us. She is the only one Watroc will listen to – he almost ate *us*. He is on an eating rampage. And perhaps Phoebe can encourage Watroc to get a message to Azghar or Calidus ... or even to Angie. I know we need all the fighting power with us but I also feel we should have a warrior here to protect the children. There are dreamons all over the place – it was hard for me to get through them," Madgwick said.

Horrigan sighed and stepped forward with Belugg in his arms. "I will stay with the children."

Zazkia and Quewin sat straighter and nodded to each other. "We think you can leave us here. All of you go, including Horrigan. We can hide if there's any trouble. Right?" she asked the group of kids. They nodded.

Horrigan put Belugg down. "That is settled, Belugg will guard you."
Belugg growled and trotted to the entrance.

"Or not," Horrigan muttered as he walked after the creature.

34

Khrow and Jeff stayed in Watroc's mouth as he waddled down the corridors. It was slow going because it seemed as if the dragon wanted to charge and eat every dreamon that happened to cross his path.

Khrow hammered his fist on Watroc's tooth until the dragon stopped and popped his mouth open. "We are not there yet. Why are we stopping?" Watroc complained.

"I know, but we need to breathe!" Khrow sucked at fresh air.

"I can't anymore – must get out." Jeff choked and held his hand in front of his face, but it did not help. His hand was filled with glump.

Khrow glanced around at the empty room then he stumbled out of the dragon's mouth followed by Jeff who staggered to his knees.

"Great job – Watroc – great job," Khrow said as he gasped for air.

"You carry on. I need to catch up with those dreamons we passed earlier," Watroc said and eyed the door.

Khrow stared at Watroc as if he had just grown an extra pair of horns. "No! You are taking us to the hostages."

"I am hungry and I haven't eaten anything ALL DAY LONG." Watroc growled and narrowed his eyes. His bottom lip jutted out in a pout.

"You were eating a dreamon when we met you just now – so suck it up. Do you want to get back to Phoebe or not?" Khrow hissed back at Watroc.

"AGGGGHHHHRRRAAAAHHHH!" Watroc roared. A stream of green flame escaped and scorched the ceiling.

Khrow shuddered at the foul air that came from Watroc's mouth and his eyes started to water. "All right. The corridors are getting a little tight for you to navigate anyway. We will continue on foot."

"Thank you, thank you," Jeff muttered.

With a few directions from the green dragon, they parted ways. They peered around the corner and then nimbly darted into the corridor. Behind them the thuds of the dragon moving in the opposite direction were intermingled with screams, indicating that he managed to snag a few dreamons as snacks.

"At least it will be a distraction," Jeff said as the last scream faded.

They hurried through the passages, steadily making their way down to the dungeons. With a quick turn here and there, they finally entered a dark room that had a strong wet, earthy smell. It was not guarded.

"It's strange there are no guards," Jeff said as he peered down the narrow, gloomy dungeon passages.

"Arrogant. They think that no one knows they are here and they are right. No one does," Khrow murmured.

They eased the dungeon door closed behind them. Khrow took the torch off the wall and strode towards the first row of cells. Jeff almost bumped into Khrow when the warrior stopped mid stride and stared at the cells. They found everyone. Every single cell was crammed with adults from the village. A few small children cowered behind skirts. The villager men stood staring at them with fierce expressions.

Khrow put his hands up. "I am Khrow, and this is Jeff. We are Sandustian warriors and we have come to help you."

Jeff's chest puffed out and he beamed. *Khrow called me a Sandustian warrior.*

The villagers rushed forward, questions tumbling out.

"Hush hush! One at a time and quietly!" Khrow said as he worked on the lock of the cell.

Jeff did not need to be told what to do; he moved to the next cell and started to pry the lock free.

"The children! Some managed to escape into the forest but we think the monsters got them," one mother gasped as she grabbed Khrow's arm.

"Our fellow warriors found some kids in the forest. I don't know exactly how many kids, but they are safe for now. Where are the elders?" Khrow asked.

"That evil dreamon took them all," a young woman said.

"Flying comets. Okay – we will come back for them, but let's get everyone out of here first. We need to form groups of ten; the first group will follow me. The second will follow Jeff. Got it? The others remain in the cells but the doors must stay closed so that it is not easily noticed anyone is missing," Khrow commanded as he took charge.

Two men from the village pushed their way to the front. "No, we've got this. We know this place better any anyone." He signalled out eight men and women. "Make sure everyone here escapes to the forest." He pointed to another four adults. "Search for any children still in the building." He counted another ten from the group. "We will go mount a rescue of the elders. Byllerazians, do not get caught. Once everyone is safe, send some fighting men and women back to the castle as we will need extra fighting power. Everyone knows what to do?" He received firm nods. "Right! Let's get to it." He turned back to Khrow and held his hand out. "I am Yogor. Thank you for coming to our rescue."

Khrow stood with his eyebrows raised as the young man thwarted his authority but then smiled and shook Yogor's hand. "Unfortunately it is just us at the moment and, of course, Watroc the dragon is on our side. He does his own thing and doesn't listen to anyone anyway so we will have to wing it with him. We stumbled across your situation by accident but what is of concern is that no one else knows what is happening here. So can you tell us why the dreamons are here and what they are looking for?"

"They said they want the key to the source. They believe the key is here," Yogor said.

"Is it?" Khrow asked.

"We don't know but the elders might know. It is never revealed where the key is at any given time." Yogor said with his hands on his hips. He glanced around at the other villagers around him as if seeking confirmation.

Jeff's eyes narrowed. *He is not telling the truth but then, they don't know us ... would I volunteer information to someone who has conveniently rescued me? Key ... where have I heard that before. Oh yes! I remember!*

As the men and women huddled together and discussed their parting instructions, Jeff pulled Khrow aside and whispered into his ear, holding his hand in front of his mouth to avoid anyone reading his lips. "I remember something important. When we were in the chamber, Uzas claimed he had found the location of the *key*. The key is a puzzle, cryptex or something that when solved will reveal the exact location of where our Sandustian dust is created. That is what Uzas wants – our dust – that's why he captured Madgwick. He wanted a warrior *with* dust. He must think the key is here!"

Khrow nodded as he listened to Jeff's murmurs. "If I remember correctly, that key has it's own brand of magic and not everyone can open it. But what if they *do* know where it is?"

Jeff shrugged. They turned back to Yogor and the rest of the people who had stopped talking.

"We think the elders are being held in the great hall. We are ready when you are. We will require stealth; no offence but we are hoping that your smell does not give us away," Yogor said with a wrinkled nose.

"We had the pleasure of travelling inside a dragon's mouth, which is the safest way to travel because who is going to question a dragon? We know first-hand what the smell is like – we will try and stay away from breezes," Khrow replied with a little smile.

They hurried around corners and slipped through narrow archways that

Khrow and Jeff would never have even seen had they been on their own. The group was very silent and Khrow raised his eyebrows at Jeff, which seemed to indicate he was impressed at the way the ten men moved so silently through the vast rooms and corridors. They reached a spiral stone staircase and nimbly ran up the stairs that led to the tower. They went a few floors before they came to a stop in front of an arch.

How big is this place? Jeff wondered.

Yogor led with Khrow right behind him. Yogor held his hand up to stop the group. Then he held up two fingers and pointed left, held up another two fingers and pointed right. The men scattered in the indicated directions and disappeared down the corridors. Yogor hunched down and crept through the door in front of him. It was dark and gloomy as if someone had forgotten to put the lights on. They lined the wall and crawled down towards the landing and a wooden rail. This was the visitor's bay where they could see the hall beneath them. If they stayed hunched down then they could remain out of sight from the crowd below.

Slowly they inched forward until they could peer over the rail.

35

Jeff rose slowly to peer over the rail. His mouth dropped open as he viewed the scene below. With wide eyes he looked over at Khrow and swallowed when he saw Khrow's face. His jaw was clenched and his lips were in a tight line. A purple glow gleamed from eyes were narrowed into slits.

Jeff tried to count how many dreamons were in the room. *At least fifty, I can't see who is below us but at least we don't have to worry about our smell because they stink worse than us!*

Dreamons dressed in black drawstring pants with red veins shooting across their bare torsos stood behind each of the twelve elders. The elders were on their knees with heads bent forward; their black cloaks lay in a puddle around them. The brutes took turns at abusing the old men, slapping them through the face or toppling them over with a blow to the head or shoulder. Each time the dreamon hissed with glee and hauled the bleeding and bruised elder back to his knees.

"Hurt ... hurt ..." The dreamons that lined the walls hissed and chanted as they swayed to a rhythm that only they were attuned to.

One of the elders was dragged to his feet by two monstrous beasts, with each brute holding the elder up with a single hand under the armpit.

Jeff gasped when he saw Uzas.

Uzas hovered around the elder as if he was floating. His blood red cloak seemed heavy and swayed as he moved. Uzas laughed with a cruel and high pitched mechanical sound. His shoulders heaved with mirth. His features were hidden beneath his cowl that hung low over his face. He waved his grey skeletal hands in the air to hush the hissing of the dreamons. The silence was instant.

"The key." Uzas spoke calmly as if he had all the time in the world. "I know that the key is here and I want it. It will reveal the location of the source to me – I want it. You will also give me access to that cave in the mountain."

Uzas pointed a finger at the elder and the old man screamed in pain. Uzas had the ability to inflict pain through energy; this ability had been gifted to him by the witch Zorka before her demise.

Yogor grinned as he watched the torture. The other Bylleraz men and women in the group did not seem too concerned that the frail-looking man was screaming in pain.

"What is so funny?" Khrow whispered with drawn eyebrows.

"This is the great hall – magic does not work in this hall. Not even for the dreamon in red, but he does not know that. The elder is acting … and doing a believable job," Yogor whispered.

Khrow frowned. "Maybe, but I see a lot of beaten and battered old men. I think they are feeling the effects of the physical abuse," he muttered in response and shook his head.

Yogor's grin dropped. The magic might not affect the elders but the physical attack was another matter altogether.

"The key is not here," an elder on his knees shouted out. Blood was mixed with his spit as he spoke. "We do not know where the key is. The moutain does not allow just anyone to pass and it's the magic within the mountain that decides who may enter. Not even all the elders may enter. Access to the cave is not ours to give."

"I will have access – find a way to open those doors. The dust must be in there and the key will open it. IT IS THERE. I KNOW IT IS," Uzas shouted back. His cloak snapped as if on a breeze.

"It is not. But even if it were, we would never tell you – you will have to kill us first," another elder said before being knocked over the head by the dreamon standing behind him.

"Destrooooy ... destrooooy," the dreamons chanted as if energised by the violence in the air.

"Kill you? I have NO intentions of killing you, my lovely people. But what am I going to do? What to do? ... I know! I will *take* one child every hour, for as long as I am denied the location of the key," Uzas said as if he were having a normal conversation.

"Leave the children alone – they do not deserve to die! They are just children," an elder gasped, his eyes wide with horror.

"Oh no. You misunderstand me – I am not a monster. I am a loving leader. I will not *kill* any children – not a single one. I love them. I *love* children. But for each hour that I do not get the key – I will change one child into a dreamon. A loyal subject to me. His or her memories will be wiped away and then once a year I will send them to patrol around Bylleraz so that you can weep at the sight of your dreamon offspring."

The dreamons shuffled and hissed as they swayed.

Khrow crunched his knuckles as he clenched his hands into fists. "We'd better make sure no children are left in the castle," Khrow whispered to Yogor.

No sooner than he said that than a dreamon marched eight children into the hall. They were not crying but their faces were tear-stained and their eyes wide as they gazed around at the dreamons. They ranged from five to eight years of age. The small group huddled together to keep away from the dreamons' clutches.

"One hour from now and we shall start with the youngest," Uzas said. "I will retire for an hour." He swept out of the room like a gale force wind, his cloak floating behind him. The door slammed shut.

Khrow beckoned Yogor and the others to leave the room; they crawled out silently. They reached the doorway when Yogor held his hand in the air to ensure no one spoke. Uzas and Zlo came to a halt just a few feet away from where they stood pressed against the wall in the shadows.

"Zlo. Where is that dragon? He is supposed to do my bidding but all he has done since he got here is EAT. I have tried to calm his mind with a spell but all I can pick up is parsley, garlic, lemon and … and chives and the words SMELLY and *YUM* … what is yum? What is going on? Why does that dragon not obey my commands? And does he think that *we* are smelly or that *he* is smelly?"

Zlo shook his head and spread his hands out. "Perhaps the spell takes time to penetrate … it is a *dragon* after all. He has been here a few days already and all he has done so far is a lot of roaring and eating. I will send a team to find him," Zlo said. He leaned forward slightly and sniffed the air around Uzas and then under his own armpits. He shook his head and then shrugged, making the black veins that pulsated across his torso ripple. They moved down the hallway and disappeared around the corner.

Yogor peeked out of the doorway, saw that the coast was clear, and quickly led the team down the hallway and into a small room. They bolted the door behind them.

"This is the worst – now we also have dragon problem!" Yogor said and slammed his fist into the palm of his hand.

Khrow stared at the ceiling as if he was thinking. He waved his hand at Yogor's comment about the dragon. "Don't worry about the dragon – Watroc is with us. What worries me is that we can't use magic … not even our dust. Correct?"

"That is correct," Yogor answered.

"We will have to fight them with hand to hand combat. I am worried about the black-veined dreamons – they can kill and that is not part of magic so they will be able to use that."

Jeff stepped forward. "What about Watroc? Angie once told me dragon's magic is stronger than witch spells and ancient enchantments. They are the most powerful magical creatures. *He* may be able to use his magic in the hall and free the children." Jeff spread his hands as he tried to make his case.

"Watroc does not listen to anyone when he is hungry and I don't think the dreamons are particularly tasty or filling," Khrow said.

"He will if he thinks it is what Phoebe would want him to do. We have to try," Jeff said.

"I agree. It's the only shot we have. Jeff, you go and find Watroc – convince him to help free the children and maybe even the elders … without him eating anyone that is not a dreamon."

Yogor signalled to a slender young man with black curly hair and blood red cheeks. "Rake, go with Jeff so he does not get lost."

He turned back to Khrow. "Rake knows this building inside and out and will make sure their movements remain undetected as they search for the dragon."

Jeff spun on his heel and hurried to the door. He glanced over his shoulder when Khrow called out to him.

"Do not get caught and do not get eaten."

Jeff nodded, gave a thumbs up and left the room with Rake.

36

Jeff sprinted down the corridor with Rake who knew exactly where he was going. They sidestepped a few dreamon patrols and hid in empty rooms as dreamons marched past. Rake ushered Jeff into a large cupboard and closed the door silently as the next patrol came around the corner. Then he opened a panel at the back of the closet and they stepped into a different corridor.

"Shortcut," Rake said as they ran down the deserted halls, following the screams that echoed around the hallways.

An arm flew out of the room and into the corridor, bouncing against the wall.

"I think we found him. I will wait here," Rake said as he peered around the corner at the horned green monster causing chaos.

Jeff took a deep breath and nipped into the room. He leapt over Watroc's tail, dived beneath and rolled sideways as the tail swung to and fro. The white tail spikes gouged the floor, ripping the carpet as it slid from side to side. *I must get in line of sight so that he doesn't think I am sneaking up on him – that is my only chance. This was such a dumb idea,* Jeff thought, he swallowed hard and cleared his throat. "WATROC," he called, but the dragon was too busy pulling a screeching dreamon apart to hear him.

"WATROC!" Jeff shouted again. His eyes widened and he backed up when he saw the dragon lift his massive neck. His head tilted so that a piercing green eye with a bright yellow iris glared unblinkingly at him.

Jeff's breath caught when he saw the eye narrow.

"What do you want? Heart of Calidus," the dragon growled.

"We need your help in the great hall ..." Jeff started.

"No. I am busy," Watroc said and turned back to his snack.

"Watroc, the elders are being tortured and we cannot fight them with our dust," Jeff said loudly. *I don't even have dust so what am I saying!* We need your help!"

"NO. I have not eaten anything decent in days," Watroc hissed.

Jeff glanced at Rake who gave an I-don't-know shrug. Rake was keeping watch for dreamons in the corridors.

Jeff clenched his teeth. *Why must Watroc be so bad tempered and stubborn*, he thought as he shook his head and clenched his fists. He had to make the dragon come with him. It was their only chance.

"WATROC. There are children! They are ..." He didn't get any further.

"I AM UNDERCOVER! I AM SUPPOSED TO EAT ALL THE DREAMONS," Watroc roared.

"Watty?" A soft musical voice spoke next to Jeff.

Jeff was so focused on the dragon he had not heard anyone come up from behind. He yelped and spun around holding his hands in front of him in a warrior position. It was Phoebe.

They had arrived and just in time.

"Phoebe!" Jeff gasped and gave her a hug as they rocked back and forth. They had been friends for a very long time and had shared many adventures together.

Behind her stood Horrigan, Nequam, Madgwick and Nyx, a warrior he had seen in Sandustian. With them was a small dog that looked like a French bulldog. Jeff frowned at the dog but then looked at the warriors standing in front of him.

"Jeff." Horrigan nodded and crossed his muscular arms over his chest. His black leathers and muscle shirt looked dirty and were covered in dog hair. His eyes gleamed bright purple.

"Hey, Jeff-O," Nyx chimed with a wide smile. Her eyes were shining a deep purple, indicating that she was an experienced warrior. She was also dirty as if she had been crawling around in mud.

Jeff's eyes narrowed at the name alteration. *This one must be the annoying one,* he thought and twisted his lips as if he wanted to laugh, but this was not the time for mirth.

Madgwick grabbed him by the shoulders and gave a small shake. "Glad to see you are still in one piece," he said.

Nequam and Rake embraced like long-lost friends.

Watroc dropped his head for Phoebe as she stroked and gently pulled his whiskers straight. The dragon started to hum with a deep rumbling sound coming from within his stomach.

Jeff explained very quickly what they saw: "They are in this huge hall; the elders are being tortured for the whereabouts of the key. Uzas has a group of children that he has threatened to turn into dreamons if they do not give up the location of the key. Khrow has gone to the hall but there is a problem ... the great hall blocks all magic. We don't have much time before Uzas takes the first kid. We were hoping Watroc would be able to use his dragon magic." Jeff shoved his hair off his forehead.

"Of course he will, won't you Watty?" Phoebe crooned to the dragon.

"Can I eat them?" Watroc growled.

"Not the kids but you can eat all the dreamons you can still stomach," Phoebe promised.

"Rake, what is the quickest way back to the great ...?" Jeff started to ask but was distracted by Watroc who suddenly froze.

His tail stopped moving and he tilted his head to the side as if listening to some ancient call. Then without another growl or roar, Watroc started to flap his wings. The force from the wings pushed everyone to the floor, clinging to each other to stop from sliding around and crashing into the walls. He reared his head and blasted a torrent of flame through the roof.

Watroc flew out of the building.

"Where is he going?" Horrigan asked as he pushed to his feet, staring at the hole above them.

"I suppose that way," Phoebe answered with a grin.

The small group followed Rake along the corridors but it seemed that at every turn there were dreamons waiting to battle and slow their progress towards the great hall.

"I suppose the surprise attack is now out of the question," Nyx muttered as she wrinkled her nose from the dreamon stench.

Nyx and Horrigan flew into battle with their dust changing into weapons in mid-flight, clearing a path for Nequam, Madgwick and Phoebe to move forward. At the next corridor, Nequam groaned as another host of monsters stood waiting with swinging arms.

"We're never going to reach the great hall like this," Nequam groaned.

"I think that is the whole point," Madgwick replied and raced into the waiting brutes.

Within minutes Nyx and Horrigan joined the fight, their dust flying in all directions as they attacked the dreamons. Soon the dreamons lying on the floor and the bruised and battered team nodded to each other to confirm everyone was still in one piece. They looked dishevelled but ready for the next battle. They were going to have to fight their way to the great hall and that particular room was a long way off.

37

Khrow and Yogor with his small team made their way back to the great hall. They gathered in a small hidden area near the entrance. They hushed each other as they whispered in urgent tones. Hands flew as they tried to convey the need for silence as they all tried to talk at the same time.

"We must try and attack while Uzas and Zlo are away. They will not expect it," Yogor whispered to the women and men huddled around him.

Khrow shook his head and leaned forward. "No. We must wait for Jeff and Watroc. The dragon could change the whole fight for us, besides we do not know how many dreamons are in that room. We only saw those in front but from the chanting we heard, there could be hundreds. I have fought dreamons before; if we go in there now we will lose. We have to wait!" Khrow stood next to the group; his head low as he tried to make eye contact with Yogor.

"There is no guarantee that the boy will find the dragon and if that dragon will even listen. Rake and boy could be dead as we speak. The longer we wait the more the elders are being beaten. We go now," Yogor replied. The group bobbed their heads as he spoke. As one, they turned and stormed into the room yelling the Bylleraz war cry.

Khrow blew the air out of his lungs and shook his head. He closed his eyes and then leapt into the room after them. He tried to gather his dust but there was no response, as though a magic wall was erected between him and his dust. He somersaulted over a dreamon and as he passed overhead he clasped the brute's neck and brought the monster to the floor. He punched a fist into the dreamon's face to knock him unconscious. He spun around and sidestepped to the right; he grabbed a dreamon by the arm and used the momentum to swing the monster around on his axis to land on the floor. Khrow landed with a knee on the torso. When he looked up his eyes widened as he saw scores of dreamons lining the wall. There were a lot more than what they had seen from above. They were totally outnumbered and one by one the party of Bylleraz fighters began to fall. Khrow dipped and dived but his strength was running out. He was fighting four dreamons at a time. Yogor lay unconscious on the floor in front of an elder.

Dreamons streamed through the archways as if a silent alarm had been rung and soon the party was overwhelmed. Khrow was dragged to the front by four dreamons.

"CLOSE THE DOOR!" Zlo shouted as he and Uzas entered the room.

The double doors slammed with a definite thud. A golden spark laced around the edges, initiating the spell of the great hall to magically seal the door. There was no way out but also no way in. The walls seemed to move and sway at the hundreds of dreamons that stood inside the hall.

Uzas floated to the group of children and yanked a five-year-old boy by the arm from the group of huddling children. "Make one more move against me and I will end this child's life. I do not want to do it but you will leave me no choice so you decide and make that decision now." His high-pitched voice pierced the air.

Zlo and a few other dreamons watched with evil grins on their faces. The boy stood with his eyes closed, his nose wrinkled and holding his breath.

Khrow was forced to kneel on the floor near the elders and alongside some of the Bylleraz fighters. One or two of the fighters lay groaning on the floor. About eight dreamons lay motionless on the stone. They were lucky none of the brutes that subdued the men were black-veined dreamons. It had been a hard fight but the monsters won this battle.

"I know the key is here and I want it now or the children will pay the price," Uzas said. His dirty yellow fingernails pressed into the boy's neck and blood dribbled down.

One of the elders shuddered and with a look amongst them, they nodded. One elder sighed and pushed to his feet. The dreamon behind him held him steady. He walked to a stone pillar and touched a circular stone that no one even noticed until the elder touched it. The stone opened with a slow grinding noise. The elder took out a shiny golden cryptex.

He held it out above his head, "We will not negotiate with our children's lives. Here, take the key. Open the cryptex and break the seal on the parchment to obtain the secrets you desire. But beware that the seal has its own magical spells and attachments that not even we know how to solve." The elder whispered but his voice carried through the room.

Uzas released the boy and flung him to the side as if he were nothing but a rag doll.

The boy fell beside an elder who immediately pulled him close in an attempt to protect him.

Uzas seized the cryptex and held it up in the air like a trophy. "This is the key! This will give me the location of the source and immortality. Was that too much to ask for?" Uzas crooned at the elders but the elders just glared at him.

Khrow stared at the wall behind Uzas; something was happening to the bricks. The stone was changing from grey to black and then deep red. It seemed to be curling away from the centre as if made of paper and being singed in a flame.

A red blob of stone dripped onto the floor like molten glass. Blobs fell to the ground in red hot puddles in a steady flow.

Uzas turned and saw the melting wall. "What is this – what is happening?" Uzas shouted and waved at his dreamons to investigate.

The dreamons hurried around looking up and along the walls. One screamed in pain as he touched the wall.

Watroc's head popped into view. He curled his lips back as he flashed a toothy grin at the crowd staring up at him.

Khrow winced when he saw a foot in a shoe still lodged between two of the dragon's teeth.

"Oh, it's my beautiful spellbound dragon. I command you to come to my side," Uzas said and raised his thin, grey, bony arm into the air.

Watroc swayed from side to side as if trying to resist the call of Uzas. He swung his head to and fro, pretending he was trying to break free from the bond that tied him to the evil monster.

A single puff of dark green smoke floated from his nostril in a small circle. Watroc turned to glare at Khrow. His green eyes narrowed and then he pulled his lips back to reveal his rows upon rows of teeth.

"A bit dramatic," Khrow muttered. The dreamon behind him slapped him on the shoulder to silence him.

Watroc raised his head and the rumbling inside his belly became so loud everyone stopped talking. Then he dropped his head and blew a steady stream of green smoke towards the sealed door. The smoke spiralled in patterns, twisting and intertwining like a dance as it captivated the dreamons' stare, making them nod their heads in sync with the spirals. It was so mesmerising no one noticed the dragon had moved to stand between Uzas and the children that were huddled in the corner of the room.

The instant the smoke touched the doors they blasted open like a popped balloon. In the corridor stood Jeff, Madgwick, Horrigan, Nyx, Nequam, Phoebe and the Bylleraz youngster Rake.

"Seize them," Zlo shouted and the dreamons converged on the small group standing in the corridor.

"Seizzzze … seizzze" the dreamons chanted as the moved forward.

There were so many dreamons Khrow could no longer see the group that had come to the rescue. He flexed his muscles and opened his hands but his dust was still unresponsive. Watroc growled behind him and in a low crouch he turned in anticipation of being roasted or eaten alive by a dragon. But the dragon was busy with his own magic. The magical block did not seem to apply to a dragon's magic.

Watroc blew a thin thread of fire onto the stone floor. The glowing green flame spun and turned until it connected to complete a green circle. Smoke tendrils curled and danced as it rose from the circle of green fire.

Out of the corner of his eye, he saw Phoebe slip past the dreamons and crawl along the floor, under chairs and darting behind curtains until she was close to the children and the circle of green fire. It was as if she knew exactly what Watroc was doing.

Khrow darted to the side and smashed his fist into a dreamon rushing towards the girl.

With a few hurried hand motions, Phoebe summoned the children and the elders to her side. With bewildered looks the elders scurried and crawled across the floor. She whispered frantically in their ears, cupping her hand over her mouth as she spoke. Her finger darted back and forth as she pointed at the circle.

Watroc began to hum.

With dragon's hum and dragon's roar,
A circle of fire I wish to draw
With flame and fury I fling my might
To bewitch this passage of magical flight

The circle flared up and Phoebe pushed the children towards the circle of flames. An elder's eyes popped open wide as if he had just understood that this is a magical exit for the children. He pushed two children towards the fire, not giving them a chance to be afraid. As they crossed the line a bright whoosh flared up and they were gone.

Uzas turned, his cloak swirling around as he screamed in a high-pitched screech, "MY PRISIONERS!"

"GO," Khrow yelled at the elders as they gathered around the children to protect them. Khrow was fighting the dreamons who were trying to get

217

to the children.

An elder lifted two children into his arms and dropped them into the circle. With another bright whoosh they vanished.

Emboldened by Phoebe and the elders' urging, the rest of the children jumped into the flame. The elders stood side by side with grim smiles. None of the elders had chosen to escape but the threat against the children was gone.

38

The dreamons yelled as they charged forward. They divided ranks to the left and right along the sides of the room as they tried to encircle the warriors.

A dreamon tried to throw a lightning bolt, which resulted in a loud crack with a sizzle. "The lightning will not work," he shouted to Zlo who was engaged in blows with Khrow.

They were on an equal footing: the warriors could not use their dust and the dreamons could not use their lightning: the magic block was absolute. Even without the dust, the warriors were very accomplished in hand-to-hand combat but there were so many dreamons they would overpower the small group of warriors in a short time. That did not stop the warriors from flying into battle.

The elders hit dreamons over the head with torches and candlesticks, but they were not warriors and the dreamons were not particular about who they beat with their fists. The elders supported each other as they tried to stand but were slowly being forced into a corner.

"Protect the elders!" Khrow shouted, as he sank into a lunge and put a fist through a rushing dreamon's stomach.

Horrigan reached the elders, ripping the dreamons away from them. Horrigan's purple gleaming eyes flashed as he struck a dreamon with a fist. He brought the creature's head down and kneed him in the jaw. The dreamon staggered away trying to recover his breathing. No sooner than Horrigan disposed of a dreamon, another two took his place. Horrigan kicked a dreamon away from Belugg.

Belugg had transformed into a dragon-dog. Wide black wings had sprouted from his back; the tips were sharp curled talons. His soft tail had changed into a thick black tail with scales and spines that stood up menacingly. The cyflith mouth was filled with teeth that hung over his bottom jaw like a sabre-tooth tiger. He gouged the dreamon's ankles with a powerful swipe of his horned tail, forcing them to collapse in pain. As they hit the ground, Belugg flapped his wings and lunged for the throat. He was small but vicious and was not considered part of the dragon family for nothing.

Nyx leapt into the air, swinging above a dreamon and caught him with her thighs, placing him in a choke hold and bringing him crashing to the floor. The dreamon hit his head on the stone and was knocked out cold. As Nyx rose from her victim, dreamons ploughed into her from all sides. She anticipated the blows but was on the defensive and had to back up to remain standing. She tried to sidestep but could not fight them all at once. A blow hit her on the head and she went tumbling.

While fighting the dreamons with one arm, Horrigan dragged Nyx behind him.

Khrow was slowly backing up towards where Horrigan was standing. The dreamons around him lay groaning and twitching from his punches and kicks. His glowing eyes were a deep purple and he was at last taking his pent-up rage out on the dreamons. He screamed as he hit and kicked. Khrow grabbed a dreamon and gave him a head butt causing the dreamon to stagger back.

Madgwick threw the dreamon over his shoulder and stamped on his throat. The creature lay groaning on the floor. Madgwick sprang two steps up a pillar and somersaulted over another dreamon, pulling him down as he landed.

Nequam, Rake and a few fighters from the village fought as bravely as they could. They spun and twirled as they tried to stay one step ahead from the attacking monsters. But these were dreamons and they were very strong and brutal. Nequam and the fighters around him were forced into retreat.

Jeff and Phoebe each had a chair in their hands and smashed them over dreamons' heads and backs as the brutes stumbled. Jeff could feel his heart beating as he watched the dreamons gaining ground. The fighters were being pushed into a corner.

"What is he doing now?" Jeff shouted from the side. He had a chair in his hands and was hitting another dreamon over his back.

Madgwick and Khrow both spun around to look at Watroc. It was never wise to fight with your back to a dragon … especially if the dragon was hungry.

Watroc swung his head further and further from side to side and there was a deep grumbling sound that bounced around the room. He reared his head up and growled so loudly everyone clutched their ears. It sounded like a thunderstorm brewing inside him. With the noise at its peak, Watroc opened his jaw wide and released a torrent of fire so strong it looked like a gigantic blow torch intertwined with ribbons of green and blue.

As the scorching flame hit the ceiling, the stone blasted away like twigs.

Everyone dived for cover but it was not necessary. Watroc's dragon fire was so hot the stone rained down in ash. Watroc kept his flame on the ceiling until the blue skies could be seen beyond the jagged edges of the roof.

It's big enough for a dragon, Jeff thought.

As suddenly as he started, Watroc clamped his jaws shut. The glow of his flame made his throat and neck seem like there was an internal laser display. The torch of fire flamed out as if someone or something had blown out a candle with a quick puff. It was like a signal to the fighters below that the laser show was over and the fight could commence.

Watroc lunged down and grabbed a mouthful of screaming dreamons, kicking and twitching in his jaw.

"WAATROOOC!" Phoebe screamed while everyone was watching the show. A dreamon called Vobeq had crept behind Phoebe and wrapped his black-veined arms around her. He lifted her easily off the ground. Phoebe tried to kick and struggle but the dreamon was too strong.

Watroc stopped mid-chew and with a gulp the twitching dreamons disappeared down his throat. He lowered his head at Vobeq, narrowed his eyes, and lifted his lips to reveal his blood-soaked teeth.

"STOP OR SHE DIES!" Zlo screamed. Blood and spit sprayed as he screamed. His nose was broken and one eye was swollen shut. "HE WILL RELEASE HIS BLACK VEINS ONTO HER" he shouted as he shuffled towards the dreamon and Phoebe.

Watroc growled and stomped but Khrow held his hand up to the dragon. "WAIT. The veins only require but a split second to latch onto her. STOP, WATROC."

Jeff bit his lip as he watched Phoebe struggle in her captor's arms.

The dreamons surrounded the group. The fight was over, the fighters were battered and bruised and outnumbered. They were herded and shoved to the centre of the room. Watroc stood and stared at Phoebe as she was held off the ground in Vobeq's clutches.

She stared at Watroc, and then nodded as if he had said something. Even if he tried to pry her away using dragon magic, the chance was huge that those fearsome veins would try to escape obliteration by using the girl as a survival option.

The dreamons dragged the warriors to kneel in front of Uzas. He laughed with a high-pitched hysterical sound that made his cloak bounce. The warriors breathed heavily as they glared at him.

He stood in front of Madgwick and lifted the bloodied warrior's chin with his index finger. The long, dirty, pointed fingernail dug into Madgwick's skin. "You were *dead*, warrior – I want to know your secret on how you came back." Then he stopped in front of Jeff. "You. I want to know how you managed to capture my lightning and *where* you went." He turned around waving the cryptex in his hand. "We will leave now. I have the cryptex and *she* will be able to open it and find the source."

She? Jeff wondered. Did Uzas mean Phoebe, or someone else?

The dreamon leader continued, "Our mission has been successful. We will take the dragon and all the Sandustian warriors with us; take the girl to keep the dragon under control. Pitiful," he pointed at Jeff, "Include this one. The others you can ..." Uzas stopped talking as a movement above him caught his attention.

Silent black smoke trailed down in spirals from the gaping hole where the bright blue sky seemed like a button. It looked slow and lazy but there was an ominous feel about this smoke that just appeared out of nowhere.

The dreamons shuffled forward but then stopped as they too gazed up at the hole in the ceiling.

"What evil is this?" Uzas demanded, clutching the cryptex close to his chest.

39

Black smoke? Jeff thought as he stared at the smoke tentacles that beckoned like fingers as it drifted down from the ceiling. *Black smoke! Trezz.*

"Trezz is coming!" he whispered to Madgwick.

The black smoke swirled and circled as if assessing the room. Then it stopped and took form in front of them.

Trezz stood in the middle of the room; his hair was tied in a ponytail, very similar to how the warrior Rig preferred to tie his hair. Trezz looked around and his bright blue eyes landed on Madgwick and widened. With a puff of smoke he disintegrated and formed directly in front of Madgwick, a smoky hand hovering over Madgwick's heart. "My brother," Trezz said when he had become solid.

Madgwick's mouth hung open and then he grinned. "Your looks have improved."

Trezz's face seemed pale in the glaring torchlight, making his thick jagged scar stand out. The scar ran down his face from the corner of his left eye across his cheek to the bottom of his chin. "Yours too," he responded with a small twist of his lips. Then he winked at Jeff. "The smell too – no doubt." Trezz twisted his neck to the right and cracked his knuckles. "It's time for revenge." He turned on his heel to glare at Uzas.

"YOU!" Uzas screamed. "Kill him. Kill the Nytezard!"

"Come." Trezz smiled at the dreamons and crooked his finger; his face was so contorted with smoke he looked evil. He lowered his head and opened his arms as if to welcome the onslaught.

"Nytezard … Nytezard … kill him … kill him," chanted the dreamons lined along the walls.

The dreamons rushed Trezz but the Nytezard was no longer there. He had dissolved into black smoke and encircled the dreamons. The dreamons screamed as they slapped and fanned the smoke away but it was no good. The Nytezard smoke filled their eyes and trailed out of their mouths. It was lethal and the dreamons dropped to the ground. Smoke trailed around dreamons like a giant snake and those who could still crawl tried to creep towards the exits. The smoke moved faster than one could blink. Now and then an arm or a leg appeared as the smoke absorbed the dreamons. With the Nytezard attack on dreamons, the warriors threw off the dreamons holding them and fought for freedom.

Vobeq held Phoebe off the ground in a lock grip; he felt hot air above him, looked up and gasped. Watroc was standing right above him. His tooth was an inch from the dreamon's face. A blob of saliva fell onto his head and down his back. He staggered back still holding Phoebe in his arms. Her legs scissor kicked as she tried to get loose from the deathly grip.

"Watroc, WAIT. You *know* what you have to do. Do that first!" Phoebe shouted to the green dragon.

A green glow started to shine through Watroc's scales. He started to rumble deep inside his throat.

The warriors were still grouped together in the centre of the room with the dreamons standing five rows deep around them. Trezz, who was still in smoke form, circled around the warriors, villagers and elders ensuring the dreamons did not touch the group.

Jeff spun around; they were still surrounded by the dreamons. Even with Trezz, they were outnumbered.

"Phoebe," Jeff yelled, staring at his friend who was still in the clutches of the monster.

Uzas laughed. "You are alone, Nytezard, you cannot beat our numbers and …" He stopped mid-sentence as a thunderous screech and a violent THUD shook the building.

Dust and stones fell from the gaping hole that Watroc had opened before.

Everyone looked up – including Uzas.

Azghar peered over the edge and roared. Azghar was an air dragon and twice the size of Watroc or even Calidus. His midnight blue scales were scattered with sapphire gems that shimmered as he moved. From his head right down his back were white pointed spines. He narrowed his eyes and opened his mouth to release bright blue steam that puffed down into the hole like a cloud.

Watroc released his magic and blew a green cloud of steam up into the hole towards Azghar.

The two clouds drifted into each other, mingling like two lost friends. Then the smoke clouds exploded causing a shockwave that pulsated down and around the room with a loud BANG. The dreamons and warriors alike staggered from the force, grabbing onto each other as they tumbled to the floor. Only Trezz, who was still in a smoke form, remained standing.

Khrow felt heat in his hands as his dust flowed through him. He yelled at Horrigan and Nyx. "The dragons have combined their magic and broken the hall seal!" He started hurling cannon balls at the dreamons with such might they went straight through the dreamons causing them to evaporate on impact.

Horrigan dropped his hand and a long silver glittering sword grew in his hand. He twirled it around his head like a ninja and then attacked.

Nyx pulled a silvery arrow and let her arrows loose, her braided hair flying from the power of her draw.

The doors of the great hall burst open, slamming against the walls on either side. Sandustian warriors stood in the doorway. Harley's message had been received.

Kojo stood in front of the Sandustian warriors. He looked mean and intimidating in his black bandana. His black skin glowed and his dark shirt stretched over his back. His muscles flexed as his dust weapons sizzled in his hands, ready to attack. Other warriors stood behind him with grim smiles on their faces: Sinjin and Mootwo grinned at the dreamons as their dust bounced in their hands. Stardust, Talon, Nimrat and Wax leapt into the hall with their dust swords held high above their heads. The Sandustian warriors were there in full force and raced into the hall, silver dust flying in all directions.

Kojo saw Khrow and Madgwick fighting in front and his purple eyes widened and glowed. "KHROW! MADGWICK!" his normally soft voice boomed.

Azghar dropped into the great hall with a THUD and knocked down a tall pillar as he landed. He lunged and grabbed dreamons that were bunched together in his jaw; he tore them apart as he spun around. His tail caught a few more pillars and they tumbled to the ground.

Tied onto his back was an ugly olive green sofa. It was covered in bright yellow diamond shapes and had fluff sticking out of the seams. Sitting crossed-legged as if she was having a cup of tea was the crazy witch Angie. She wore a broad rimmed blue hat with massive yellow daisies tucked into the hat band. The flowers were about the size of a dinner plate and almost hid her face. Her green eyes were covered with bright yellow goggles and her red streaky hair hung down her back in curls and waves.

Harley, her magical broom, flew through the hole and immediately started to beat a dreamon over the head. His tail twigs bristled and his handle gleamed as he whacked the dreamon.

She didn't seem to notice the horde of dreamons still surrounding the small group in the middle. Leaping down off her ugly sofa, she rushed to Madgwick, knocking him onto his back as she lunged at him and almost sat on his chest as she grabbed his ears. "You are alive! I knew it. I KNEW

IT. ALIVE!" she yelled into his face.

The air was knocked out of Madgwick's lungs and he tried to draw breath. There was no extra air to talk.

She clambered to her feet with a curt, "You smell bad. I mean – really bad. Is that new cologne? We need to have a serious talk about your taste when we get back to Sandustian. Now stop lying about, Madgwick. You are dead for a few days and end up being smelly and a complete slacker. UP."

Madgwick shook his head and stuck his fingers in his ears as if to release the pressure of her yells.

She skipped towards Jeff and pinched his cheeks until he thought they were going to stay like that. "I knew you would do it. You are so clever to have figured it out – don't know about the smelly thing you and Madgwick have got going on but we need to nip that in the bud right away. Now, *lazy* both of you – get to work," Angie said.

Jeff said nothing but stared at Angie. *Huh?* he thought.

Azghar huffed and the attention was brought back to the situation at hand. He lifted his lip and showed his teeth. A single smoke ring shot out of his left nostril.

Angie looked at Uzas. "Let the girl go and surrender."

"ATTACK!" Uzas screamed and started throwing lightning bolts at the warriors.

The fight was on but this time the odds were on the warrior's side. The dragons were there and they gulped the lightning as if were nothing but strings of jellispickles.

Belugg was still transformed into a dragon-dog. His charcoal coat gleamed and his black wings flapped as he flew from dreamon to dreamon. He grabbed at the dreamon flesh with his sharp teeth that hung over his bottom jaw. The dreamons tried to toss him to the side but the spikes on his spine made it impossible to grab him without being speared.

Except for Madgwick and Jeff, the warriors had full power and destroyed the dreamons one by one.

"Retreat!" Uzas ordered as he watched his army of dreamons being slaughtered.

Uzas gave the signal and the dreamons started jumping into their lightning bolts. This was their preferred way of travel.

Jeff and Nequam ran towards Phoebe, jumping over fallen dreamons and blocks of stone that lay crumbled on the floor.

Trezz turned back to Uzas and pointed his finger at the dreamon leader. Smoke trailed out of his fingertip. "I will find you – I will avenge all the evil you have done to my folk and to my friends."

Uzas stared at Trezz and said, "I will wait for you, young Nytezard." And then with a bright lightning bolt he was gone.

Within seconds and what seemed like a hundred light flashes the dreamons were gone but the stench remained.

Vobeq, still holding Phoebe in an elbow lock off the floor, jumped into a lightning bolt and the two of them were whisked away with a crackle and snap.

"PHOEBEEEE!" Jeff screamed.

Watroc spun around and stared at where Phoebe had been an instant before. His eyes narrowed.

Within seconds Azghar and Angie stood next to Watroc. A rumbling noise like a jet engine increasing power could be heard from Azghar and Watroc. When the noise had reached a level where everyone held their ears for protection, they opened their jaws and a flame shot towards the back wall where Phoebe had been held captive by the dreamon.

The blue flame from Azghar and the green flame from Watroc collided to form a torrent of fire. Angie waved her arms in a windmill motion and sent purple dust flowing into the green and blue flame. The flames sparkled and with a loud crack a black hole the size of doorway appeared.

Angie yelled over her shoulder, "We will keep it open, go in and fetch her. NOW."

Jeff rushed forward but Angie shook her head. "No Jeff. Not you – that dreamon inside of you is still dormant from Calidus's spell. But he could awaken if you go inside there."

The scar pulled to the side as Trezz grimaced. He whooshed past the dragons and disappeared into the black space, half in form and smoke. His black smoke blended with the darkness of the portal and within seconds he had vanished.

The warriors, elders and villagers watched the space waiting for movement. Nequam stood next to Jeff and placed a hand on his shoulder.

The dragons threw their fire at the doorway, not relenting for a second and kept the portal steady as they waited for Trezz. Their rumbling noise echoed around the room.

"Come on … come on," Jeff breathed as he watched. He did not know how long the dragons could keep their flames going.

No one said a word. Everyone watched and waited.

Then Phoebe's voice came wafting out of the portal: "My jacket is going to stink forever – totally ruined!"

She appeared to be floating within the black smoke that was transporting her out of the dark space. Where the smoke was lethal to the dreamons, the girl was not harmed at all. She was chatting away with Trezz as she drifted toward them.

The moment her feet touched the ground, the dark space winked out of sight and the dragons' flames abruptly stopped. The sudden drop in noise almost hurt as everyone still stood in silence.

Watroc pushed forward until his face almost touched Phoebe's. She stroked his whiskers and the dragon shivered as if he had a sudden chill.

"There, there, it's all okay, I am back. Trezz destroyed that dreamon that grabbed me." Phoebe said with a sniff.

Angie patted Phoebe as if she had to make sure every part of her was in order. "Yes, she seems to be in good shape. I did recommend Trezz use essence of lavender but I doubt that would have made any difference here.

He is also bit smelly," she announced to everyone staring with held breath.

Trezz shook his head at Angie. "I am not smelly – it's not me. It's the dreamons." Trezz turned to face Madgwick and Khrow. His features were still contorted by smoke as he grinned. His blue eyes gleamed. "I know where they go when they vanish in lighting. This is going to be so much fun."

40

The Sandustian warriors sent word to the elders that Bylleraz was free from the dreamon hold.

Galagedra arrived with a number of elders to consult with the Bylleraz elders. Deep grooves ran across Galagedra's face like a jigsaw puzzle. The wrinkles around his blue eyes deepened when he smiled. His midnight blue robe swayed as he strode through the hall. His robe was tied with a simple yellow sash that dangled down the front.

They inspected the great hall ruins left from the fight and the dragons' assault. The battle would not have been won without the dragons and warriors. With a bit of hard work and a touch of magic here and there, the great hall would be restored in no time. Azghar promised to reinstate the magical seal for the hall.

Galagedra stood with his hands on both Khrow and Madgwick's shoulders; he ruffled Jeff's hair and then shook his bowed head. "We will talk at length back home."

The elders and Galagedra discussed the cryptex. The warriors stood by and listened.

"The parchment inside the cryptex is sealed with magic. Only a very powerful witch or wizard will be able to open it but at all costs, we must get the parchment back. The secret of the key is vital to keep the location of the source safe. I regret we handed the cryptex to that evil monster but we had to save the children from being turned into dreamons. Once turned into dreamons they would be gone forever. We were not prepared to take that chance on a young life," the elder said, wringing his hands.

"It is totally understandable and we will send forth warriors to trace the cryptex and the parchment. It will be returned to Bylleraz," Galagedra said.

"Uzas mentioned a *she,* so there is someone else involved. Perhaps … a witch?" Nyx said.

Horrigan slapped his fist into his palm, "Widzema! That would explain the shimmers at the entry to Bylleraz."

Galagedra nodded but seemed deep in thought.

Azghar hummed as he and Belugg sat a little way from the warriors. Belugg howled and yapped, his tail wagging as he and Azghar rubbed their noses together.

The warriors moved away from the elders and started preparing to depart from Bylleraz.

Angie sat on her ugly olive green sofa and glared at Watroc as he snickered and laughed every time he looked at her sofa.

"It's a good colour. I miss the pink but it's a good colour. Love the diamonds," Phoebe said as she sat on the cushions and patted the arm rest.

Angie wagged her finger at Watroc. "Stop laughing. This is my new upgraded sofa. Not as comfortable as the other one but Azghar *apparently* does not like pink. Trezz looooooves it," Angie said and smiled broadly.

Trezz turned his back on Angie and rolled his eyes.

Jeff leaned on the sofa. "Angie … did you know that we were out there somewhere?" he asked.

"Well sort of, it made sense when the dust formed an arc over the moon and then Azghar and I concluded there was a slight, ever remote but slight chance you were in Khadruz." Angie sniffed.

"But how?" Jeff asked.

"Well, the moon was already there and then dust came and made a pattern-like formation …" Angie began with her hands flying as she described the dust over the moon.

"No. I mean how did you know?" Jeff asked with a shake of his head.

Khrow, Madgwick and the other warriors stopped so that they could listen.

Azghar sniffed and lowered his head. "It is an ancient binding enchantment. Khrow was bound to Jeff when he gifted his dust to Jeff. Khrow would be stuck in Khadruz until such time that Jeff either died or released him with dust – that link has now been broken. Jeff is bound to Calidus – that magic bond is unbreakable. Calidus was following the path that was preordained for Jeff. Jeff had to depart to follow Khrow. Calidus opened that passage for him. Madgwick, well he is bound to ..." Azghar rumbled on in his deep voice.

"EEEECK. A wuunack!" Angie screamed, sprang to her feet and threw some dust into the air that scattered everywhere. The warriors started to cough.

Khrow, Madgwick and Jeff spun around to see if there were any wuunacks scurrying around. When the dust had settled, Angie and Azghar had moved on to talk with Galagedra.

Madgwick stood watching the warriors. A small figure came to stand next to him with a broad smile. It was Fitghet. He was the creator of the Sandustian magical dust and had arrived with the elders. Although his home town was Bylleraz, he resided in Sandustian with the elders. Madgwick smiled at Fitghet, the smile did not reach his eyes. He was happy to be back and alive but there was a hole where his dust had resided within.

"My dust was sent away," Madgwick said with a shrug and dipped his head.

"I know – twice," Fitghet said.

"Twice?"

"Yes, the first time you sent it away to protect it rather than yourself, and the second time when Angie released it to protect you. And so, warrior – you are worthy," Fitghet said. He dug his hand into his coat pocket and pulled out a little bottle of blue swirling dust. He held it out to Madgwick.

Madgwick stared at the bottle with wide eyes as if he could not believe this was real.

"Go on. Open it," Khrow said with a smile.

Madgwick looked at the group around him: Trezz, Jeff, Khrow, Horrigan, Nyx, Phoebe and Nequam. They smiled and nodded.

Smiling, Madgwick pulled the cork and released the dust.

The dust emerged out of the bottle that looked like blue smoky fingers. Slowly it rose. Then it spiralled around, with patterns within patterns. Silver glitter sparkled and shone like little stars as it raced around. Then suddenly it slammed straight into Madgwick's chest. The warrior fell backwards from the force but it looked like he was aglow. Madgwick flexed his hands and the dust darted in and out like it was playing. Madgwick's eyes shone a deep purple.

Jeff smiled as he sat on the ugly green sofa with Phoebe and they watched Madgwick welcome his dust back. He didn't have any dust but both Khrow and Madgwick were alive and that was worth it.

Fitghet turned to Jeff. "Young warrior. Galagedra said your dream-catcher abilities have been magically blocked as it is too risky with the dreamon dormant inside of you. But, we have decided that you are a worthy warrior, and therefore have been granted your own magical dust – created only for you. I have not yet started to make it but it will be ready at the next full moon. We will meet at the enchanted pool in the forest where you will be joined with your dust." Fitghet smiled at Jeff's face.

"It will be a grand ceremony," Galagedra said with a smile.

My own dust.

Jeff covered his mouth with his hands as the warriors slapped him on the back and ruffled his hair. Full moon was in a few days' time.

Horrigan and Nyx waved as the warriors were about to make their way back via the gate that the Sandustian elders had opened. They had decided to stay with Phoebe; Nequam was going to introduce her to the villagers. They would bring Phoebe home when she was ready. Belugg would be waiting for Horrigan when he got back to Sandustian. The cyflith and Azghar wanted to spend time together.

Watroc had to leave with Azghar as he was needed to free Calidus. Khrow and Madgwick would travel with Watroc. The dragon stood staring at Phoebe as she waved him goodbye with a huge smile that showed her shiny braces.

Jeff sat on Azghar's neck and was tied by glittering dust. He did not want to sit on the sofa with Angie.

"Angie. Do you know where Calidus and Rig are? " Jeff asked. He gave Angie and Azghar word-for-word detail of what Rig and Calidus had said.

"Oh I think so and Trezz can follow Calidus' smoke trail. We have not had a dangerous mission for a long time. I think you might need some extra training when you get your dust. I will help there."

"Angie, I was almost killed on my last mission," Jeff said.

"Bah ... wuunacks and Soop. Like that was really dangerous – oh come on. Wait until you see where we are going next. It's going to be so much fun. We will leave straight after your dust ceremony."

Jeff stared at Angie as if she had just grown two purple glittery horns.

"I will also be going," Madgwick said with a nod.

"Me too," Trezz said from his smoky form that was still wafting around.

Azghar rose into the air and hovered as they waited for Belugg's wings to emerge so that the cyflith could join them in the air for the journey to Sandustian.

They were heading home.

www.ingramcontent.com/pod-product-compliance
Lightning Source LLC
Chambersburg PA
CBHW020104180626
46812CB00006B/2463